T0314746

Bello:
hidden talent rediscovered

Bello is a digital-only imprint of Pan Macmillan,
established to breathe new life into previously published,
classic books.

At Bello we believe in the timeless power of the imagination,
of a good story, narrative and entertainment, and we want to
use digital technology to ensure that many more readers
can enjoy these books into the future.

We publish in ebook and print-on-demand formats
to bring these wonderful books to new audiences.

www.panmacmillan.co.uk/bello

Richmal Crompton

Richmal Crompton (1890–1969) is best known for her thirty-eight books featuring William Brown, which were published between 1922 and 1970. Born in Lancashire, Crompton won a scholarship to Royal Holloway in London, where she trained as a schoolteacher, graduating in 1914, before turning to writing full-time. Alongside the *William* novels, Crompton wrote forty-one novels for adults, as well as nine collections of short stories.

Richmal Crompton

THE OLD MAN'S BIRTHDAY

First published 1936 by Macmillan

This edition published 2015 by Bello
an imprint of Pan Macmillan
20 New Wharf Road, London N1 9RR
Basingstoke and Oxford
Associated companies throughout the world

www.panmacmillan.co.uk/bello

ISBN 978-1-5098-1027-7 EPUB
ISBN 978-1-5098-1025-3 HB
ISBN 978-1-5098-1026-0 PB

Copyright © Richmal Crompton, 1936

The right of Richmal Crompton to be identified as the
author of this work has been asserted by her in
accordance with the Copyright, Designs and Patents Act 1988.

All rights reserved. No part of this publication may be reproduced,
stored in a retrieval system, or transmitted, in any form, or by any means
(electronic, mechanical, photocopying, recording or otherwise)
without the prior written permission of the publisher.

This book is a work of fiction. Names, characters, places, organizations
and incidents are either products of the author's imagination or used fictitiously.
Any resemblance to actual events, places, organizations or persons,
living or dead, is entirely coincidental.

This book remains true to the original in every way. Some aspects may appear
out-of-date to modern-day readers. Bello makes no apology for this, as to retrospectively
change any content would be anachronistic and undermine the authenticity of the original.

A CIP catalogue record for this book is available from the British Library.

Typeset by Ellipsis Digital Limited, Glasgow

This book is sold subject to the condition that it shall not, by way of
trade or otherwise, be lent, hired out, or otherwise circulated without
the publisher's prior consent in any form of binding or cover other than
that in which it is published and without a similar condition including
this condition being imposed on the subsequent purchaser.

Visit **www.panmacmillan.com** to read more about all our books
and to buy them. You will also find features, author interviews and
news of any author events, and you can sign up for e-newsletters
so that you're always first to hear about our new releases.

Chapter One

OLD Matthew Royston opened his eyes, stretched his long lean frame, then sat up in bed with a jerk.

Mellow golden sunlight poured through the slats of the Venetian blind, gleaming on the polished surface of the mahogany wardrobe, dancing along the rows of little brass knobs that decorated the old-fashioned bedstead, playing around the framed texts that broke at intervals the trellised pattern of the wallpaper, blazing with its full force on the enlarged photograph of Matthew's wife that hung over the bed.

The photograph had been taken shortly before Harriet's death, and it showed with relentless fidelity the tight mouth and severe humourless eyes that had spoilt her good looks.

The old man glanced round the room, and his lips, under their raggy, drooping, white moustache, curved into a faintly ironic smile. It always amused him to wake up in this Victorian bedroom, which had hardly been altered in any detail since Harriet had arranged it as a bride more than sixty years ago. The thick white mats that she had crocheted before her marriage still lay on wash-hand-stand, chest of drawers, and bedside table. On the mantelpiece stood photographs of their children at various stages of growth—Catherine and Charlotte as little girls in long-waisted dresses with enormous sashes round their hips and tall black button boots; Margaret, an elaborately trimmed hat perched above a curled fringe, standing stiffly upright holding a muff; George in a knickerbocker suit with curls down to his shoulders; Richard as a baby, his dimpled arms bare, his chubby cheeks half hidden by huge shoulder bows. . . .

Between the photographs was massed a heterogeneous array of

the curios that Matthew had sent home during his wanderings—coral from Corsica, cloisonné and ivory from Pekin, a jade Buddha from Ceylon, grass fans from the South Sea Islands, and some gleaming black figures carved patiently and elaborately by an unknown Japanese craftsman out of coal. These were flanked, on one side by a lustre of Bristol glass, on the other by a tall vase, whose surface Catherine and Charlotte in their childhood had covered with used postage stamps, an artistic achievement of which Harriet had been very proud.

In Harriet's lifetime a case of stuffed birds had stood in the centre of the chest of drawers. Its removal was the only change the old man had made in the room since her death. He loved birds and had always disliked the dusty lifeless little figures perched so unnaturally on the branch of dead wood.

The door opened, and Gaston, his valet, entered. He was an incongruous figure in the smugly conventional bedroom—short, stocky, with a round, closely cropped head, and so bow-legged that his legs, in their tight black trousers, seemed to form an almost complete circle. One eye was permanently closed, and from it a long scar ran down his cheek to the corner of his mouth.

Matthew was never quite sure at what point in his adventurous career Gaston had attached himself to him. Gaston said that Matthew had saved his life. Certainly the two had gone through many vicissitudes together, and, when Matthew had returned to England and settled down to respectability, Gaston had accompanied him.

He drew up the Venetian blinds with a rattle, adjusted the Nottingham lace curtains, then, walking with his curious straddling gait to the marble-topped wash-hand-stand, placed on it a can of hot water.

Harriet's photograph seemed to gaze down at him in prim disapproval, and her expression seemed to be reflected on the faces of the two faded angels who presided in stiff attitudes over the text "Watch and Pray," above the mantelpiece.

The contrast between himself and his surroundings never struck Gaston as in any way odd. Surroundings meant nothing to him;

he had always taken them for granted. Had he been articulate enough to put his thoughts into words, he would have said that his job here was to protect his master, as he had protected him on the diamond fields and the African veld—there against thieves and murderers, here against a highly respectable family who wished to take charge of the old man and order his life for him; there with knives and fists, here with lies, stubbornness, and a servility of manner that was his most trusted and unfailing weapon.

He took down the old man's clothes from the wardrobe and laid them out in silence. Gaston never wasted time in greetings or comments on the weather. Finally he turned to the bed.

"Will you get up for your breakfast?" he asked.

He spoke English well but with a slightly foreign accent. He spoke several languages well but none without a slightly foreign accent. He was not sure himself what his nationality was, though he believed that he was "partly Spanish." His earliest memory was of being kitchen-boy in a not very reputable inn in Marseilles.

"Of course," said Matthew rather sharply. "Why shouldn't I?"

Gaston shrugged. "Last night——" he began.

Old Matthew interrupted him curtly.

"Go and get my bath ready."

Gaston went out.

Old Matthew lay in bed, his straggling white eyebrows drawn into a scowl. Gaston's reference to last night had irritated him. It always irritated him to be treated as if he were an invalid. He was perfectly well except for slight attacks of—"wind round the heart" it was called, he believed. The attacks of late had been rather frequent and severe, but so far, with Gaston's help, he had succeeded in hiding them from his daughters, managing always to reach his room before the acute stage of the attack came on.

Matthew was not afraid of pain. In the old days he had often cauterised his own wounds, holding the red-hot metal in the flesh till it sizzled and steamed. It was not the pain that frightened him. It was the thought of his daughters' discovering the attacks and "getting their claws into him." That was how he always thought of it. "Getting their claws into him." Taking possession of him, invading his privacies, ordering his life, making him lie in bed and consult doctors. ... One of his boasts was that he had never consulted a doctor in his life. He hated the whole tribe of them.

He had held out so far, but could he hold out to the end? He was ninety-five to-day. Old age lay before him, old age with its degrading helplessness, its intolerable dependence. A chill crept over his spirit at the thought. Then his fighting instinct came to his aid, and he threw back his head with a defiant snort like an old war-horse sensing battle. Let them do their damnedest. He was still a match for all of them.

He got out of bed and studied his reflection carefully in the full-length mirror of the wardrobe. He stooped a little more than he used to, but he had never carried his lean wiry figure very erect. His lackadaisical appearance had misled many people who had failed to reckon with the alertness of his blue eyes. Those eyes were now as alert as ever, though the lids sagged and long white eyebrows curled over them. His head was almost bald, his wrinkled skin of a greyish but not unhealthy colour. Beneath a raggy white moustache his mouth was grim, humorous, somewhat sensual. He looked an old man, feeble and stooping, but in the eyes and mouth and even in the frail bent figure there lurked something indomitable.

He had his bath, dressed, then went into the adjoining room, which had once been his dressing-room and was now his sitting-room. Neither Catherine nor Charlotte nor any of the maids were allowed to enter his rooms without his permission. Gaston alone dusted, tidied, and cleaned them. That again was a constant grievance of his daughters'. They would hover about the open door, trying to discover signs of neglect that would give them excuse for insisting on the right of entry.

But Gaston was too clever for them. Even Catherine's keen eye could not find a speck of dust or so much as a mat out of place, for Gaston, despite the lawless life he had led, had a cat's love of cleanliness. Charlotte was easy-going, and, left to herself, would have established friendly relations with Gaston, but Catherine and Gaston had hated each other from the moment they met. Gaston's very appearance was in Catherine's eyes an affront to the whole

4

household. She prided herself generally on her servants' appearance. Her maids were comely without achieving actual prettiness (Catherine distrusted actual prettiness in maids), studiously correct and respectful in manner. Her father's valet should have been a neat, submissive little man, who would have co-operated with her in managing Matthew for his own good, not this monstrosity who encouraged the old man's obstinacy and, as she frequently complained, "gave her the creeps" whenever she looked at him.

Indeed, their first sight of him always astonished visitors, and Catherine's thin lips would tighten as she explained shortly: "An old servant of my father's."

Charlotte, on the other hand, had a habit of sentimentalising everything around her.

"He's a dear old man," she would say. "My father saved his life in Africa, and he refused to leave him afterwards. He's most pathetically devoted to us all."

And she would actually see him as a dear old man, most pathetically devoted to them all, till she next met him, and his one eye would shoot a gleam of malicious triumph at her from its drooping lid. For his continued presence in the house was a triumph, and they were all aware of it. Catherine had fought unavailingly for years to get rid of him. She frequently gave him notice, more to relieve her own feelings than with any other object, for she knew that he would blandly disregard it. Occasionally she tried to provoke him to some open insolence, which her father could not overlook, but she never succeeded in breaking down his defences of ironic suavity.

As Matthew entered the room, Gaston was taking the breakfast tray from a housemaid at the door. He never permitted any of the other servants even to set foot in the room, and his anger, if he found that they had done so, was the more terrifying as it was expressed by hideous grimaces and unintelligible curses.

He straddled back to the room, set the dishes upon the table, and pulled out the old man's chair. Then he whipped off the dish-covers and, seeing that the sun fell on his master's face, went over to the window to draw the curtains slightly forward. His clumsy bow-legged figure moved with astonishing silence and agility about the room.

It was a formidable meal to which the old man sat down—steak and tomatoes, bacon and eggs, hot roll, toast, butter, marmalade, and coffee.

In the days of his wanderings he had often lived contentedly on coarse biscuits and tinned beef—and at times on little enough of those—but all his life, when circumstances allowed, he had been gourmand and gourmet combined. On returning home to settle down, he had dismissed Harriet's cook, whose professional horizon was bounded on all sides by rice pudding and shepherd's pie, and had set to work to find one more to his own liking. He had finally engaged a thin dyspeptic woman who had been trained by a well-known French chef, and who gave even to the preparation of an ordinary family dinner an almost fanatical zeal.

Harriet was aghast when she heard how much salary he had arranged to pay her, but she shrugged her shoulders and said nothing. Beneath Harriet's intolerance and narrowness of outlook was a certain shrewdness, and from the beginning some instinct had taught her to avoid conflict with her husband.

The old man ate voraciously for a few minutes, drained his coffee cup, then leant back in his chair to survey the room.

The warm sunshine and the strong coffee had given him an exhilarating sense of well-being and confidence. Gone were the vague fears of old age that had troubled him a few minutes ago. He was an old man, but he wasn't the sort of old man they could relegate to the chimney corner. Everyone who knew him was slightly afraid of him, in spite of—or perhaps because of—the fact that he seldom lost his temper. And he was hale and hearty enough. He had never had a day's illness in his life. . . .

Gaston poured out another cup of coffee, but the old man still leant back in his chair, surveying the room. It was the only room in the house that failed to conform with the Victorian ideal. It was devoid of all superfluous ornaments, swept clean—despite Catherine's protests—of the table-covers and vases and

6

antimacassars that broke out like a rash over all the other rooms. The furniture consisted of the battered mahogany table on which the old man was breakfasting, his shabby leather arm-chair, its once smooth brown surface worn to a fawn fluffiness, another less shabby arm-chair that the old man never used, a leather sofa, and a writing-table. Along the walls ran low bookcases with open shelves, containing a strange assortment of books—books on travel, technical books on gold prospecting, biographies, a few books of poetry, a large number of French novels of the less reputable kind.

These last were prominently displayed, chiefly for Catherine's benefit, lying on top of the bookcases, on the window sill, and on the writing-table. The old man took a mischievous delight in shocking his eldest daughter.

He lived mostly in this room, seldom appearing in the elaborately furnished drawing-room downstairs, over which Catherine and Charlotte presided. Here he would read, dream, smoke, or play backgammon or poker with Gaston.

This last shocked Catherine more than anything.

"Father, dear," she said reproachfully, "there's no need for you to play games with a *servant*. If you'd like a game of cards any time, we can ask the Vicar in and have a nice quiet game of whist."

Catherine, who was aggressively "churchy," was continually trying to bring Matthew into the fold of St. Adrian's, on whose Council she was a redoubtable figure. Once indeed she had managed to inveigle him into a private interview with the Vicar, which she had vaguely hoped would transform him into a regular churchgoer. Matthew found his visitor a quiet, likeable little man, obviously ashamed of Catherine's manœuvre and determined not to presume on it. They had talked together on impersonal topics quite amicably for an hour or so, but the meeting had never been repeated.

Gaston was bringing in his post now. Nothing of much interest. Bills, receipts, his copy of *Le Journal*. He detested English newspapers but read *Le Journal* through every day.

As he was opening it, there came a knock at the door, and Gaston stepped into the corridor, holding the door almost closed behind him. The old man could hear his daughters' voices, arguing, expostulating; then Gaston's, suavely respectful. Gaston returned, his one eye gleaming triumphantly.

"It was Mrs. Moreland and Miss Charlotte," he explained. "They wanted to see you. I said you had not yet finished your breakfast."

To his master, whom he adored, Gaston spoke curtly, seldom even according him the conventional "sir," but to his master's daughters, whom he hated, he was always obsequiously respectful.

Matthew nodded.

A moment later he heard their voices in the garden, and, though he had not yet finished his breakfast, he rose from the table on an impulse and went over to the window to look at them. Charlotte was scattering crumbs upon her bird table on the lawn (it was typical of Charlotte that she fed the birds in midsummer because it was pleasant to go into the garden to do so, but generally omitted it in winter because then it was cold and wet), while Catherine, standing by, gave voice to her grievances in sharp clear tones. Matthew caught the words "father" . . . "that man" . . . "intolerable." . . .

He stood watching them. . . .

Strange that Charlotte, fat, imperturbable, absorbed in her domestic routine of jam-making, fruit-bottling, pickling, preserving, tradesmen's books, and spring cleaning, should be the spinster; and that Catherine, tall, angular, prim, and intolerant, should be the married woman. Catherine, however, despite her primness and angularity, was good-looking, with well-turned features, a slightly Roman nose, and fine brown eyes. Her mouth spoilt her, of course. It was small and pinched, as if in constant disapproval.

At the thought of Catherine's marriage a grim smile flickered beneath old Matthew's raggy moustache. Her husband, James Moreland, had been dominated from childhood by his mother, a woman after Catherine's own heart, narrow, unimaginative, rigidly self-righteous. His mother and Catherine had tacitly arranged the match between them. His mother had considered Catherine a suitable wife for James, and Catherine had considered James a suitable husband for herself. James had had no say in the matter. For twenty years he was as completely under Catherine's thumb as he had been under his mother's. For twenty years he remained to all appearances the pious youth who had been handed over by a dominating mother to a dominating wife. He had figured largely upon all the local committees connected with good works. He never smoked or drank or used bad language. Like Catherine he frequently expressed disapproval of the loose tendencies of modern times. Then he had had a stroke, and for the next five years he had lain in bed, his limbs paralysed but his tongue loosened. For the stroke had apparently destroyed, not only his fear of Catherine, but also the inhibitions that had formerly held him in bondage. And thereupon James Moreland, churchwarden, member of various societies for the suppression of ungodliness in every form, an authority upon correct procedure in all matters ecclesiastical, showed himself suddenly the most lewd and ribald of libertines. Lying helpless in bed, he would pour forth an apparently inexhaustible flow of stories that made Catherine turn purple with ineffectual rage. James, who had once trembled at her displeasure, now merely laughed at it. His face lost its narrowness and sharp contours, becoming rotund and jovial.

Matthew had formerly avoided his son-in-law, but now he began to cultivate him. For James, with his inhibitions gone, was good company. It afforded the old man sardonic amusement to imagine by what subterfuges he had acquired his secret store of knowledge during those long years of apparent subjection to his wife's rule. Business trips to Birmingham and Manchester had, of course, often cloaked visits to Paris. He had not infrequently sat, he told Matthew, under Catherine's very nose, reading French novels inside the binding of the Parish Year Book. Matthew lent him such French novels of doubtful repute as he had not already read, and the two of them passed many hilarious hours together. Then, to Catherine's secret relief, James died, and Catherine, suffering from that feeling of frustration that assails a managing woman when there is no one at hand to manage, decided to return to what she called the shelter of her father's roof. Old Matthew, with only the easy-going Charlotte in attendance, was indeed the obvious outlet for her energy. She returned in the role of disconsolate crêpe-hung widow that she had assumed upon James's death. The role was not consciously insincere, for, with that strong-mindedness which had always been her most marked characteristic, she had completely wiped the last five years of James's life from her memory. She remembered the quiet little man who had obeyed her implicitly for twenty years, not the ribald libertine who had outraged her sense of decency for five.

Her possessiveness, thwarted for so long by the transformed James, turned with renewed force upon Matthew. But Matthew was a match for her. And James was his chief weapon. At a reference to James's later period Catherine would retreat promptly and in good order from any position she had taken up. To do Matthew justice, he never made such a reference till Catherine had deliberately opened hostilities.

He returned to his breakfast and *Le Journal*. Gaston had cleared away the bacon and eggs, and had placed before him one of Cook's freshly made rolls, warm from the oven. Fresh roll, golden country butter, home-made marmalade. ... Old Matthew savoured them with lingering enjoyment.

At last he had finished, and Gaston cleared the table, putting the tray on the service wagon in the corridor outside. Almost immediately came Catherine's sharp imperious tap at the door.

"Let 'em in, Gaston," said old Matthew.

Chapter Two

GASTON opened the door, and Catherine entered, followed by Charlotte.

"Many happy returns of the day, father," said Catherine, kissing the air near his right ear. "You slept well, I hope?"

Matthew, grunting affirmation, presented his left ear to Charlotte, who pressed a full moist kiss upon his cheek.

"*Dear* father!" said Charlotte. "This is a very happy day for us all."

She smiled mistily upon him, seeing him as a lovable old man, mild, affectionate. So vivid was the picture in her mind that she almost saw a patriarchal white beard covering his aggressive chin and descending to his waist. The phrases "the evening of his day," "the sweet serenity of old age," "the gentle radiance of a well-spent life," flashed through her mind. She continued to smile mistily. . . .

"Now, father——" began Catherine.

"Sit down, my dear," old Matthew interrupted her, drawing forward his own arm-chair, though he knew quite well that she never sat in arm-chairs. He had exquisite manners and frequently used them to keep his eldest daughter at bay. She took her seat on the upright chair at the table where he had breakfasted. Charlotte stood by the window, looking down at the garden, her thoughts a lush tangle of sentimentality.

An old-world garden (Charlotte adored the expression "old-world") . . . the dear old home in which they had all grown up . . . the home in which dear father had lived (with intervals) ever since he married dear mother . . . and now he had reached a serene old age, the evening of life. . . .

"Father——" began Catherine again, rather sharply.

Again he interrupted her, moving a chair forward for Charlotte. "My dear . . ." he said.

Charlotte sat down, realising that he himself would not sit while she stood. The misty smile increased in mistiness. . . . Such beautiful old-world courtesy, such loving devotion to them all. . . .

Not till she had sat down did the old man take his own seat in his shabby leather arm-chair.

Catherine was frowning impatiently. He had deliberately made such a formality of their visit that she had almost forgotten what she had intended to say. Or rather, what she had intended to say immediately on coming into the room, seemed now hardly worth saying. But she set her lips grimly and said it.

"Father, I was looking at your breakfast tray outside. Really, I don't think you ought to have those heavy breakfasts now. A brown bread roll and milk would be much better for you. I've often told Cook not to prepare those heavy meals for your breakfast. I told her that at the most a little boiled fish . . ."

"She obeyed you, my dear," said the old man in a tone of ironic politeness. "You mustn't blame her. I sent it down again. Gaston orders my meals."

She flushed with exasperation, but continued stubbornly:

"I'd never *dream* of eating such a breakfast as you had to-day. A little brown bread and butter and marmalade and one cup of weak China tea is all I ever have, and I'm sure I look and feel perfectly well."

"I congratulate you on your régime and its success," said the old man suavely.

Catherine drummed her fingers on the table, her whole figure tense with irritation. He was so maddeningly obstinate. . . . James had been so different, so easy to manage, so ready to agree with her. Then she swerved away from the memory of the meek dutiful James, lest it should escape her control and extend to the James who had been neither meek nor dutiful. Her drumming fingers touched the paper that lay outspread on the table. She glanced down at it, and the lines round her mouth deepened. To Catherine the French language in any connection whatever suggested immorality.

"There's an excellent leading article in this morning's *Morning Post*," she said. "I meant to bring it with me. I'll send it up later."

"That's good of you," he said, "but, as you know, I never read the *Morning Post*."

"It would do you more good than those French newspapers."

"Doubtless you are right, my dear."

His blue eyes mocked her from beneath their bristling white eyebrows.

She was like Harriet in many ways, he was thinking, but she lacked Harriet's shrewdness. Harriet had never joined issues unless she were confident of victory. Catherine, dignified, obstinate, imperceptive, would return again and again to a hopeless attack. She had no sense of proportion, and Harriet, for all her narrowness, had had a certain sense of proportion.

"The Vicar's lent me a book that I'd like you to read, father," she was saying resolutely. "It's a most interesting account of the way the Church is tackling the slum problem."

Charlotte turned dreamily from the window. She had been listening only vaguely to the interesting conversation that dear father and dear Catherine were having about the *Morning Post* and the slum problem. She had been looking down at the garden, creating an imaginary scene in which dear father had played Hide-and-Seek with her among those bushes when she was a little girl. He had been so fond of his children. At least she supposed he had. In Charlotte's mind real memories had been so completely ousted by imaginary memories that hardly a single one remained. . . .

But she mustn't waste any more time in dear father's snug little den, though of course he loved having her there. She had a busy day in front of her.

"Well," she said, "I must be going to see about this party. . . ."

And suddenly old Matthew remembered his birthday party. He was going to have the whole of his family to dinner to-night. He had suggested it himself on an impulse, and Catherine had disapproved of the idea from the first. It was Catherine's disapproval, of course, that had made him resolve to carry the arrangement through in the face of her opposition, despite the fact that his first enthusiasm had waned somewhat as the day drew near. He was really too old for dinner parties, though he would not have admitted it to anyone. He preferred to sit by the fire in the evening, to doze or dream or read or play poker and back-gammon with Gaston.

But he and Catherine had had the most protracted battle over Stephen. Stephen was the old man's grandson. His father, George (Matthew's elder son), had died of influenza a fortnight after his wife Anne in 1927. Catherine always spoke of their deaths as "merciful," because they took place before Stephen met Beatrice Ware. Stephen and Beatrice had been living together on a farm in Wiltshire now for two years, living of necessity "in sin" because Beatrice had a husband whose meteoric career as a drunkard and spendthrift had ended abruptly in a mental home. Catherine insisted that Stephen was now "dead" to them. Matthew had always found Stephen slow and stupid, but Catherine's attitude had irritated him so much that he had insisted upon giving the dinner party chiefly in order to invite to it Stephen and Beatrice, whom he had never seen. He had issued his ultimatum with his usual air of sardonic politeness.

"I invite whom I please to my own house, Catherine, but I have no wish to cause you unnecessary pain. If you don't wish to meet any of my guests, of course you need not do so. You could perhaps go to James's people for that night?"

She had made no further objection, only pursing her lips whenever the subject of the dinner party was mentioned.

"So good-bye for the present, father dear," said Charlotte brightly. "I'll try and find time to peep at you again later on."

She waved a plump hand and withdrew. Old Matthew remained standing, as a hint to Catherine, which, however, she disregarded.

"I wondered if you'd like to have the Vicar to your dinner party to-night, father," she said.

"A kind thought, my dear," said Matthew, "but surely somewhat late in the day. For the Vicar, I mean."

"I think he's free, and I think he'd come," went on Catherine.

"I consulted him about Stephen and that woman, and he said that in the circumstances I wasn't justified in staying away from your birthday party, though of course he doesn't condone sin."

"I hope not, indeed," said old Matthew, assuming a righteous air.

"But I think it would be nice to have him," persisted Catherine.

"It's a family party, my dear."

"The Church should be represented at all family gatherings."

"You shall represent it, my dear. I can think of no one more adequate."

"Don't be so absurd, father," said Catherine sharply. "And I'm sure Enid would like to meet him, because she said that Mrs. Markson had been asking her about the Wantage schools for her daughter, and she knew nothing about them. The Vicar would be able to tell her."

"Wantage," said the old man dreamily. "James once told me a good limerick about Wantage. How did it go now?... 'There was a young lady of Wantage ...'"

Catherine furled her banners and withdrew hastily but in good order.

"Well, I'd better go and help Charlotte now. We've a lot to get through this morning. Rest as much as you can, remember."

She swept out of the room with dignity unimpaired.

The old man took a pipe from the mantelpiece, lit it, and sat down again on the shabby leather arm-chair, moving it slightly so that it should stand in the full light of the sun, which now poured with increasing strength through the open window.

The comfort of it seemed to steal through his old body, enriching his blood, giving warmth to his very bones. Ninety-five. He was ninety-five to-day. Despite himself he could not help feeling rather excited at the thought. His mind went back over his life, trying to patch together its inconsequences, to make something coherent of it. His memories of his boyhood were vague and episodic. His mother had died when he was a child, and he remembered only a handsome, rather severe-looking woman, whom he associated with feelings of awe rather than affection. His memories of his father were clearer. He had been a charming indolent man, who, inheriting a small estate that was growing more impoverished each year, had lived in a world of make-believe, refusing to face realities. Matthew's boyhood had been spent to the correct accompaniment of nurses, ponies, tutors, and public school, while his father's affairs became daily more entangled. Finally, rather than face bankruptcy proceedings, he had committed suicide, leaving Matthew at seventeen to face the world penniless and alone. Matthew had dropped the shackles of respectability without regret. Even as a child there had been in him a strain of lawlessness that had caused his parents some anxiety. He made his way out to Africa, picking up a living by various and sometimes strange means. He consorted with tramps and outcasts. He took part in several rather shady transactions. He killed a man in a fight in a hotel at Bulawayo and lay in hiding for a month afterwards. He had innumerable women, mostly of a flashy, dare-devil type. One had tried to kill him with a knife, and he still bore the scar on his chest. Through all his adventures he was upheld by a surging, full-blooded joy of life. Once he had found his feet he made money easily and spent it as easily. In 1869 he joined a small party of diggers on the banks of the Vaal river, and he had made his fortune and returned to England before the real diamond rush began.

He never knew what had made him choose Harriet as a wife. It may have been that something about her recalled faint memories of his mother. It may have been that an old unsuspected heritage of respectability, frustrated for so long, found outlet in his marriage. It may have been that the marriage appealed to that incalculable streak of humour in him. Certainly, when he left her, as he did for long periods, to racket round the world again, taking hairbreadth risks of life and fortune, the thought of his family at home, living in an ultra-respectable atmosphere of church-going, parish visiting, and At Home days, vaguely amused him.

Harriet bore him six children in less than eight years, performing that duty with the same efficiency and calm dignity with which she performed all her other duties. In 1886 he returned to Africa in time to take his part in the gold rush. He entered into the adventure with his old zest, winning and losing several fortunes in quick succession, always retaining his exuberant joy of life. He took part in the Jameson Raid and in the South African War. After that he began the series of travels from which he sent home the curios that stood on the bedroom mantelpiece. Towards the end of his married life he had spent more time in England, but even then his home had seen little of him. He rushed about England (with Gaston always in close attendance), involved in innumerable hare-brained schemes, some of which abutted dangerously on the shady side of the law. A hundred times his affairs trembled on the brink of ruin, but his luck held out, and he was a comparatively rich man when he retired. On returning for occasional visits home, he had never failed to bring presents for his wife and children—Catherine, Charlotte, Margaret, George, and Richard (the youngest, Penelope, died in infancy)—though he seldom gave them a thought when he was away from them. He was not fond of children, and in surrendering his own to Harriet's upbringing he felt that he had relinquished all further claim on them.

Except for his long absences from home, which she never appeared to resent, Harriet had few causes of complaint against him. Having chosen her as his wife, he treated her with unfailing deference, giving her undisputed sway over the household. She never knew the real man, of course, but probably she never wished to know the real man. He had given her a home to manage, children to bring up, an established position in the town in which she lived. By doing that, he had done all that was expected of him. In return she showed him the conventional obedience of the Victorian wife, which, however, he was careful not to try too far. After her death, old age seemed gradually to lay its hand on him. One by one he let go his schemes, and made his permanent home at Greenways, the Victorian house just outside Danesborough that Harriet had chosen as their home before their marriage.

His mind searched back into the past, and, suddenly, as if a dam had been broken, a torrent of disconnected memories began to crowd upon him—a girl in Rio de Janeiro, who had nearly poisoned him by putting a love potion into his coffee; a tramp just outside Jo'burg, who, spending the night in the same ditch as Matthew, had drawn a volume of Horace from his bundle of rags and sat placidly reading it by moonlight; the captain of a cargo ship on which Matthew had worked his way to Hong Kong, who had gone mad suddenly and murdered several of the crew; a drunken miner, who had lurched into a hotel at Kimberley and, throwing a diamond as big as a marble on to the counter, had demanded a champagne bath; a captive witch doctor, who had escaped from prison, leaving the knot of his bonds still tied and the door still locked.

The room seemed to be full of people, crowding upon him, suffocating him. An odd terror possessed him. He rose with an effort and, going over to the bookcase, took out the copy of *Arabia Deserta* that he had been reading the night before. The austere unemotional prose always soothed and stimulated him:

An hour after middle night we halted in a deep place among the dunes; and, being now past the danger of the way, they would slumber here awhile. Rising before dawn we rode on by the Wady er-Rummah; which lay before us like a long plain of firm sand, with much greenness of desert bushes and growth of ghrottha: and now I saw this tree in the daylight to be a low weeping kind of tamarisk. The sprays are bitter rather than—as the common desert tamarisk—saline: the Kasîm camels wreathe to it their long necks to crop mouthfuls on the march. The fiery sun soon rose on the Nefûel horizon: the Beduins departed from us towards their menzil; and we rode forth in the Wady bottom, which seemed to be nearly an hour over. I heard then a silver descant of some little bird that, flitting over the desert bushes, warbled a musical note which ascended on the gamut and this so sweetly that I could not have dreamed the like.

The sound of the opening of the door interrupted him. He looked up sharply.

Gaston entered, holding something beneath his coat. Closing the door, he brought out a small struggling cat, its right side almost torn away.

"Stable cat," he announced succinctly. "He has been fighting. Mrs. Moreland says have him destroyed, but he is a nice cat."

Matthew took it upon his knee, and, as soon as the little creature felt the gentle old hands upon it, its struggles ceased.

"Get some hot water," said Matthew.

"Nice little cat," said Gaston again as he went into the bedroom.

Matthew's hands continued their careful explorations. The glaze of fear left the greenish-yellow eyes.

Gaston returned with the hot water.

"No ribs broken," said Matthew. "He'll be all right."

"Mrs. Moreland say have him destroyed."

"Dam' nonsense!" said Matthew.

They laid the cat upon the hearth. Gaston brought a bottle of strange-smelling liniment from his room, and together the two old men washed and dressed the wound. Often they had tended their animals' hurts like this in the years of their wanderings.

"Remember that dog you had called Hector," said Gaston, looking up, "the one that fought with the leopard? Four ribs broken, he had, hadn't he?"

"Aye," said old Matthew.

Then the telephone bell began to ring.

Chapter Three

MARGARET rang him up first. Her voice sounded, as always, clear and musical, with a faint underlying hint of weariness.

"Many happy returns of the day, father."

"Thank you, my dear."

"How are you?"

"Splendid."

"Well, I'll see you to-night. Don't get overtired. . . . Good-bye."

"Good-bye."

Margaret was not one of those women who never know how to bring a telephone conversation to an end. Old Matthew had always liked her the best of his children, though he had never known her well. He suspected that no one had ever known Margaret well. A passionately reserved child, she seemed to have forged an impregnable armour for herself against the world before she was out of the nursery. She had been the beauty of the family, with blue-black hair, violet eyes, a fine pale skin, and exquisitely moulded lips. Even now, though she was over sixty and had a grandchild of seventeen, she was still beautiful, still wore that look of rather disdainful fastidiousness that she had worn as a girl, still carried her slender figure gracefully erect. Her lips had lost their expression of wistful sweetness and were set in a line that was hard and rather bitter, but they were still lovely.

Old Matthew sometimes felt slightly remorseful about Margaret. She had been sacrificed so ruthlessly to Harriet's ambition. From the beginning Harriet had destined her beauty to that Victorian ideal, a "good match," and Victor Lessing, rich, handsome, well connected, had been marked down as her husband before the girl had even met him. But—Margaret herself had not been unwilling. Young, inexperienced, romantic, cloistered in unnatural seclusion, for Harriet kept her daughters under strict and constant supervision, she had been carried away by the man's extraordinary good looks. Later, his weakness and sensuality showed plainly enough in his face, but in those early days the glamour of youth still hid them.

Helped and encouraged at every turn by Harriet, he had swept her off her feet. She had lived in a roseate dream, from which she had awakened abruptly to find herself tied for life to a shifty wastrel.

A woman less sensitively proud might have borne with him more easily, but to Margaret marriage with a thoroughgoing villain whom she could have hated would have been less intolerable than marriage with a man she could only despise. Her reserve had hardened quickly into bitterness, and when he died, twenty years later, she had felt neither sorrow nor relief. . . . To her he had died a few months after their marriage.

Her son Harold had inherited his father's good looks, together with his conceit and slightly pompous manner. These were combined, in Harold, with a diffidence and self-distrust that had never troubled Victor, but that nevertheless had their roots, too, in vanity.

Matthew had never cared for the boy, and he suspected that to Margaret he had been as great a disappointment in some ways as his father, though his career had been eminently respectable, and he was now one of Danesborough's leading solicitors. He had married young, choosing, with unusual perspicacity, a good-tempered, stupid little woman who had adored him consistently from their first meeting till her death two years ago.

Harold, who had a fair histrionic talent, had played the role of disconsolate widower to the admiration of the whole town, completing it in the usual way by marrying again before the year was out. Ruth, of course, had been the ideal wife for him, but old Matthew, who watched his family pretty shrewdly despite his detachment, felt less certain about Helen. She was, he suspected, too much like Margaret to suffer Harold gladly. Moreover, her engagement to Philip Messiter had been broken off only a fortnight before she became engaged to Harold—a fact rather suggestive of Harold's having "caught her on the rebound," as the gossips said. Harold's daughter, the seventeen-year-old Penelope, probably formed a factor in the situation, but what sort of a factor old Matthew was not quite sure.

Margaret lived with her unmarried daughter, Enid, just outside the town in the rather pretentious country house that Victor had chosen. Enid was vivacious and popular, and Charlotte often said how fortunate Margaret was to have such a daughter to help keep her young and cheerful. It was Enid who was speaking on the telephone to him now. She had evidently taken the receiver from her mother's hand. Her voice sounded, as usual, hearty and unnecessarily loud.

"Hello, grandfather. Are you still there?"

"Yes."

"Heartiest congrats. What does it feel like to be ninety-five?"

Her resonant laugh came crackling over the wires.

"Pretty much the same as it did to be ninety-four," replied the old man.

"Oh, don't tell *me*! I bet you're as proud as Punch. It's simply *great*, isn't it?"

He could imagine her, large, blonde, handsome (for she had her share of Victor's good looks), her unfashionable Venus de Milo figure looking bulky and clumsy despite its careful tailoring, smiling animatedly into the telephone, while Margaret stood near, her brow wearing that slight frown that Enid's exuberance always brought to it. He sometimes wondered if Enid ever guessed how much she jarred on her mother.

"I hope you'll have a simply topping day," she went on.

Enid, of course, was one of those women who can never stop talking into a telephone once they have begun.

"Thank you, my dear. Good-bye."

"Oh, don't go just yet. Tinker wants to kiss his paw to you down the telephone and wish you——"

"Good-bye, my dear," said the old man firmly, and replaced the receiver.

Pity the girl hadn't married. She must be well over forty now. A fool, but not really a bad sort. With a husband like Victor Lessing, Margaret was lucky to get off so easily in her children. They were both fools, but Victor had been more than a fool.

The telephone bell was ringing again. Matthew took up the receiver.

It was Richard this time. His pleasant, cultured, hesitating voice seemed faint and far-away after Enid's heartiness.

"That you, father? . . . Many happy returns. I didn't know whether to ring up or come along, but Catherine said you ought to be kept quiet this morning."

"Catherine be damned!" snapped the old man irritably. "I'm not in my second childhood yet."

"Of course not, of course not. She didn't mean that. . . . Look here, I'll come round now at once, shall I? Or do you think perhaps I'd better wait till a little later? Are you going out? . . . Well, don't stay in for me, but I'll come round some time this morning, and if you're out I'll wait for you."

He sounded, as usual, terrified of committing himself even on so small a detail as a visit to his father. The slightest decision meant to Richard hours of vacillation, of restless uneasy swinging to and fro between alternatives. Above all, he dreaded responsibility of any sort. He shielded himself from it carefully, building up elaborate defences behind which he lived, fraying his fine spirit to shreds over the veriest trifles.

"Yes. Come along when you like," said Matthew. "I shall probably be in."

"You wouldn't like . . . Look here, I could come and lunch with you if you'd care to have me. . . . Is anyone else coming? Or perhaps I'd better not, as you're having such a crowd of us to-night. What do you think?"

He could imagine Richard at his end of the telephone, small and square and immaculately neat, his face wearing that look of comical distress that it always wore when the need of any decision presented itself to him.

"Just as you like," said Matthew rather dryly. "I shall be in to lunch, and no doubt there'll be enough food for you if you come along. . . ."

"Of course, of course. Well, look here. . . . Perhaps I'd better not if Mrs. Perrot's ordered my lunch here. I'll find out and let you know, shall I? It was stupid of me not to have found out before I mentioned it. . . . I'd love to come, of course, and I daresay whatever it is would keep till to-morrow, in any case. . . ."

Richard, in his charming little refuge of a sitting-room, among the first editions and antiques that he had collected so carefully and with such unerring taste, working himself up into a fever over the question of whether he should lunch with his father or not, Mrs. Perrot probably hovering solicitously outside the door, anxious only to save him from this torment of indecision. . . . For Mrs. Perrot, Richard's landlady, was his most loyal and devoted ally in his fight against reality. She protected him zealously, making for him all the decisions affecting his daily life, inventing a thousand fictions to save him from the bugbears of responsibility and effort.

The anxious hesitating voice continued: "I'll ask Mrs. Perrot if she's made any definite arrangement for lunch, and if she hasn't——"

Matthew took pity on him.

"You'd better not come in any case," he said firmly. "I daresay Catherine and Charlotte will have enough to see to with to-night."

He heard a faint sigh of relief.

"I suppose so. . . . Well, I'll come round some time this morning to see you."

"Very well. Good-bye."

"Good-bye."

Matthew returned rather thoughtfully to his chair. Richard had been the most promising of his children. George, the other son, had been steady, hardworking, level-headed, but Richard, even as a child, had been brilliant. Everyone had prophesied a distinguished career for him. Certainly his record at school and college had justified the prophecy. He had won every prize for which he had entered. The scholarship from Danesborough Grammar School to Harrow, from Harrow to Cambridge, had been taken almost as a matter of course. The double first at Cambridge seemed to be only the beginning of the triumphal progress to which he was destined. And then quite suddenly it had all fizzled out. There was some ingrained streak of indolence in him, inherited probably from Matthew's father, that had had no chance against the "tumult and the shouting" that had accompanied his school and college successes. He needed someone always at hand to spur him on, to encourage, applaud, inspire. School and college had provided the right atmosphere, the right touch of mingled compulsion and encouragement. Without it he became suddenly like a pricked balloon.

It had been agreed that he should read for the bar after leaving college, but he decided to take a holiday abroad first. It was a reasonable enough decision, for he had worked very hard for his degree examination. He took, however, a longer holiday than he had intended. He wandered about Europe, visiting churches, picture galleries, and museums, picking up a desultory knowledge of several languages, reading incessantly, perfecting a taste that was naturally that of a connoisseur. When he came home people expected that he would now settle down to read for the bar, the first step in the "distinguished career." But the thought of returning to the atmosphere of study and examinations terrified him. He was already a confirmed dilettante. He decided to write. ... While he was abroad he had evolved a new theory about the origin of European art, but several more years of study and travel were necessary before he could actually start on the work. Harriet, who held the purse strings and whose ambition had early picked out Richard and Margaret as destined to enhance the family prestige—the one by his brains, the other by her beauty—objected strongly to this plan, and would probably have succeeded in forcing him back into the groove she had chosen for him, if a timely legacy from a godmother had not given him financial independence. He went abroad again, travelling, studying, following up obscure clues of language and culture.

While Matthew, the adventurer, was ruffling it in the New World, risking life and fortune at every turn, defying the law with dare-devil impudence, Richard, the scholar, was bending his shortsighted eyes over manuscripts and records in the museums and libraries of Europe.

He came home finally with a trunk full of notebooks whose contents were to be incorporated in his book. But he did not start on it at once. There were various threads to be followed up in England. He amassed a library of books bearing on the subject and set to work to read them through in his dreamy desultory fashion. At first he lived at Greenways, but Harriet, who was bitterly disappointed in him, objected to his books, to his unsociable ways, to his irregular hours, and to what she called his "finickyness" about food. He, on his side, objected with equal vehemence to her domestic arrangements—he said that her maids were perpetually turning out his room or clattering about in the passage outside—to the shepherd's pie and rice pudding that formed the staple dishes of her menus, and, though he had perhaps as little to hide as any man in England, to her habit of going through his pockets and opening his letters. They parted without rancour, and Richard found rooms in the town. It was a kind fate—or perhaps an unkind fate, according to the way you look at it—that took him to Mrs. Perrot's. Mrs. Perrot was a sort of cushion into which he sank more and more deeply as the years went by, a magic cushion of inexhaustible softness that never let him feel the hard contact of reality. Mrs. Perrot had worshipped him with a mixture of reverence and motherliness from the moment he appeared on her doorstep—shy, agitated, stammeringly asking if he could see her rooms, adding, in sudden terror lest he might have definitely committed himself to anything, that he wanted to see them for a friend.

From that moment Mrs. Perrot considered it her highest mission in life to serve and protect him. She knew no greater joy than when Richard, after partaking of one of his favourite dishes, cooked by her to a nicety and flavoured as only she could flavour a dish, would lean back in his chair, draw a deep breath, and say: "Excellent, Mrs. Perrot. Really excellent."

Richard, though he ate little, was as great a gourmet as his father.

She took him seriously, too, as a literary man. During his hours of reading the whole house was muted to a reverent silence. His sitting-room was done out regularly and thoroughly, but it was done out in the early morning by Mrs. Perrot herself, wearing bedroom slippers, tiptoeing silently to and fro, replacing everything scrupulously on the exact spot where she had found it. The books that overflowed everywhere would have annoyed some housewives, but not Mrs. Perrot. She dusted them carefully, and the fact that, peeping into them, she found them wholly unintelligible, only increased her respect for them. The years passed by quickly and uneventfully for Richard in Mrs. Perrot's house. He had intended to set to work upon his book immediately on moving in, but he finally decided that it was unwise to begin it so soon after his study of the subject. Better let the whole thing settle down into perspective first. So he proceeded to let it settle down into perspective and betook himself meantime to the study of early Castilian literature. After thirty years it was still settling down into perspective. So were various other books that Richard had planned since. Whole cupboardfuls of notebooks, in fact, their pages covered with Richard's small scholarly handwriting, were settling down into perspective. Though he still made exhaustive notes on everything he read, he had long since stopped talking about the books he was going to write. Not that he had ever talked much about them, for Richard, despite his gifts, had always been singularly modest. Latterly, he had also stopped travelling abroad. He was still deeply interested in European culture, but the discomforts of foreign travel now outweighed their interest, and Mrs. Perrot's cooking had spoilt him for hotel food.

This picture of his son flashed quickly through old Matthew's mind as he turned slowly away from the telephone, and his thin lips curved into their faintly ironic smile.... There was no contempt in the smile, for somehow it was impossible not to like Richard. He was indolent, but he was not mean. Indeed he could be extremely generous as long as his generosity involved him in no responsibility. And he was, of all the men whom Matthew had ever met, the most fastidious in mind and body. Matthew, in whose life fastidiousness had played little part, could respect it in other men. When Richard's thoughts turned to sex, if they ever did turn to sex, he did not see, as Matthew saw, a rather bedraggled procession of his old mistresses. There *had* been a woman in Richard's life—or rather, a girl—but, though there was no doubt of his love for her and hers for him, he had shirked the responsibility of marriage, and had put off proposing for so long that the girl, conscious that everyone in the town was laughing at the situation, her pride wounded beyond bearing, had accepted a rival suitor. Richard had been heart-broken, but quite definitely relieved. It was the same with his friendships. Half-unconsciously he longed for friends, and he could have had friends in plenty, for he was a pleasant companion, interesting, well read, with an attractive touch of shyness, but he shrank from intimacy, with its accompanying burden of responsibility, and he contented himself with a large circle of casual acquaintances kept rigidly at arm's length.

Still smiling faintly, the old man sat down again in his shabby arm-chair. He had certainly fathered an ill-assorted brood: Catherine, Charlotte, Margaret, George, and Richard. His grandchildren were no better assorted—Enid, Harold, and George's four children: Isabel, Stephen, Milly, and Paul. He had not seen Stephen for a long time. He was going to see him to-night. Stephen and Beatrice. He had never seen Beatrice. "That woman," Catherine always called her. . . . A good, solid, plodding, stupid sort of fellow, Stephen. Rather like George. Funny that none of his children or grandchildren or great-grandchildren had inherited the devil in him. His great-grandchildren seemed a pretty tame bunch—Harold's Penelope (called after Matthew's youngest child, who had died in infancy), Isabel's Daphne, Milly's three: Philippa, Mark, and Leslie. Paul had no children, though, like Harold, he had married twice. Brave fellow! Deserted by his first wife about a year ago, he had had the temerity to marry again last month. Anthea had been a pretty handful, and Lilian looked like being another. The old man did a swift calculation. Fifteen of them—children, grandchildren, great-grandchildren. It wasn't bad, he thought complacently. And his great-grandchildren were almost of marriageable age. He might yet live to see his great-great-grandchildren.

Gaston entered and bent over the little cat.

28

"He's asleep," said Matthew.

"He will be all right now."

"Aye," said Matthew.

The telephone bell rang again, and this time it was Daphne's voice, shy and sweet and rather breathless.

"Is that you, great-gran?"

"Yes."

"Oh, it's just——" she broke into her nervous little laugh, then went on: "We wanted to wish you many happy returns of the day. Is it dreadful of us to worry you? Aunt Catherine said she hoped we wouldn't all be badgering you over the telephone all morning, but we did so want to—Pen's here. May she speak to you?"

Penelope's voice: "Hallo, great-gran. Many happy returns of the day."

The cousins' voices were strangely alike. Both had something of nervous uncertainty in them, something suggestive of youth feeling its way timidly in an unknown world.

"Thank you, my dears," said the old man, with a softening of his usually brusque voice. "It's very kind of you."

"Oh *no*!" He didn't know which of them was speaking. "Of *course* it isn't." The nervous little laugh, so it must be Daphne. "Pen and I are going into the town to do some shopping. . . . Oh, mother wants to speak to you. Here she is."

Isabel's voice, brisk and rather high-pitched. "Is that you, grandfather? Many happy returns of the day. Run away, children. Shut the door as you go, please. . . ." A short silence during which Isabel was evidently waiting for the two girls to depart. The sound of the door closing. Then Isabel's voice again, sunk to a shocked conspiratorial note, with an undercurrent of relish.

"Have you heard, grandfather?"

"Heard what?" he snapped rather irritably.

"About Stephen. He's here."

"Where? At your house?"

"Grandfather, of *course* not. In the town, I mean."

"Well, why shouldn't he be? He's coming to my dinner party to-night."

"Yes, I know." There was a faint reproach in the lowered voice. "But he came last night."

"Speak up," snapped the old man. "I can hardly hear a word you say."

"But, grandfather dear," went on the lowered voice, "I don't want the whole *house* to hear."

"Why not?"

"Well, I told you. About Stephen. Does Aunt Catherine know?"

"Know what?"

"About Stephen. That he spent last night at the White Swan. With that woman."

"I can't say whether Catherine knows or not. I haven't asked her."

"Well, the whole *town* must know by now."

"Then you can stop muttering about it and speak up."

"No, but, grandfather, I *do* think . . . I mean, considering what people here feel about what he's done, I do think that he needn't have come flaunting himself and the woman here for a whole day before he's invited."

The old man was on the point of a sharp rejoinder when he pulled himself up. Irritating as Isabel was, one must be gentle with her. Alone of the Roystons, real tragedy had touched Isabel.

Just over a year ago her husband and two of her three children had been drowned yachting. Daphne was the only survivor.

The tragedy seemed to have changed Isabel as completely as his stroke had changed James. Before, she had been a devoted wife and mother, absorbed completely by the affairs of her home, a worshipper of that conventional respectability that was in her eyes its best safeguard. Since the tragedy she had become hard, cynical, pleasure-loving, neglecting her home, filling her life with outside interests of the more trivial kind—dress, bridge, cinemas, parties. It was curious that at this threat of invasion from the world to which Stephen and "that woman" belonged, even her voice seemed to have lost its new hard drawl and to have become the voice of the old Isabel, the fluttering mother hen.

"What harm has it done anyone?" said old Matthew. "After all, my dear, he's your own brother."

"I know, but he surely realises that we can't consider him as a member of the family at all as long as he's living with that woman. And as to the harm,"—the reproach in her voice became less tentative—"the harm was done, if you don't mind my saying so, grandfather, by your asking them in the first instance. It wouldn't have mattered so much if it had happened in term time, but with Daphne at home——"

The old man laughed dryly. It was notorious that, since the death of her husband and the other two children, Isabel had neglected Daphne shamefully, leaving her to her own devices throughout the holidays, obviously relieved when the time came for her to go back to school.

She hurried on nervously, as if she guessed the meaning of his short dry laugh.

"And there are Pen and Pippa. . . ."

"I've no doubt that Harold and Milly can look after their daughters without your help, my dear."

"Of *course*," she said. Her voice now sounded hurt and distant. "I'm sorry, grandfather, if I've taken too much upon me by ringing you up to tell you this. I only did it because I thought it my duty. After all, as a family we are respected and looked up to in the town, and one can't gloss over the fact that Stephen and this woman are——" She hesitated.

"Living in sin is the expression your Aunt Catherine uses," supplied Matthew.

She laughed, as if both exasperated and amused.

"You're in one of your teasing moods"—she sounded suddenly more human than she had sounded since she began the conversation—"so I won't talk about it any longer. I'm sorry I bothered you about it, anyway, on your birthday. I only thought you ought to know. Good-bye, grandfather dear, and once more many, *many* happy returns of the day."

She rang off, and almost at once Catherine and Charlotte entered. It was clear that they knew about Stephen. Catherine's small mouth was tightly set. Charlotte looked unhappy and bewildered. The rose-coloured spectacles through which she liked to view the world had suddenly ceased to function. Impossible, however hard one tried, to sentimentalise immorality. Generally one could ignore it, but not when it appeared on one's front doorstep like this, demanding admittance.

Catherine's eye fell upon the little yellow cat, and the corners of her mouth took a grimmer, more downward curve.

"I thought I gave orders that that animal was to be destroyed," she said.

"You did, my dear," said the old man. "I countermanded them."

Despite the courteousness of his tone, there was a steely glint in his eye, and Catherine decided to leave the little yellow cat alone. In any case she had things of greater moment to discuss.

"Stephen's here," she said.

"I know," said the old man quietly.

"He stayed at the White Swan last night."

"I know."

Something of her assurance left her. How on earth did father know? He was so secretive. It was one of his worst faults. . . .

"He's here now at the front door with the woman. They're asking to see you."

"Show them up, then."

"Listen, father," she said majestically. "Stephen did what he did deliberately, with his eyes open. You ought to make a difference between him and the rest of the family. Let me say that he can come to-night—as you've invited him—but you don't want to see him till then. Or let me say——"

"He was such a nice little boy," put in Charlotte tearfully.

"Show them up, Catherine," said old Matthew peremptorily.

"If you *must* see them, father," said Catherine, "at least see them downstairs in the drawing-room. Don't have them up here into your sitting-room. Let them understand that——"

The old man waved her unceremoniously aside and went on to the landing. Leaning over the balusters, he called:

"Come on up, my boy. Come up, both of you."

Chapter Four

THE first thing that struck Matthew about his grandson was that he had surprisingly improved. Thick-set and stocky though he was, he now held himself upright, moved easily, and looked you straight in the eye when he spoke. He had lost the sullen sheepish expression that Matthew remembered as his chief characteristic. Again Matthew's lips curved into their ironic smile beneath the raggy white moustache. Odd to think that while he was living a life of blameless respectability he had worn a hang-dog, shamefaced air, and that now, when he had outraged conventional morality, he held his head erect and met your eye without flinching. Of course, George had been partly to blame for the boy's sullen manner in the old days. George had had old-fashioned ideas of discipline and had been somewhat heavy-handed in his methods with his sons. He had always got on well enough with Paul, but between him and Stephen there had smouldered continually the secret antagonism that so often separates a father and his eldest son.

Stephen was speaking without self-consciousness or embarrassment.

"It's awfully good of you to let us come to see you, grandfather. This is Beatrice. . . . I don't think you've met her before."

Matthew turned to the woman, and the first thought that flashed into his mind was: She's better dressed than any of them. They won't like that. . . . Yet you couldn't call her "smart"—a favourite adjective of his womenkind. Her clothes were too plain, and she wore them with too easy an air. You can always tell from a woman's bearing, thought the old man shrewdly, whether she's accustomed to the sort of clothes she's got on, or whether she's dressed up for the occasion.

She put her slender gloved hand into his. He noticed that it neither clung nor lay inert in his clasp. Its pressure was as quick and friendly and unaffected as the smile that lit up her pale oval face. Breeding, thought the old man, with an odd secret thrill of pride, forgetting for the moment that she, at any rate, was an alien to his family. Breeding. They've both of 'em got it. Only breeding could have taught them just how to tackle a situation like this. And they don't even know that they are tackling a situation. They're just being themselves. . . .

"Sit down, my dear."

She smiled again faintly as she sat down on a chair by the window.

A bewildering series of impressions had flashed through old Matthew's mind since he had looked at her. She's only a slip of a girl. . . . No, she isn't even young . . . she's old. . . . Her hair's quite white. . . . No, she isn't old. . . .

He lowered himself into his own chair, motioning Stephen to the sofa.

"It's good to see you again, grandfather," began Stephen.

The old man shrugged.

"You might have come to see me any day these last two years, as far as I'm concerned," he said.

"Thank you," said Stephen simply.

It wasn't just the coming of maturity that had altered the boy. It was something more fundamental than that. It was as if he now carried in himself some deep spring of happiness that could never be tainted or dried up. It wasn't that he seemed assured, it was that he seemed—the old man searched in his mind for words—independent of everything around him. Outside things didn't matter to him any longer.

"We drove down yesterday," he was saying, "because we wanted to come and see you before this evening and thank you for asking us."

The old man grunted. He could just see the woman out of the

corner of his eye. She sat silent and motionless, making none of those little fidgety movements that women generally make. She didn't even seem to be listening to the conversation. He longed to turn his head and look at her again. He had only had that odd contradictory impression of youth and age. A young girl with white hair. He turned his head very slightly, but she was looking down at the garden and he could not see her face.

"And how's all the family?" Stephen was saying. "It's a long time since I saw anything of them."

"I don't suppose you'll find they've altered much," said Matthew. "It isn't the sort of family that alters much."

Stephen looked at him and smiled, thinking how different they all were from the old man. He never talked of his past life, but details of it had inevitably leaked out.

"None of us are like you, are we?" he said. "It's as if you'd used up all the adventuring strain in the breed and hadn't any left to hand on to us."

Again the old man grunted, not ill pleased by the remark.

"I saw that Harold had married again," went on Stephen.

"Aye."

"What's she like?"

"Helen? I don't know. . . . Harold shouldn't have chosen a woman like that. He should have stuck to Ruth's type. Everyone knew what Ruth was like."

"I suppose Pen's almost grown up now."

"Aye. Eighteen or thereabouts."

"Daphne, too. . . . I was terribly sorry for Isabel. I wrote and she answered, but——"

He stopped short. Matthew could supply the rest. Isabel's letter, though gracious enough, had let him see quite plainly that she desired no further communication with the brother whom she looked upon as a black sheep.

"Milly wrote at Christmas," went on Stephen. "I imagine she finds it pretty difficult to manage on Arnold's salary with those three children."

"She'd find it pretty difficult to manage on anyone's salary," said old Matthew. "She's a born muddler, is Milly. She's Richard without his fastidiousness and common sense. Lucky for her she married a fool. She'd have driven a sane man to drink years ago."

"How old will Pippa be now? About sixteen?"

"I suppose so."

"I see old Paul occasionally. It was a pity about Anthea. I liked her."

"Aye. Everyone like Anthea. Bar your aunt Catherine, of course. But she'd worn Paul's patience pretty thin by the time she left him."

"What's his new wife like?"

"Lilian? She's a good housewife, but not an easy woman to live with, I reckon."

The old man was talking absently, throwing sidelong glances as he talked at the woman by the window. A strange sweet excitement that he couldn't understand possessed him. He rose abruptly and took up his position on the hearthrug facing her.

"Come over here and let me look at you," he ordered curtly.

She came across the room to him, pulling off the hat that shaded her face, and stood before him for his inspection.

He placed his hands on her shoulders and looked at her in silence. Her level gaze met his steadily.

Her hair was thick and glossy, falling about her ears in soft curls, but it was silvery white; her skin was fine and delicate, of a clear transparent pallor as if a light burned through alabaster; her eyes were the deep blue of cornflowers, widely spaced with dark sweeping lashes; her lips curved into a faint enigmatic smile. Oddly enough, the white hair emphasised instead of detracting from her youth. Not more than thirty, he guessed. She held her small head so proudly that she seemed at first sight taller than she really was. His eyes travelled slowly downwards. . . . A lovely body—slender, nervous, thoroughbred. He turned suddenly to Stephen, then looked quickly away. Stephen was watching her, and, for all his experience of life, Matthew had never before seen such stark worship in a man's eyes.

Suddenly the woman stirred beneath his hands, breaking the spell that seemed to hold the three of them silent in the little room.

"Well," she said, "are you satisfied? Our hair always goes white before we're thirty. My mother's was white when she was twenty-six. I'm thirty-two."

Her voice was clear and musical, with something appealingly childish in it.

He smiled and released her shoulders with a slight pressure, then moved her chair from the window and set it next to his.

"Come and sit where we can see you," he said. "Don't hide yourself over there."

She sat down, and for a brief second her eyes met Stephen's. The look they exchanged sent an odd pang of loneliness through the old man's heart. Against his will the drab procession of the women he had loved moved dustily across his memory. He made a quick movement of revulsion as if to dismiss it.

"And how's Uncle Richard?" Stephen was asking.

"He's the same as ever," said the old man.

"Still reading up for the book he's going to write?"

"Aye."

The old man was not watching Beatrice, but he was conscious in every nerve of the graceful motionless figure beside him. Serenity, that was it. It seemed to surround her like an atmosphere. She wasn't the sort of woman to ask for pity or even sympathy, so probably only God and herself knew what she had gone through with the brute who was still officially her husband, and yet out of all the stress and turmoil of it she had brought this radiance of serenity, so that as she sat there, silent, remote, warmth and light seemed to steal from her over the old man's soul. And that odd sweet excitement that he couldn't understand still held him. His heart was beating unevenly. Beneath the horde of memories that jostled each other through his mind—innumerable adventures in love, war, business, politics—a more distant memory was stirring, a memory so elusive that, try as he might, he could not capture it. It was connected with Beatrice, somehow. He turned to her again, examining her with narrowed eyes. Striking-looking. Beautiful, perhaps. But he had met a hundred women more striking-looking, more beautiful, who had left him wholly unmoved.

What was there about this woman of Stephen's that made her different from any other woman he had ever met? It was that mysterious, incalculable something, he supposed, call it glamour if you will, that can make even ordinary prettiness, even downright ugliness, more potent than the most perfect beauty the world has ever known. Glamour . . . it informed every line, every motion, of her body. Glamour. . . . The far-off memory stirred into faint life, flickered for a moment in the shadowy corners of his mind, then vanished, leaving him with a painful sense of frustration.

Stephen was talking about his farm in Wiltshire, but the old man was not listening. Though the memory still eluded him, the excitement connected with it was deepening. He looked at the woman beside him. She had roused the ghost of this memory. Surely she could bring it to life. His eyes fastened themselves upon her, as if to wrest the secret, whatever it was, from her by force. She turned to him with parted lips.

"Yes?" he said eagerly.

"I thought you were going to say something."

"You remind me of someone," said the old man slowly. "Someone I knew a long time ago and then forgot. I can't think who it was."

She gave him her faint shadowy smile, then withdrew again into the fastnesses of her detachment.

Stephen went on talking about his farm. A sort of panic seized the old man. It seemed to him desperately important that he should remember. Feverishly he dug down into the scrap-heaps of his memory, finding things that he had lost years ago and had no desire to rediscover . . . a drunken woman with red hair who had struck him in the face in a café in Beira; sunset over the African mountains; a voice he had heard one night singing within a walled garden, agonisingly sweet. . . . Junk . . . junk . . . junk. . . . But he *must* find it. His very life seemed to depend on his finding it. In the intensity of his emotion his hands gripped the arms of his chair till the knuckles showed like bare bone.

"Beatrice has made the garden," Stephen was saying. "She has a wonderful hand with flowers. Green fingers, they call it down our way."

Again the woman turned to him with her shadowy smile, and at once it seemed to the old man that the room was full of the scent of white jasmine.

Then quite suddenly he remembered.

He had met her when he was a boy of seventeen, attending his first dance. He had never seen her before, did not know who she was, but, as their eyes met across the crowded room, this strange sweet excitement, whose ghost now held the boy's ghost, had surged over him in an irresistible flood. She was not really beautiful—a pale slender girl in a white crinoline, her shapely head wreathed in tiny rosebuds, very young and shy, with soft dark eyes and childish lips—but for the boy, at any rate, all the glamour in all the world encompassed her. He found a mutual friend to introduce him to her, and she gave him her one remaining dance. He moved in a dream, hardly knowing what he did or said, till the time came when he could claim her. As soon as the music of their dance began he approached her with beating heart and flaming cheeks, and, as he put his arm timidly about her waist, his pulses pounded deafeningly in his ears. It seemed sheer sacrilege even to touch her. As they waltzed she told him in her gentle childish voice that she was sixteen and that it was her first dance. When the music stopped he said:

"Shall we go out on to the terrace? It's quite warm."

His voice was breathless with the consciousness of his daring, but he wanted so desperately to get her away from these crowds of people. He wanted so desperately to have her for a few moments, at any rate, just to himself.

"Yes . . . I'd love to."

Her voice, too, sounded oddly breathless and urgent, as if to her also it were somehow vitally important that they should leave these chattering crowds and go where they could be alone together.

Outside, the deep blue sky was powdered with stars, and in the darkness the trees that bordered the terrace seemed like kindly shadowy giants, protecting them. They stood by the stone balustrade, the boy's eyes fixed half timidly, half ardently, on his companion.

Her sweet pale face seemed to gleam through the dusk. Her nearness sent a wave of almost intolerable ecstasy through him. His whole being worshipped her with a love that was free from the least taint of sensuality. He did not even want to kiss her. He only wanted to kneel at her feet and kiss the ground she stood on, then die for her in some romantic spectacular fashion. Her eyes met his, soft and starry with the dawning wonder of her answering love. Neither spoke. He never knew how long they stood there in the summer night looking at each other in silence. Then the music struck up again within the house.

"I must go now," she whispered, but still remained there motionless, as if held against her will by some spell.

"What's your name?" he said unsteadily. "Your Christian name?"

"Hope. What's yours?"

"Matthew."

"Matthew," she breathed softly.

Then she turned away, slowly, reluctantly, as if with an effort.

"Don't go," he pleaded.

"I must. It's the next dance."

"Tell me where you live," he said urgently. "Let me come and see you."

She gave him her address and added, "When will you come?"

"May I come to-morrow?"

"Yes, to-morrow," she whispered. "Come tomorrow. You won't forget?"

"*Forget!*" he said.

She flitted away from him through the darkness like a ghost. Except during the dance, he had not even touched her hand. He lay awake all night thinking of her, imagining that he was rescuing her from incredible dangers, dying for her in a hundred heroic ways. In his most ardent dream he only knelt before her and kissed her hand.

The next afternoon, after an hour spent on his toilet, he set out to the address she had given him. The servant who answered the door told him that Miss Hope was in bed. She must have caught a cold at the dance. The doctor said that there was a slight congestion of one lung, but it was nothing serious.

The next afternoon he set out again. By the porch door of his home grew a bush of white jasmine, and on an impulse he picked an armful of the scented blossoms, stripping the bush roughly in his haste. The same maid-servant answered the door. She took the armful of flowers he thrust at her, then burst into tears. Through her sobs she told him that Miss Hope was dead. The congestion had spread to the other lung during the night, and, though they sent for the doctor at once, she had died in the early morning.

The boy stumbled blindly away from the house, a thick black mist before his eyes. He walked for miles over the countryside, not knowing where he went, praying only for death.

He lay awake all night in sick panic, trying to face the long and dreary waste that his life must be without her. At dawn came a sudden shattering vision of her in her youth and shy sweet loveliness, and he buried his head in his pillow and wept with a child's heart-broken convulsive sobs.

In the morning he received a letter from her mother.

"She spoke of you frequently during her short illness, and just before she died she asked me to send you her love. We have put your white jasmine in the coffin with her. Will you come and see me some time?"

But he never went to see her. He shrank from going to the house again. Rebellion and misery tore at his heart. He couldn't bear it. Over and over again he told himself that he couldn't bear it. At times his dull wretchedness would quicken to a sort of madness, and he would run into the woods and lie there outstretched, beating his head against the ground. He dreaded and longed for the nights, when her memory seemed to return to him most vividly, and he would lie in torment, sometimes dry-eyed, sometimes finding relief in tears.

Then came the crash of his father's fortune and the break-up of the world he knew. He went abroad, and in the turmoil and stress of his new life he forgot the tragedy of his first love. But it had lived somewhere apart in his mind, perfect, inviolable, untouched by the sordidness that had grown up around it, waiting all these years till this answering grace and loveliness should wake it from its long sleep.

He roused himself with an effort.

"Of course, wheat-growing's a difficult proposition nowadays," Stephen was saying. "Grazing seems to be the only hope for us."

Beatrice's blue eyes were fixed on him, full of gentle solicitude.

"You're looking tired," she said. "Stephen, I think we've stayed long enough."

Yes, her voice had been like that—clear and musical, with that oddly childish inflexion. Her eyes, too, had had this same childlike gravity and candour.

Again the scent of white jasmine seemed to fill the room.

"Do you smell jasmine?" he said suddenly. "White jasmine?"

"I smell honeysuckle," said Beatrice. "That's a climbing honeysuckle just outside the window, isn't it? Perhaps that's what you smell."

He shook his head.

"No, it's jasmine ... white jasmine."

Stephen went to the window and looked out.

"There is no white jasmine that I can see," he said.

"No, of course not," said Matthew, and again that strong sweet excitement surged over him. He sat there, surrendering himself to it, hunched upon his chair, silent, motionless, an old man in the throes of a boy's first love.

Suddenly the door opened, and Catherine entered, followed by Charlotte.

"Well, Stephen," Catherine greeted her nephew distantly, then turned to Beatrice.

"How-do-you-do, Mrs. — Does one call you Mrs. Ware or Mrs. Royston?"

She's been thinking that out downstairs, said the old man to himself.

There was a slight hardening of Stephen's face, but he answered quietly, "You call her Mrs. Royston, aunt."

Old Matthew glanced at Beatrice. She gave no sign even of

having heard the words. She still wore her air of remoteness and serenity. It was Catherine, not Beatrice, who looked flushed and embarrassed by the question. A sudden exaltation seized the old man. You can't hurt her, his heart sang out triumphantly. She lives where your claws can't get at her. . . .

She was taking leave of him. The slender nervous hand lay again in his. He looked up at her and seemed to see her for a moment through a sudden mist—a young girl in a white crinoline with a wreath of rosebuds round her dark hair. Then the mist cleared, and he saw that she was Beatrice, Stephen's wife (yes, damn them, she was more a wife than thousands of legally married women).

"I hope we haven't tired you," she was saying in the voice that came from the most secret heart of his memory. He had to make a conscious effort of will to prevent the mist creeping over him again. She wasn't the girl with soft dark eyes and dark cloudy hair. Her hair was white, her eyes were cornflower blue. . . .

"Don't bother to come down with us, aunt," said Stephen.

They went out, closing the door quietly behind them.

The old man felt strangely breathless, as if he had been running for a long time. He sat there, trying to get his breath without letting Catherine see that he was in any distress. Once give her an opening and she'd be on his track, taking possession of him, "getting her claws into him."

But Catherine was in no mood to notice his symptoms. She was poking the fire viciously with a trembling hand. Her face was flushed and angry.

"It's outrageous!" she said. "If only they'd seemed *ashamed*——"

The old man gave a hoarse triumphant laugh. Catherine turned to him. What a queer noise! Father had been very queer lately. Insisting on inviting Stephen and that woman, for one thing. Old men over ninety often got queer. She must try to make him see a doctor. He ought to be made to take more care of himself. And really he ought not to have all the family business on his hands. Old men of that age often gave power of attorney to one of their children. It was best for everyone that they should. Especially if they were beginning to get queer.

43

Charlotte stood at the window, watching Stephen and Beatrice walk down the drive to the big iron gates. She still looked forlorn and miserable. Then suddenly the look of misery vanished from her face.

"After all," she said, "her husband might die any day, and then they could get married."

Chapter Five

"Poor old darling!" said Enid as she put down the receiver. "He's pretending not to be all cock-a-hoop because he's ninety-five. Ninety-five!" Her loud rather jangling laugh rang out. "I only hope I don't live to be ninety-five."

"If you do you'll probably be as proud of it as your grandfather is," said Margaret quietly, without looking up from her needlework.

Enid bent down to the small Highland terrier that had risen from the patch of sunlight on the hearthrug at the sound of his name and was standing at her feet, looking up at her and wagging his tail expectantly.

"Well, 'ickle boy Tinker, what's 'oo smilin' about? What's 'oo's 'ickle joke? Wouldn't 'oo's cross old grandfather let 'oo kiss 'oo's 'ickle paw down the telephone? It was a s'ame, it was."

The terrier wagged his tail again and returned to his patch of sunlight.

Enid began to wander restlessly about the room, whistling untunefully.

Margaret sat, her head bent over her embroidery, her whole being tense and rigid with the effort to control her irritation. It was an irritation of which she was deeply ashamed. Enid was a good daughter, dutiful, devoted. She was indeed too much devoted at times, for she would frequently give up an evening's entertainment lest her mother should feel lonely at home without her, never guessing that Margaret looked forward with secret pleasure to the peace and solitude of the hours when she was absent.

She crossed over to the mantelpiece and stood there, tapping her foot on the fender. Margaret's brows contracted sharply at the sound. She was on edge to-day, she didn't know why, and when she was on edge Enid's restlessness jarred on her intolerably. It was only a surface irritation, as she assured herself a hundred times a day. Deep down in her heart she liked and respected the girl. She was wholesome and straightforward, modest about her outstanding prowess in games and her popularity in the town.

"I'd hate to be old," said Enid, and laughed again—a harsh, self-conscious laugh. "I used to think I'd hate to be middle-aged, but I'm that all right now."

"You're only forty-two, my dear," said Margaret.

"That's middle-aged. . . . I suppose that once you're over forty you get more and more ashamed of your age till about seventy, then you suddenly begin to be proud of it. . . . When's Stephen coming, by the way?"

"Some time this afternoon or evening, I suppose."

"Aunt Catherine's *furious*. I believe she tried to get Uncle Richard to put his foot down about it. Fancy Uncle Richard putting his foot down about anything! After all, if the woman's husband's mad and they can't be married, I don't see why people need get up on their hind legs. . . . The old man himself wasn't a model husband, by all accounts."

Margaret said nothing. Something in her, irreparably hurt by her own marriage, shrank from discussion of marriage in any connection.

Enid mistook her silence for disapproval and flushed slightly. Really, mother was absurd, treating her like a child, refusing to discuss Stephen and Beatrice Ware with her, when everyone talked about that sort of thing quite openly nowadays. But Enid's irritations never lasted long. Her blue eyes were already roving speculatively round the room.

"Mother, let's alter this room round a bit, shall we? I'm so tired of it as it is. Let's try the sofa by the window."

"Just as you like, my dear," said Margaret rather wearily.

That was another of Enid's restless habits. She simply couldn't leave a room alone. She was continually changing the position of the furniture, or altering the whole scheme of decoration. Margaret, on the other hand, hated change. She thought sometimes, rather

46

guiltily, that nowadays her affection for things was stronger than her affection for people. She had come to love room after room, only to watch their contents being ruthlessly dispersed by Enid, for, as if to compensate for the secret exasperation the girl caused her, she yielded to her every whim.

At present the room was disconcertingly modern: light wood, unstained and unvarnished, chromium plating, unframed mirrors, oddly shaped chairs, impressionist pictures, mats of fantastic designs on the parquet flooring.

Margaret felt slightly ill-at-ease in it, for she had taken deep pleasure in the mellow surfaces of old wood, polished till they shone like crystal, the thick pile of the Axminster carpet, the soft tints of the water-colours that had hung on the walls. She suspected that Enid herself, solid, hearty, and matter-of-fact, did not feel really at home among its hard bright angularities. It was, she suspected, a defiant gesture in the face of middle age.

Enid had taken up her position on the hearthrug, leaning her six-foot figure against the mantelpiece.

"I suppose I ought to be getting along," she was saying.

"Where are you going?" asked Margaret.

"I've a meeting of the dramatic society at twelve."

"Oh yes . . . of course."

Enid was secretary of the dramatic society, and the best secretary the dramatic society had ever had. People never discussed Enid without using the word "capable."

"And I'm calling in to see Brenda Collin on the way."

Margaret said nothing. She disliked Brenda Collin and thought that Enid's habit of forming sentimental friendships with young women made her slightly ridiculous.

Enid strode suddenly across to the window and looked out.

"I believe that was Stephen who passed just then. . . . There's a woman with him. Quite old. She's got white hair. They're turning the corner. They must be going to Greenways. I say, they've a nerve, haven't they? They won't get much of a welcome from Aunt Catherine." She shrugged her large shoulders. "Well, I'll go and put on my bonnet."

She left the room and returned a few minutes later, in one of the well-fitting tailor mades that were the only possible wear for her figure.

"You know I'm lunching with Harold and Helen, don't you, mother?" she said.

"Yes. . . . Give them my love."

Enid hesitated.

"Won't you be lonely all by yourself? I could easily put them off, you know. They only asked me out of politeness. I could ring up and——"

"Oh no," said Margaret. Ever since she heard of the invitation she had been looking forward to the unbroken peace of the morning . . . the quiet luncheon over a book . . . the respite from having to brace up her nerves continually against Enid's boisterousness. Then she bit her lip, afraid that she had spoken too eagerly, and said more slowly, "I shall be quite all right, my dear. Of course you must go."

Enid still hovered irresolutely in the doorway.

"You see, I'm going to the Rectory tennis party this afternoon, and it does seem a shame to leave you alone for so long."

"No, dear, I shall be *quite* all right."

"I'll come home to change after lunch, of course, but you ought to rest this afternoon, so as to be your brightest and best for grandfather's beano to-night."

"I'll rest after lunch. . . . Good-bye, dear."

"Good-bye."

Enid went out, followed by the little Highland terrier. Her voice was heard in the hall.

"No, 'ickle Tinker-boy, 'oo tan't turn with Mummy to-day. Mummy's doin' to see Bwenda an' Bwenda's dot a nasty gweat big dog that eats 'ickle Tinker boys all up . . . Mummy's so sorry, darlin'. Be good 'ickle dogsie. Bye-bye."

The front door shut with a resounding slam.

The tenseness of Margaret's form relaxed and she drew a long deep breath.

Enid strode down the sunny street, thinking about Stephen and the woman who had been with him. Her white hair had shown plainly beneath the small blue hat. ... Enid felt an obscure satisfaction at the thought that the woman was old. Her own hair was slightly faded, certainly, but there were only a few scattered, inconspicuous grey hairs in it. She was in High Street now, and she threw a covert glance at her reflection in a shop window, noting her handsome, highly coloured face and large, well-proportioned figure. There was no complacency in the glance, for Enid had never admired her own style of good looks. Still—she wasn't middle-aged yet. Not really middle-aged. The tiny nagging fear sank temporarily to rest.

Passing a little hat-shop with the name "Marie" in neat gold letters over the door, she heard someone call her name and turned to see two girls coming out of it. They were both members of the local hockey club, which Enid had captained ever since she left school.

With each of them she had in the past formed one of those short-lived, passionate friendships that were her chief emotional outlet, but she was now on terms of easy camaraderie with both. Her infatuations never ended in quarrels or alienation. They drifted back gradually and naturally into the friendly acquaintanceship from which they had grown, leaving no ill feeling on either side. ("Old Enid's a bit sentimental, you know, when she gets a crush on you, but she's a real good sport, all the same.")

She greeted them in her strident jovial voice.

"Hello, Pam. ... Hello, Margery, my infant. What are you doing with yourselves?"

"Shopping, darling," said Pam. She had auburn hair and deep blue eyes. "Ordering the fish and fruit for dinner like good little girls."

"And trying on every hat in Marie's in the intervals, I bet," said Enid with another loud laugh.

"Well, we *have* just been in," admitted Margery, a slender blonde with a dazzling complexion and a provocative upturned nose. "They've got a marvellous black felt that makes me look like Greta Garbo. Except for my nose, I mean. Come in and see it, Enid darling, then you can tell Michael that it would be a sin not to buy it for me."

"You don't need me to help you wheedle a hat out of Michael," said Enid. "You could wheedle a whole warehouseful out of him in five minutes."

"I know," said the girl demurely, "but I want an excuse for trying it on again."

"You married women haven't anything to do, it seems to me," said Enid breezily, "but wander about the town shop-gazing. It's we unmarried ones who do all the work."

"Well, Enid darling, half your own family's wandering about the town shop-gazing. We've just met Pen and Daphne."

"Oh yes, the babes came home from school yesterday. I must remember to stand them an ice-cream or something."

"And Mrs. Chudleigh . . ."

"Milly? Good Lord, is she about?"

"Yes, with Pippa. We met them in Barrat's. They were getting some artificial flowers or something for Pippa to wear to-night. She's going to some sort of bean-feast, isn't she?"

"Oh Lord, the whole lot of us are. It's my grandfather's birthday, you know. He's ninety-five. He's having the whole family to dinner."

"Gosh! How grim!"

"Yes, won't it be! Aunt Catherine, Uncle Richard, Milly, and all the merry throng. Milly will be wearing the grey silk that she dyed red last year, only unfortunately it only dyed in patches. Parts proved immortal, as it were. And Uncle Richard will be on the brink of a nervous breakdown at the very thought of coming out in the evening at all. Ma Perrot will probably have put on his goloshes and tied his chest protector round his neck and slipped a hot-water bottle under his arm."

"It sounds *heavenly*. Don't die of over-excitement, will you, darling?"

"I'll try not to."

"I hope there'll be champagne."

"If it depended on Aunt Catherine there wouldn't be, but, the old man being the old man, I expect there will be. And a good brand. He knows a thing or two about wines. Too painful if it were a case of 'Roystons, Roystons everywhere and never a drop to drink.' "

They screamed with laughter.

"You're *priceless*, Enid. Go on about your family. We love hearing about it."

Enid hesitated. She wanted to make some easy, laughing reference to Stephen and the "family skeleton"—she felt that to do so would banish this odd depression that hung about her and that she connected with the glimpse she had caught of Stephen and Beatrice Ware—but the words refused to come.

"Have some coffee with us, darling," went on Pam. "There's still heaps of the morning to fill in."

"Can't, infants. I've got a date with Brenda Collin."

The vague depression vanished completely at that. Brenda might be disapproved of in Danesborough, but she was young and gay and smart and attractive, and the fact of their close friendship proved that Enid, too, partook in some degree of these qualities. She couldn't, at any rate, be frumpy and middle-aged.

"Oh, Brenda Collin!" said Margery with a little grimace. "We never see anything of you nowadays, Enid. You're always with her."

"Nonsense!" said Enid, highly delighted. "You probably see a good deal more of me than you want to. By the way, you're both joining the hockey club again in September, of course. I'm drawing up the eleven in good time."

They hesitated and glanced at each other.

"Darling, we can't this year. We're so terribly sorry."

"Why on earth not?"

"Didn't you know? Pam's presenting Humphrey with a son and heir or daughter and heiress, as the case may be, early next year."

"You sweet lamb! Are you really? But what a bore! You're the only decent centre-forward I've ever had. I tell you what I'll do. I'll put in Joan Manning for the time being, and you can rally round again next year. . . . Now what about you, Margery? You're not presenting Michael with anything, are you?"

Margery screamed a shrill denial, then fluttered her dark lashes in a way that Enid had found irresistible in the days when she had the "crush" on her.

"Enid, darling, don't be cross with poor little Margery. She loves hockey and she 'dores you, but she has got such a lot to do now she's an old married woman, and last night her nasty old husband said, 'I hope you aren't going to join that damned hockey club next year.' You see, it means Saturday afternoon, which is all the poor lamb gets at home, so he made me promise not to. Darling, we're so terribly sorry to desert the dear old club, but you do understand, don't you?"

"You're a couple of lazy little blighters," said Enid heartily, "but, as things are, I suppose I'll have to let you off."

"You're not cross with us, are you, pet?"

"Yes, I am. I sweat blood trying to get a decent hockey team together, and then you go and let me down like this."

Her mock scolding recalled the infatuation that had been one of the thrills of their adolescence, and they giggled delightedly, feeling themselves romantic care-free schoolgirls again.

"You're a horrid old bully, Enid. As if we could help our husbands being such pigs."

"Rubbish! You're a couple of mouldy little slackers, that's what it is. Anyway, I'm not letting you off altogether. I shall rope you in and make you work like blazes for the dance and entertainment in December."

"Of course, darling. We'll work ourselves to skin and bone for you."

"I can see you!"

"You wait, then. . . . Anyway, do come and have coffee with us just to show you don't quite hate us."

"I do quite hate you. . . . No, seriously, lambkins, I must fly, or Brenda will be champing. . . . Well, good luck, Pam. I suppose I must start putting away my Saturday pennies for a christening mug. Start it on hockey in good time, won't you?"

They screamed ecstatically at the joke and stood watching her as she strode away from them.

"She's a good scout, old Enid," said Pam.

But there was a note of patronage in her voice, and, promptly forgetting her, they fell to a confidential discussion of husbands and maids and tradesmen and housekeeping in general.

The warm glow that the friendly encounter had left in Enid's heart gradually faded. It was a nuisance about Pam. A good centre-forward was so difficult to get. She wanted a new right-wing, too. Her last year's right-wing had left Danesborough.

She must find out if any of the High School eleven were leaving this term, and rout them out to join the club. She seemed always to be routing out girls to join the club, and then, as soon as she'd routed them out and licked them into shape, she had to start it all over again. She enjoyed the routing out and licking into shape, and she enjoyed the infatuations that generally accompanied the process, but she was beginning to grow just a little tired of it all. Generation after generation of jolly girls, leaving school, joining the club, getting married, leaving the club. . . . Even the infatuations were beginning to lose their thrill. One sentimental schoolgirl was, after all, very much the same as another. A woman like Brenda Collin was different. . . . It was her friendship with Brenda that had made all her other friendships seem empty and colourless.

Suddenly she saw her cousin, Milly Chudleigh, with her elder daughter, Pippa, on the other side of the street. What a sight Milly looked! Really, considering the position that the Roystons held in Danesborough, it was the limit the way Milly went about dressed like a charwoman, though most charwomen nowadays managed to dress a good deal more smartly than Milly ever did. Arnold's salary, of course, must be pretty small, because, though Milly always tried to make out that his post at Derrick and Sanders' was a very important one, everyone knew that really he was only a clerk there. But it wasn't a question of money. Milly was the type of woman who would have looked dowdy whatever her husband's salary was. Her house was dreadful—the beds unmade till late afternoon, the remains of some meal always on the dining-room table, dust everywhere, nothing in its proper place. Fortunately for both of them, Arnold could see no faults in Milly even as a housekeeper. Arnold, of course, was a worm—and a self-important, conceited worm at that—but there was no denying that he made Milly a good husband. He was, as are so many worms, a paragon of virtue. He did not drink or smoke or use bad language, he gave his whole salary to Milly to muddle away on her inefficient housekeeping, and he would uncomplainingly take the general servant's place when, as so often happened, they were without one—carrying in coals, cleaning grates, scrubbing the steps. An uxorious husband, he was an overbearing, dictatorial father, and Milly, who adored him, upheld his authority, never taking the children's part against him, however unreasonable he showed himself.

Enid glanced across the street again. Pippa looked almost as shabby as Milly in her dusty crumpled school coat and shapeless school hat. Why on earth couldn't Milly buy the child some decent clothes to wear in the holidays now that she was sixteen? Under the shadow of the cheap unbecoming hat Pippa's face looked unhealthy and sullen. All Milly's household looked unhealthy. They lived chiefly on tinned food and tea.

Feeling slightly ashamed of herself for the action, Enid turned to look into Merridew's window, so that Milly should not see her and cross the road to speak to her. In order to quiet her conscience, she assured herself that she needed some new golf-gloves and had in any case meant to buy them at Merridew's. Milly had now passed on and all danger of recognition was over, but, in order to complete the quieting of her conscience, Enid went into Merridew's and bought the golf-gloves. Then she strode on down the street, whistling between her strong white teeth.

"Hallo, Aunt Enid!"

She wheeled round.

Pen and Daphne looked very smart and pretty, Pen in grey and Daphne in pale green. Their school uniforms were almost as unbecoming as Pippa's, but no one ever saw them in Danesborough. They generally went about together in the holidays, though they did not go to the same boarding school. Pippa, who attended Danesborough High School and was two years younger than Daphne and one year younger than Penelope, was excluded from the companionship more by her own will than theirs. They made frequent overtures of friendship, but she rejected them brusquely.

"Hello, my lambs!" answered Enid heartily. "So you're back in the land of the living. What are you doing with yourselves this morning?"

"Shopping," said Daphne.

She was tall and slender, with a pale oval face, heavily lashed hazel eyes, sensitive lips, and a shy uncertain smile.

"I called for Daphne," said Penelope, "and we rang up great-gran together to wish him many happy returns of the day, and then Aunt Isobel drove us out because she wanted to speak to him alone."

About Penelope, too, there was the appealing awkwardness of youth. Her tallness and thinness gave her a slightly coltish air, her grey eyes were solemn and wondering like a child's, the corners of her lips drooped wistfully.

"Probably wanted to tell him what a rotten report you've had," said Enid, turning to Daphne. "I suppose your report is rotten, by the way. I never had one that wasn't."

The two girls laughed dutifully.

"Got your best bib and tucker ready for tonight?" went on Enid in her resonant chaffing voice.

"We're going to the tennis party at the Rectory this afternoon first," said Pen.

"Oh yes, of course. We'll all be meeting there. Roystons, Roystons everywhere." She wondered whether to repeat the joke that had been so successful with Pam and Margery, decided that it was inappropriate, and went on: "When do you go back, by the way? Or is it tactless to ask so soon?"

"It is rather," smiled Daphne, "but I go back on September 18th and Pen on the 21st. It's our last term, you know. We're both leaving at Christmas."

"Good Lord! Are you really? How old are you?"

"I'm eighteen, and Pen's seventeen."

"Quite ancient, of course. . . . Well, look here, you'll both have to join the hockey club when you leave."

"Oh, *may* we? We'd simply love to."

A faint wryness invaded Enid's smile, as she looked into the future and saw them in a few years' time rather nervously saying how *terribly* sorry they were to desert the dear old club, but that now they were married . . .

"What do you play?"

"I play left-wing, and Pen plays back."

"Curse you! What I want is a good centre-forward."

"Monica Black plays centre-forward. She's at Roedean now, but she's leaving at Christmas. She lives only about two miles out of Danesborough. I'm sure she'd love to join."

"Good. I'll rout her out."

"You play centre-half, don't you, Aunt Enid?"

"Yes," said Enid absently.

"And don't you play for the county?"

"Only golf. I gave up county hockey last year. I found I hadn't time to keep it on with all my other jobs."

The admiration in their eyes lightened the vague heaviness that still hung about her spirit.

"Well, I can't stand gossiping with you children all day," she said breezily. "I'd take you to have an ice somewhere, but I've got a date this morning. We'll make it some other morning, shall we?"

"Thanks awfully. We'd love to."

"Well, I'll see you at lunch, Pen, shan't I? Bye-bye, infants."

She went on down the street with her long loose stride.

"She sets your teeth on edge sometimes, doesn't she?" said Daphne, "but she's an awfully good sort really."

Chapter Six

THE strange depression that hung over Enid's spirit refused to be dispersed. She hadn't realised that those kids were leaving school at Christmas. They would be living at home now, of course, taking their part in the adult world of Danesborough. Their presence would place her definitely and finally among the older generation. It was one thing to have young nieces away at boarding school, and quite another to have grown-up nieces meeting one wherever one went and forming the "younger set" of the town. Oh well—she shrugged her shoulders and began to whistle untunefully between her teeth.

"Hello, Enid darling! Do look at my little poppet."

A young woman, wheeling a pram, stopped beside her. Enid had a vague idea that she had once belonged to the hockey club, but could not remember her name. The pram contained a fat, unattractive-looking child.

"What a pet!" said Enid, prodding it playfully in the chest and wondering what on earth it would look like when it grew up.

"It's Auntie Enid, darling," cooed the young mother. "Say 'Auntie Enid.' Give Auntie Enid a kiss."

The child stared at Enid, pallid and expressionless. Enid bent down and kissed the flabby cheek.

"*Isn't* it a pet!" she said again with mechanical brightness.

"Who do you think he's like?" continued the mother.

Enid, repressing a desire to refer to the Zoo, said:

"Oh, my dear, I can never see likenesses in children."

"They say he's like Herbert. I'd *love* him to be like Herbert, of course."

"Yes," said Enid, trying ineffectually to remember who Herbert was. "I think he *is* rather like Herbert."

"Darling, I'm so glad you think so. I'll tell Herbert. He'll be ever so proud. . . . How's the dear old club getting on?"

"Fine."

"They were *great* days, weren't they? I often think of them. Do you remember that match against Dellingham?"

"*Rather!*" said Enid, who had played in so many matches against Dellingham that she did not remember any particular one of them.

"My dear, I shall *never* forget. . . . How on earth I managed to fall on my nose in the mud and hit a goal in one and the same movement I've never understood! Have you ever seen anything *like* what I looked like when I got up?"

"*Never!*" said Enid, who had seen too many players rising from the mud, like Aphrodite from the foam, to be able to recall any particular one. "You were *splendid*, darling."

"Oh no, I wasn't, but it was a marvellous match, wasn't it? I was trying to tell Baby about it one day last week. Of course he couldn't understand, but he looked just as if he did. He's got such an *intelligent* little face, hasn't he?" She bent down till her face was on a level with the flabby expressionless face of the child and cooed, "Mummy all over mud playing 'ocky, darling. Everyone laughing at Mummy." She stood upright and turned to Enid with a proud smile. "Isn't it marvellous the way he looks as if he understood. The way he takes everything in. We shall have to be awfully careful later on when he goes to school, not to let them push him too much. That's always the danger with these clever children."

"*Rather!*" agreed Enid again with vague enthusiasm.

"My dear, I saw old Mr. Royston out the other day. Isn't he *wonderful*?"

"Isn't he? It's his birthday to-day, you know. He's ninety-five. We're all rallying round there to-night for dinner."

"Oh, my dear, how *marvellous*! Not *really*! Ninety-five. Just think! I wonder if Baby will live to be ninety-five. I hate to think of him growing up at all. He's so sweet just as he is, isn't he?

Darling, I must fly. I hate to keep Baby waiting for his bottle. Say bye-bye to Auntie Enid, darling. . . . Wave 'oo handy."

The child continued to stare blankly into space.

"You can almost *see* him taking things in, can't you? In a way it's a dreadful responsibility having such an intelligent child to bring up. . . . Well, it's been lovely seeing you again like this. We must meet properly and have a real long talk some time, mustn't we? Come round some evening and watch Baby have his bath, will you? He's perfectly sweet in his bath. You'd *love* it. Well, *good-bye*, darling."

"Good-bye. Take care of yourself and the babe."

"Rather, and—oh, my *dear*, that Dellingham match!"

"*Great*, wasn't it? Good-bye."

Enid walked on rather slowly. What a fool the girl was! Who was she, anyway? Had she ever been really friendly with her? Dreadful to think that one forgot people like this. It somehow made one feel terribly old and mouldy. What was the matter with her this morning? She had never felt like this before. She was tired, she supposed. Tired of everything. Tired, most of all, of her own breezy and popular self. The root of the trouble was that, though this self was now what is called a "second nature" to her, it had never been wholly natural. Even as a child, Enid had realised how incongruous was her large muscular body with the shyness that was her instinctive reaction to the world around her. Almost automatically, she concealed the shyness by a defiant aggressiveness that consorted well with her appearance. Throughout her sensitive childhood she built up defences of loud slanginess, of tomboy dare-devilry, which served their purpose in that they concealed the shrinking something within her that wanted only to be concealed.

When she was hurt, as she so often was, she scared, not for the hurt, but only lest she should betray signs of it. She could bear any suffering as long as no one but herself knew that she suffered. Margaret's own spirit was so bruised and battered by her marriage that she had had little thought to spare for her children. Then Victor died, and she was left face to face with her daughter—a strapping young woman with boisterous aggressive manners and a loud defiant voice. She had made the best of the situation, bringing all her forces to bear, not on trying to understand the girl, but on trying to conceal the irritation she caused her. Enid herself was only vaguely aware of the root of the trouble. She knew that often, even when she was the centre of a noisy throng and appeared most at her ease, something within her shrank away from it in an agony of shyness; she knew that, when she sounded most self-assured, something within her was in a ferment of diffidence and self-distrust. Often she seemed actually to see a tiny Uncle Richard standing irresolute—as Uncle Richard so often stood in real life—in the middle of her heart, and the sight angered and humiliated her so much that she often criticised Richard himself with a bitterness that surprised the others. She looked upon her natural shyness as a weakness to be overcome. She had no suspicion that this repression of her real nature had caused a disharmony in her that made her restless and often, in secret, acutely unhappy.

She waved a hearty greeting to the treasurer of the golf club (Enid, of course, was the secretary) who was passing on the other side of the street. She played hockey, tennis, and golf for the town, but—again that odd depression surged over her—how much longer would she be able to keep it up? A woman's athletic form generally began to go off when she had passed forty. The depression deepened to panic. What would she do when she was too old to play games? Would she start pottering about with good works, teaching in Sunday School and giving out parish magazines just to fill in her time? As if to lend point to the question, Mr. Morrow, the Parish Church curate, a tall middle-aged man with a round boyish face, passed her and took off his hat with a flourish. She squared her large shoulders defiantly and began to whistle again through her teeth.

She glanced at her watch. It was three minutes to eleven. She was in good time.

"Call in at eleven and have a spot before your meeting," Brenda had said. She wondered if Max would be at home. He generally seemed to be at home for his wife's parties, even when they only consisted of a "spot" at eleven. At the thought that he might be there, Enid's heart quickened. . . .

From her earliest girlhood she had avoided intimate friendships with men, treating them all in a hail-fellow-well-met fashion that kept them at arm's length. They called her a "good sport," but never made any attempt to know more of her than the slangy breezy surface she showed them. Something in her manner, friendly enough though it was, seemed to set a definite barrier of casual acquaintanceship beyond which they must not pass. The girl was acutely sensitive about her large body, and aware that it made any man who walked with her or danced with her look slightly ridiculous. Moreover, the secret self that lived imprisoned within her was deeply romantic, but, knowing how incompatible was romance with the massive hoyden body that governed it, shrank in terror from any approach to it. It was that hidden romantic—traitor in the citadel of her hard good-fellowship—that drove her to find outlet for it in the succession of sentimental friendships with young women at which Danesborough smiled good-humouredly.

But with Max Collin it was quite different. For one thing, he was the first man who had not made her conscious of her size. He was a handsome blond giant, broad-shouldered, broad-thighed, a good head taller than Enid herself. When with him, for the first time in her life, she felt feminine and—not small exactly but, at any rate, not conspicuously large.

Danesborough disapproved of the Collins. They were London people and had never even attempted to identify themselves with the little country town in which they now lived. Max was an engineer and had a good post in Ballaters', but he never seemed to take it seriously, laughing at it and Ballaters' and Danesborough indiscriminately. He and Brenda drank a good deal, and frequently went up to London to dances or had friends down from London to stay with them.

It was Brenda's smallness and ravishing prettiness that had first attracted Enid. She had black hair, sparkling black eyes, and a complexion whose dazzling fairness made you forget the rather loose mouth and weak chin. If Enid had known then all that she knew now about Brenda, of course, she would never have made overtures of friendship, but the knowledge had come so gradually that, by the time it was fully here, the care-free sophisticated atmosphere of the Collins' house, with its undercurrent of cheerful contempt for convention, had become as necessary to her as a drug. As to Brenda and young Guy Richards, the actor, who came to stay with the Collins so frequently—well, over and over again Enid had assured herself that if there really *had* been anything in it Brenda surely wouldn't have hinted so broadly that there was. She was merely trying to shock her. . . .

Max himself opened the door to her, large, smiling, serene.

"There you are, darling," he said. "We've been waiting and watching for you for the last half-hour."

His saying "darling," of course, meant nothing. He called every woman he spoke to "darling"—a habit that had shocked Danesborough indescribably.

"Brenda said eleven and it's only just struck."

Enid's breeziness always dropped from her when she was with Max Collin. She became quiet, with an odd suggestion of shyness in her manner, as if her real self were peeping out from its prison. Her voice, when not raised to its usual strident note, had a pleasing musical timbre.

"There's an awful fug in the lounge. Let me help you off with your coat. Not brought Tinker? You should have done. Brenda's chained up the hound."

Towering above her, he drew the tweed coat from her shoulders. She tried not to realise that he was taking longer than he need have done over the process, and that his hands touched her far more than was necessary; tried, too, to ignore the thrill that shot through her at the contact.

Then he put his arm firmly round her waist and went into the lounge with her. That, again, meant nothing to Max Collin. He put his arm almost automatically round the waist of any woman with whom he found himself.

"Here comes the sun!" he announced her cheerfully.

The little lounge was thick with cigarette smoke. At first it seemed to be full of people, too, but soon Enid realised that there was only Brenda, Guy, and a girl with a white face and henna-ed hair, who was sitting on the floor on a pile of cushions, flourishing a long jade cigarette-holder, and whom Brenda introduced as "Frankie".

Guy Richards was a handsome, rather effeminate-looking youth, with an obviously treasured wave in his hair and carefully manicured hands.

"Whisky or a cocktail, darling?" Max was saying.

Enid chose a cocktail, and Max went to the little cocktail bar in a corner of the room (it was the cocktail bar that had finally damned the Collins in the eyes of Danesborough) to mix her a dry Martini.

When he had handed it to her, he raised his own glass, and his eyes met hers so meaningly that she looked away quickly, the colour rising in her cheeks.

Suddenly the girl called "Frankie" got up and announced that she had a headache and was going to lie down. No one made any comment. She went out, slamming the door.

"She's going this afternoon, thank God," said Brenda. "No one asked her to come. She invited herself, the blasted little cat. Max fell for her once, and she thought he'd do it again. It's taken her three days to find out her mistake. She's as peeved as hell."

Max had taken his seat by Enid on the settee and had slipped his arm round her waist again. Brenda raised her glass.

"Here's luck," she said, and her eye met Enid's across the room with a long and rather peculiar look. "Now let's tell Enid about our plan," she went on. "Enid darling, we've made a lovely plan, so do be nice and accommodating about it. Max has got next week off, and a friend of Guy's has got a cottage at Coniston that he's lending us, and we want you and Guy to go there with us for the week. You will, won't you? We all three want you awfully."

"But"—Enid laughed nervously—"I've got such heaps of things on hand just now."

"Rot! You know you can easily manage a week."

"Be a sport, darling," pleaded Max.

As he spoke, his arm round her waist tightened, drawing her nearer. She tried to resist the pressure, but was helpless. His touch seemed to relax every nerve and muscle in her body. Again a knife-like pang, unbearably sweet, shot through her.

"No, I can't," she said breathlessly. "Honestly, I can't."

"Of course you must," persisted Brenda. "Well, look here. Max has to go to the works in two jiffs, so we won't waste time arguing about it now. Come to dinner to-night, and we'll talk it over."

"To-night? Oh darn! I can't. There's a bean-feast at my grandfather's. He's ninety-five to-day, and he's having a birthday party. All the family's got to show up."

"Can't you cut it? He'll never notice you aren't there."

"No, but the others would. They'd never speak to me again."

"What luck for you! It's almost worth cutting it, then, isn't it?" They all laughed.

"No, honestly, I daren't," protested Enid. "There'd be a dreadful row if I did. The whole crew is being there. Even the family skeleton's come out of its cupboard and is walking the streets in broad daylight."

It soothed some obscure hurt in her to refer to Stephen like this.

"No! Surely the highly respectable Roystons haven't got a skeleton."

"Haven't you ever heard? It's my cousin Stephen. Paul's brother, you know."

"What did he do? Seduce the rector's wife?"

"Almost. I mean, he went off with a married woman."

"What a thrill for Danesborough!"

"Oh, he didn't actually do it here. I believe he discovered her in Somerset. About two years ago."

"Quite an ancient scandal. But a perfectly good one, of course. Come to dinner to-morrow night, then."

"Thanks awfully."

"Merely to discuss arrangements. It's settled that you're coming to the cottage."

"Well——" Enid hesitated.

"Of course it is. You'll make her come, Max, won't you? Now,

64

Guy, you're going to help me choose the stuff for those new curtains. The patterns are upstairs. Come along."

They went out together. Enid made a slight effort to free herself from Max's arm, but it tightened round her still more determinedly. Abandoning all attempt at resistance, she lay back against his shoulder. The smouldering fear that had lain in her heart all morning blazed up into sudden recklessness. She hadn't faced the fear before, though she had known it was there. Now she faced it defiantly. She was forty-two. Life as a woman would be over for her in a few years without her having lived at all. Her youth stretched behind her, arid, sterile. No man had ever even desired her. She felt bitterly ashamed of her unfulfilled womanhood and as bitterly ashamed of her shame. Well, something was being offered her now, not what that secret self, always repressed and always craving expression, had longed for, but—something. Why shouldn't she snatch at it, whatever it was, before it was too late?

Max's blond head was bending over her. A shudder went through her as his lips found hers and clung to them, pressing down on them fiercely, ravenously. His kisses seemed to drain all the strength from her body. She was trembling when he released her.

"You'll come, won't you?" he said.

His voice broke the spell. Again she made an ineffectual attempt to free herself from his arms.

"I can't think when you're holding me like that," she said with an unsteady laugh.

"I don't want you to think. I'll think for both of us——"

"You don't understand——"

"Yes, I do. You're the only woman in this God-forsaken hole worth the name of woman. You——"

Brenda's voice, upraised in a light catch of song, sounded just outside the door. He relaxed his hold but did not take his arm from her waist. Brenda entered alone.

"Time you were off to the works, my lad," she said. "Buzz off. Enid and I are going to have another cocktail."

"All right." He withdrew his arm lazily and rose to his enormous height. "Don't get too tight. See you to-morrow evening, Enid, if there's anything left of you after your wild family orgy. Keep your eye on your Uncle Richard. I bet he's one of the lads, what? So long."

Brenda got up when he had gone and closed the door firmly. Then she went over to the cocktail bar, humming lightly, and began to mix the cocktails. Neither of the two spoke. Enid felt breathless and shaken. Her cheeks were burning. How much did Brenda know or guess?

Brenda came over to her, handed her a cocktail, and sat down by her, still in silence, watching her with a faintly cynical smile. The silence seemed suddenly to acquire some horrible significance. Enid searched frantically in her mind for a casual remark with which to break it but could think of nothing. Her voice in any case would have sounded forced and unnatural. The hand that held her wine glass was trembling, and there was a strange throbbing in her throat and ears. Suddenly Brenda spoke, in an easy nonchalant tone.

"You are coming away with us, aren't you? Max wants you to, you know."

Enid said nothing. She felt dazed and bewildered, as if all this were happening in a dream. The casual, half-laughing voice went on: "Be kind to him, Enid. He's crazy about you."

"What *are* you talking about?" Enid managed to bring out in a fairly good imitation of her usual voice.

Brenda raised her glass and glanced at Enid speculatively over its rim.

"Be kind to me, then," she said. "I'm taking Guy to amuse me, and we want Max to have someone to amuse him. It won't be any fun for us if he hasn't. ..." She was silent for a moment, then spoke slowly, her gaze fixed straight before her. "Listen, Enid. ... I'm not a spoil-sport like some wives. Max wants you, and, as far as I'm concerned, he can have you. I like to have a good time myself, and I don't grudge Max a good time. He feels the same. ... We haven't slept together for years, you know."

The words were like flies buzzing round and round in Enid's head. They were meaningless. The only meaning they could have was so monstrous that it was unthinkable. Then suddenly and with an effort she forced herself to face their meaning, and again that intoxication of recklessness surged over her. Suppose that they meant—what they seemed to mean. Suppose that she did what they suggested she should do. It wasn't what she had secretly dreamed of, but—surely it was better than nothing. Better than letting her youth go by without having known anything more real than hockey matches and tennis parties. At least it would be something to remember when she was old.

"You don't know what you're saying, Brenda," she said breathlessly.

Brenda laughed.

"Yes, I do. And I wouldn't be saying it, my dear, if I didn't know that you're as crazy about Max as he is about you. I've got eyes in my head. I like you, and if it's got to be somebody—and it *has*—I'd sooner it were you than anyone else." She paused, then added irrelevantly: "Max is quite a good sort, you know."

Enid was silent. She seemed to feel again Max's arm tightening about her body, and at the memory again that sharp stab of ecstasy shot through her.

Brenda rose with her short dry laugh and carried both glasses back to the little bar.

"Well, I've said my say," she remarked lightly. "You're the world's prize strong silent woman, my dear, aren't you? Have another cigarette."

"No, thanks."

"It's settled that you're coming with us, then?"

"No . . ."

Brenda's reddened lips flickered into a cynical smile.

"I think it is," she said quietly. "However—you'll come to dinner to-morrow night, and we'll arrange the final details."

Enid rose slowly. She still had that odd feeling of moving and speaking in a dream.

"Yes, I'll come to-morrow. I must go now. I've got a meeting of the Dramatic Committee at twelve and it's always horribly punctual."

"I know. Everything in Danesborough is. Personally, I consider punctuality as the most contemptible of all the vices, don't you?"

She went with Enid across the little hall to the front door and held out her hand. Her bright black eyes met Enid's without flinching.

"Good-bye, old thing. . . . You'll have a really good time at the cottage, I promise you. Don't be a fool and back out of it. See you to-morrow night. Good-bye."

Chapter Seven

THE sunshine fell in golden splashes on the surface of the bare mahogany table, deepened the shade of the amber glasses, and seemed to creep into the glowing hearts of the marigolds that stood in the Chinese bowl in the centre.

Harold smiled genially round the table at his daughter, wife, and sister. Enid's presence cheered and stimulated him, not because he was particularly fond of her—indeed, the brother and sister had little in common—but because she was a guest, and guests always had an exhilarating effect upon him. They provided him with an audience, and he loved to have an audience.

His wife and daughter, of course, were an audience of sorts, but Pen was such a silent little thing and Helen was sometimes so nervy. Women, he knew, were peculiarly subject to nerves. . . . His first wife had not been nervy in the particular way in which Helen was nervy, but she had cried if she thought he was annoyed with her and made herself ill with worry when he had a cold or a headache or did not come home at the exact minute she was expecting him. Helen's nerves weren't like that. . . . He glanced at her across the table. How lovely she was, despite the line between her brows and the slight compression of her lips! His eyes caught hers, and he smiled affectionately, but hers slid away with a sudden dilating of their dark pupils. He tried to ignore the pang that shot through his heart at the rebuff, slight though it was. She was tired and nervy. Women were like that. One had to make allowances for them. . . . He threw a careless glance at the mirror that hung on the wall by his side. His self-assurance was very easily dispersed and needed constant nourishment to sustain it. A passing glance in a mirror was often a great help to him. Now, as usual, the sight of his handsome features, cleft chin, and slightly waving hair, restored his confidence. Of course Helen loved him. It was odd that Ruth, who had adored him from the moment she first met him till her death, had never roused in him this ache of longing that Helen roused.

Pen's grave watchful eyes were fixed on his face. He gave her his casual pleasant smile. A nice little thing, Pen, he thought patronisingly. A pity she was so quiet and colourless. He had always admired rosy-cheeked, chubby, curly-haired children, and Pen from babyhood had been disappointingly pale and thin and straight-haired. He liked children to be roguish and merry, too, and Pen had been a silent child, who always seemed to him just a little stupid. Still, he had to admit that, now she was seventeen, there was a certain style about her, though she was far from having inherited his good looks.

"Do you know this baby's leaving school at Christmas?" he said to Enid.

There was something rather more mechanical than usual in Enid's loud answering laugh.

"She told me so this morning. Makes one feel almost a grandparent, doesn't it? It'll be nice for you both to have her at home."

"Oh yes, we're still content with our solitude *à deux*, but we always have a welcome for Pen."

Helen made no answer or comment, and Enid, glancing up suddenly, caught the look in Harold's eyes—a naked hungry look like that of a dog who pleads for a bone. It's indecent, she thought, with a little shudder of revulsion, for a man to love a woman like that. Then, suddenly, irrelevantly: I will go to the cottage with the Collins. I'll regret it all my life if I don't. I won't shilly-shally any longer. I'm going. It's settled. Finally settled. After all, what's the good of keeping yourself decent just for nothing? I shall be old soon. It will be too late for anything.

"Have you heard that they've made me President of the Dickens Society?" Harold was saying.

"No."

"If there's one thing I loathe more than another," he went on with his pleasant smile, "it's presiding over meetings of any sort. I simply hate the idea of it, but——"

Helen raised her dark eyes from her plate.

"If you really don't want the position, Harold," she said clearly, "there's no need at all for you to accept it. Mr. Haynes will be only too glad to take it on."

Harold laughed nervously, and there was a slightly awkward silence. Pen's eyes, loving, anxious, were fixed on her father's face, as if noting and sharing the hurt that the cold clear voice had dealt him. Helen was looking down at her plate again, the lines between her brows and round her lips intensified. Why am I such a beast, she was saying to herself. I do try not to be. I simply can't help it. I made up my mind this morning that I'd be nice to him. He can't help being—not quite real. Not quite real and muzzy-minded. And—he cares so. That's what makes it so hateful. It wouldn't matter if he didn't care so. It was my fault for marrying him. He seemed so kind, and Philip had hurt me so terribly. I ought to have known that I didn't really love him. If only everything about him didn't irritate me so—his voice, his smile, the things he says, the way he says them ... but I *will* try to be nice to him.

"Of course you must do it, Daddy," Pen was saying. "They don't want Mr. Haynes. They want you. It would be *terribly* selfish of you not to take it."

Her eagerness to cover his humiliation made her voice breathless and unsteady.

Helen shot a glance at the girl's face—a softened, remorseful glance, a glance she had never sent to her husband, however deeply she had wounded his feelings.

She had loved her stepdaughter from their first meeting, and Pen, she knew, could have loved her in return, if Harold had not stood between them like a shadow distorting each to the other. The child fought against the new love, feeling in it a secret disloyalty to that older, more absorbing love she bore her father.

Her eyes, still fixed on him, were full of a tender solicitude. It isn't that she doesn't see his faults, thought Helen wistfully. She loves him with his faults, as a mother loves her child. That's the way she'll feel to her husband. I could never feel like that to a man.

Harold was talking to Enid again. About books now. He prided himself upon his literary taste and was apt to make it out to be rather more highbrow than it really was.

"It's a most interesting book," he was saying. "It traces the creative impulse all down history and shows how at each stage it has been influenced by material conditions and historical events." He turned to his wife with his courteous air of not wishing to leave her out of a conversation, "It's most interesting, isn't it, dear?"

Helen's eyes met his with a slight hardening of their cool depths.

"I haven't read it," she said, and added clearly, "I didn't know that you had."

Again the shaft went home, openly, cruelly. Again he flushed, smiled nervously, and said: "Oh, well——"

He seldom read the books he talked about with such fluency. It was so easy to get the gist of them out of the reviews that it seemed a waste of time actually to read them.

Again Helen threw a quick glance at Pen. I'm sorry, Pen, the glance seemed to say, I can't help it. I'm so miserable. This time the girl's eyes answered with a look of faint reproach, a look that denied the shy friendship that sprang up so easily between them when Harold was not there and neither of them were thinking of him, for even the thought of Harold could bring constraint and self-consciousness into the atmosphere.

Helen moved restlessly in her chair. She felt angry and ashamed. She wasn't always as bad as this. Sometimes she managed to control her irritation with him for days together. And now, of course, Pen, who had only come home from school yesterday, would think that she was always like this. She had been looking forward to Pen's coming—Pen, so shy and sweet and honest and young, so sensitive and defenceless. She had wanted to take care of her, and all she had done so far was to hurt her, hurt her even more than she had hurt Harold. God alone knew why the child adored him so. . . . It was Philip's fault, of course. She had felt nervy and on edge ever since she got his letter this morning, saying that he was coming to see her in the afternoon. Why did he want to see her? Everything was over between them. Surely he realised that. And Enid—why on earth had Harold asked his sister to lunch to-day of all days? As if she wouldn't have enough of his family to-night at the old man's party! She liked a few of the Roystons—she liked the old man and Paul, she didn't dislike Richard, she liked Daphne, she would have liked her mother-in-law if the shadow of Harold had not stood between them as it stood between her and Pen—but the Roystons *en masse* depressed and irritated her. Enid especially jarred on her—and to-day more than usual. Her hand went into the pocket of her jumper where Philip's letter was, and her irritation deepened to a dull despair. She had been trapped, and she could never escape. Never. . . . Enid's loud laugh rang out, and she glanced at her with a feeling that was partly envy, partly contempt. The girl sat there, boisterously healthy and care-free, without a thought in her head beyond her next golf or tennis match. You had only to look at her to see that she had never known the racking torment of love.

Harold had just asked her to go to some meeting with him the next week (Harold loved meetings), and she was saying, "I shan't be here next week. I'm going to stay with the Collins. Someone's lent them a cottage at Coniston."

Helen's lip curled slightly. Brenda Collin, Enid's latest "crush."

"Perhaps Pen will come with me then; will you, Pen?" said Harold.

"Of course, Daddy."

He smiled across at Helen.

"And what about our 'sweet stay-at-home, sweet love-one-place'? Will she come?"

Helen's figure went rigid in her effort at self-control. Because she now refused to accompany him to all the meetings of all the little societies of Danesborough in which he was interested, he had pigeon-holed her as the domesticated woman who cannot bear to leave her own fireside. She hated being pigeon-holed. She hated having tags of poetry quoted at her. She hated being addressed in the third person. She managed to smile at him, however—a stiff unnatural smile, but still a smile.

"I don't know. May I leave it open till the day?"

"Of course," he said, obviously pleased by the studied kindness of her voice.

Helen glanced at her stepdaughter and was rewarded by the sudden look of relief on the small expressive face, the sudden relaxing of the slight tense form. It was so easy to please them both, if only one could keep oneself in hand. . . .

"It would be splendid if you both came," Harold went on.

Poor Harold! She felt for the moment genuinely sorry for him. She wasn't the sort of wife he should have had. He wanted an adoring "little woman" without brains or opinions of her own, a "little woman" who would have taken him at his own valuation, listening admiringly to his views on everything and everyone, leading up to his best stories and never minding how often she heard them. Ruth, his first wife, had been like that. She had never seen Ruth, but Philip had met her once. Philip, Philip, Philip. . . . Her hand stole again to the pocket that contained his letter, and again that wave of terror and misery swept over her. Why did Philip want to see her this afternoon? What could they possibly have to say to each other that had not been said already? And to-day. It seemed the final touch of maladroitness that he should have chosen to-day—the old man's birthday, the day of the Royston gathering that she had been dreading ever since she first heard of it.

"I believe I saw Stephen this morning," Enid was saying, "going up to Greenways."

"Surely not," said Harold, looking suddenly grave and shocked.

"He's coming to-night, you know," said Enid.

"Yes, but—well, I took for granted that he'd come straight over for the dinner and then go back."

"Why?" challenged Helen.

He spread out his hands deprecatingly.

"My dear, he must know how we all feel about it."

"How do you all feel about it?"

"We naturally disapprove of his living with a woman who is not his wife."

He spoke gently, but rather stiffly, as if reproaching her for prolonging so distasteful a discussion.

"But she couldn't possibly marry him," persisted Helen.

"That hardly affects the situation," he said.

"You're all so *hard*," burst out Helen, and to their surprise they saw that she was trembling. "If they love each other . . ." she stopped suddenly, then went on in her usual voice, but a little unsteadily, "Oh well, it's futile to discuss the subject. For one thing, no two people in the world mean the same thing by love."

The maid brought in the sweets, and Harold, always careful of the proprieties, began to talk local trivialities with Enid. Pen's eyes went from one to the other, her childish form again rigid with apprehension. Helen's thoughts returned to Philip.

She ought to decide what line to take with him, but she couldn't do that till she knew what line he was going to take with her. One thing was certain. He must be made to understand that the past was over and done with. She wouldn't let him tear out her heart by taking her back to the past.

She imagined his entering the room, looking at her with his short-sighted grey eyes, an uncertain smile hovering round his long mobile mouth. The picture was unexpectedly vivid, and her heart began to beat rapidly. Again panic swept over her, the sudden unreasoning panic of something trapped. She mustn't see Philip alone. . . . She hadn't even told Harold that she had heard from him. She had tried to, but she felt that she could not be sure that her voice would sound quite natural when she said his name. Now, with the courage of despair, she spoke calmly, detachedly, without the faintest tremor in her voice.

"Harold, I heard from Philip Messiter this morning. He's coming over this afternoon. You'll be in for tea, won't you?"

He looked at her, obviously pleased at the thought that she wanted him to be in for tea, obviously also feeling no jealousy at the thought of Philip's visit. Indeed, Harold himself had more than once suggested her asking Philip and his wife over to dinner. There was very little subtlety about Harold, and so he could never perceive subtlety in a situation. Helen and Philip had been engaged and then had discovered that they did not love each other. Each of them had married someone else. That was all there was to it.

"I'm glad," he said. "Get him to come to dinner sometime and bring Mona. No, I'm frightfully sorry, but I can't possibly be home for tea. I shall have to come home earlier than usual anyway for this birthday party of grandfather's, and I'm booked up with appointments all afternoon."

"You'll be here, Pen, won't you?"

Pen shook her head.

"It's the tennis party at the Rectory, you know."

Her glance passed on to Enid.

"Do stay to tea, Enid. I hate having to entertain visitors alone."

"I'm sorry, but I'm going to the Rectory tennis party, too. And must fly home immediately after lunch. I hate leaving mother for both lunch and tea. She's so lonely all by herself when I go out."

She often said things like that about Margaret in order to try to convince herself that they were true. But now her perceptions, heightened by the emotional crisis through which she was passing, tore aside the veils of self-deceit. It isn't true, she said to herself. She likes my going out. I irritate and bore her. We both pretend that I don't, but it's only pretence. If things were different with her I shouldn't be going to Max. But I'm tired of pretending.

"I wish one of you would stay and support me," Helen was saying in her clear steady voice. "I hate coping with callers alone. Anyway, I hate having people to tea when I'm going out to dinner. Can't you possibly manage it, Harold?"

"Sorry, darling. I'm absolutely full up this afternoon."

Enid had occasionally had doubts about this marriage of Harold's, but she told herself now that they had been groundless. Helen wouldn't be begging him to come home early like this, if they weren't happy together.

Sometimes it seemed to Enid that the whole world was full of happily married self-sufficient couples, and the thought would bring with it an odd sense of desolation. She deliberately surrendered herself again to the memory of Max, imagining his arms about her, his lips on hers. I'd rather have been married and had children, she thought, but I must have something.

Harold thought complacently: Women are all the same. Want you to be continually dancing attendance. Never understand that business must have a look in sometime.

The nagging fear that lurked beneath his complacency and that he never dared to face was lulled into temporary oblivion.

Pen sat silent and motionless, her slight figure relaxed. It was all right. He was happy again. He was always happy when Helen was kind to him. Her love seemed to hover about him, forming an armour through which even Helen's unkindness could not pierce.

Helen rose with an abrupt movement.

"Shall we have coffee in the drawing-room?"

The drawing-room was the pleasantest room in the house. Curtains and chair-covers were of glazed chintz, Persian rugs lay on the polished floor, framed Chinese embroideries hung against the cream walls. And everywhere were flowers, massed on table and mantelpiece and on the spinet that stood by the door. An old brass cauldron on the floor between the windows was full of sweet-peas. The air was fragrant with them.

Helen took her seat in front of the low coffee-table and began to pour out the coffee. A feeling of anger had seized her, as if all these people were deliberately betraying her, as if they were watching her drown without putting out a hand to help her.

Harold, a vague sense of well-being pervading him, leant back in his chair and smiled genially at the three of them. He was, after all, a very lucky man. Not many men could lay claim to three such good-looking women as wife, daughter, and sister. A rush of affection flowed out towards them, a longing to feel himself as beloved by them as they were by him. Helen *did* love him. He told himself so a hundred times a day. Not, of course, in quite the same way as he loved her, but women were notoriously less passionate than men. Even Ruth at times. . . . He became suddenly anxious that they should see him as he really was. He hungered for their love and esteem.

"I met Jevons yesterday," he said to Helen, "and he said that he thought the way I'd handled the Marlow case was wonderful."

"You told me so last night," she said shortly.

He tried to recover his shattered poise.

"Did I? Well, of course, Jevons always is very appreciative of my efforts."

"He owes you money, doesn't he?" said Helen.

He was hurt again, and his self-confidence collapsed abruptly. And into Pen's slender figure there crept once more that familiar rigidity as if, though she had not moved, she were holding her arms about him to protect him.

You beast, you beast, cried Helen to herself. But I'm so miserable. I'm so terrified. If only they knew how miserable and terrified I am. . . . Determinedly forgiving, Harold smiled across at her.

"Got a headache, little woman?" he said.

Her exasperation surged over her in an irresistible flood. It wasn't any use even trying to fight against it. She rose and spoke jerkily.

"No, I haven't a headache. And I wish you wouldn't call me 'little woman,' Harold. I suppose you don't realise that it's the most offensive thing you could possibly find to call me."

He stared at her, and she felt suddenly frightened, frightened of her passion and its secret unsuspected power over her, frightened of Harold, of Penelope, of Philip, of life itself. Danger seemed to surround her on all sides.

She gave a laugh that was more like a sob.

"Don't take any notice of me, Harold. I have rather a headache. Call me anything you like. It's time you went to the office now, isn't it? I'll see you off like a dutiful wife."

She went into the hall with him and, taking a rose from a bowl on the low oak chest, put it in his button-hole.

"There!" she said, patting the lapel to make it lie smoothly.

He smiled with pleasure, but underneath the pleasure there still lingered the fear he dared not face. He took her in his arms and kissed her passionately. She accepted his kisses, tense but unresisting.

"Darling," he whispered, "you do love me, don't you?"

"Of course. Of course. . . ."

Chapter Eight

PEN opened the drawing-room door and stood hesitating on the threshold.

"I'm just going, Helen."

Helen turned from the window, walked over to the mantelpiece, and stubbed her cigarette on a small enamel ash-tray.

"You're rather early, aren't you?"

"I have to call for Daphne and Pippa."

"Well, come in and let me look at you."

The girl entered, closed the door, and came slowly across the room to where her stepmother stood. She wore a tennis frock of pale pink silk and a white linen hat. Helen looked her up and down, then, smiling, straightened the dress about the shoulders and waist. As her hands moved over the thin immature form, it occurred to her that the tenderness she felt for this child was the purest emotion she had ever felt in her life.

"Thank you," said Pen. "Is it all right now? I ought to be going, oughtn't I? I told Daphne I'd be there by three."

Pen was ill-at-ease, fighting against the influence to which she longed to yield, fighting, not sullenly or resentfully, but with a puzzled, anxious, childish loyalty. Helen was so lovely when she was like this. A sort of radiance came from her that shone right into your heart, that you couldn't keep out. If only she'd be like this to Daddy! It seemed selfish and treacherous somehow to take from her a kindness that she refused to Daddy and that would have made him so happy. He never even saw her like this. When she was with Daddy she was hard and tense and unapproachable.

There was always a faint bitterness in her voice and smile. If only she would be like this to him!

Still smiling, Helen looked down into the wistful blue eyes. It was this wondering childish gravity, this unspoilt naïvety, that had broken down her defences at their first meeting. And Harold, blind fool, treated his daughter with a patronising indifference that had something in it of contempt. "A nice little thing," he had described her, "not pretty and not much go about her. You'll find her quite easy to get on with." Easy to get on with!

"It won't take you five minutes to go to Daphne's," she said. "Stay here a minute. I've seen nothing of you since you came home. You were out all morning and then Aunt Enid came to lunch."

Pen's answering smile was tremulous, as if breaches were appearing in her defences. Strive as she might against the slightest disloyalty to the father she adored, her starved little spirit could not help warming its hands at this glowing kindness.

To Helen it seemed suddenly terribly important to keep Pen with her for even a few moments longer. She felt secure, serene, in her gentle childish presence. It was like a harbour in which she could rest between two toilsome bufferings. Behind her lay that dreadful luncheon, at which Enid's presence had somehow seemed to make Harold more exasperating than usual. And before her lay that interview with Philip from which her whole soul and body shrank.

"You know, darling," she said, "a white belt would look much nicer with that dress than the pink one. I've got one upstairs. I'll fetch it."

"Oh no, Helen, it doesn't really matter," protested Pen, but Helen had already left the room. She returned in a few minutes with a white kid belt. When she had fastened it, her hands slipped in a swift caressing movement down the slender undeveloped hips.

"What a thin little creature you are!" she said. "You're nearly as tall as I am, but there's nothing of you. You're just like a gate-post, aren't you?"

Pen laughed, and Helen realised suddenly how rare in that house was the sound of Pen's laughter.

"Oh, I'm not," said Pen. "It's only that I've grown very quickly. I'm terribly strong, you know."

"Oh, *terribly*!" mocked Helen.

The tenderness of her smile made Pen feel suddenly sheltered and cared for and beloved, as if she had been brought from a dark cold place into the radiant sunshine.

Her memories of her own mother were strangely dim, considering that she had died only two years ago. Ruth, who had shared all Harold's views unquestioningly, shared his views of Pen as a matter of course. She was a nice little thing, but unattractive. It was a pity that her hair was so straight and her cheeks so pale, and that she was so unprepossessingly shy.

Ruth had been one of those women who adore their husbands so whole-heartedly that they have no affection to spare for their children. She had indeed always felt somewhat guilty for having upset the routine of Harold's ordered life by introducing a child into it. Pen's natural self-distrust had been intensified by the atmosphere in which she had grown up. No one had ever been actually unkind to her, but she had early realised that she was an unwelcome addition to the household. Her mother had been openly bored by her society and harassed by the inevitable complications she introduced into the *ménage* at each stage of her growth. Her father, though he had no real love for children, had enjoyed posing occasionally as a devoted parent, and his visits to the nursery and fondling of the child in front of visitors accounted, perhaps, for the adoration that she had conceived for him. Later, when she came to see him more clearly, her love changed slightly, taking on an almost maternal protectiveness without losing anything of its fervour. But always something deep down in her had longed for what Helen was offering her and—now that it came it seemed wrong to take it. Pen gave a little hopeless sigh. Life was so terribly, terribly difficult. The older one grew, the more difficult it seemed to become.

Helen was still looking her up and down. The dress was certainly on the short side. A sudden sense of her responsibility came to her.

"What about clothes, Pen? I suppose you'll need some more for the summer holidays, won't you?"

"I suppose I shall. I do grow out of things so."

"Would you like me to help you, or would you rather get them on your own?"

"I'd like you to help me, please," said Pen shyly.

"You've got something for your grandfather's party to-night, of course?"

"Oh yes. That's all right. It's the washing frocks I seem to have grown out of so."

"Well, we'll go up to Town one day, just you and I, and have a shopping morning and go to a theatre in the afternoon and really enjoy ourselves, shall we?"

Sudden colour flamed into Pen's cheeks, sudden brightness into her eyes. For a moment she resembled the child Harold and Ruth had always hankered after.

"Oh, I'd *love* it." She stopped abruptly, seemed to fight with a riot of conflicting emotions, then went on, smiling tremulously. "I'd simply love it."

"We will then. One day next week."

"Thank you. . . . I ought to go now, oughtn't I?" Pen had suddenly become grave and anxious again. "Daphne will be waiting for me."

Helen glanced at the clock. It was three. She couldn't keep the child with her any longer. She'd have to face Philip now. How long would he stay? She felt a sudden desire to make sure of as early a deliverance as possible from the interview.

"What time will you be back?" she said.

"I'm not sure. Fairly early, I think. Parties at the Rectory generally end early. Mrs. Harte just turns people out."

Helen smiled.

"Well, come back as soon as you can, and we'll make our plans for our day in Town. Good-bye, my dear." Her hands touched the thin shoulders in a quick fugitive pressure. "Have a nice time."

She had never yet kissed the child, never before come so near her in any way as she had come this afternoon. Till now they had stood aloof from each other, watching each other guardedly from behind carefully built up defences.

"Good-bye."

The door closed softly. Then came the sound of the shutting of the front door and of steps running lightly down the path to the gate.

Helen stood at the window till the child was out of sight, then turned slowly back to the room. Well, Philip's visit came next. . . .

As she prepared to meet him, her features, her whole poise, seemed to alter. The tenderness that Pen had roused vanished, her eyes grew hard, her lips took on a tight bitter line. She went to the mantelpiece and stood there, staring unseeingly at the empty fireplace. Her thoughts had gone back to the past.

Her father had had mining interests in Portugal, and after his death she and her mother had led a roving life in expensive Continental hotels till her mother's death just over two years ago. After that Helen had returned alone to England. She had hated her wandering hotel existence and wanted to settle down quietly in some English country village. Her father's mining interests had been both extensive and lucrative and, rather to her surprise, she found herself a rich woman. In order to have a *pied à terre* from which to look about her, she took a furnished cottage near Danesborough, and there she met Philip Messiter and they fell in love with each other at once. Philip owned a small estate called Ravensthorpe, eight miles or so outside Danesborough, which had belonged to his father's family for several generations. He lived in the Georgian manor-house with his mother and sister and farmed the home farm himself. For years he had fought a losing battle to keep the estate together. The property was mortgaged and in shocking disrepair. Philip himself would have given up the struggle long ago. It was his mother, an obstinate determined old woman, who refused to yield. His sister was a pale shadow of her mother. Both of them had rejoiced openly, shamelessly, at the news of his engagement to Helen Grosvenor.

"We can save Ravensthorpe, after all," had been the first thing they said on hearing of it.

From the beginning, the thought of Helen's money, and all that it was obviously going to mean to him, had been like a canker at the heart of his love. He was a man who had always found it easier to confer favours than to accept them. That he should owe the restoration of his name and fortune to his wife was a bitter draught for him to swallow. Helen herself was glad and proud to be able to help her lover, but he did not make it easy for her. The fact that he, too, felt an irrepressible sense of relief whenever he thought of her money increased his secret resentment against her. He would have loved to play the part of King Cophetua to her beggar maid, but he could not bring himself to play gracefully the part of beggar man to her Queen Cophetua.

His position at Ravensthorpe had been desperate, she had saved him from failure and disgrace, and he could not quite forgive her for it. Her love had quickened her perceptions, and she did all she could to make it easy for him to accept her help, but whenever they discussed any subject in which her money was even indirectly concerned a coldness and constraint at once sprang up between them. His attitude hurt her bitterly.

"Darling," she would plead, "if only you'd see that it doesn't matter! Money's such a little thing compared with our love for each other. It's an outside irrelevant thing—just a trick of chance—and our love goes right down to the roots of us."

When he could forget her money they got on together perfectly, but any reference to it would send him at once into his shell, making him cold and distant in manner. He tried to explain his attitude to her. "The man should give to the woman," he would say, "not the woman to the man."

"But why?" she would demand, and he would be hurt afresh by her lack of understanding.

Once she told him that he was "ungenerous," and he had replied bitterly, "Oh, of course, we all know that you have the prerogative of generosity in this situation."

A secret resentment almost as bitter as his own grew up in her heart against him. He, too, might have shown more understanding. Her position was as difficult as his. She was willing to give him unstintingly with both hands, glad only of the chance of proving her love for him, and he took it grudgingly, resentfully, making a grievance of the taking. He poisoned the joy that she had in giving and thereby poisoned the secret springs of her love. Quarrels between them became more frequent. All subjects seemed to lead to her money.

"I wish you'd let me give it to you all now," she burst out once, "then it wouldn't be mine. I hate it. I want it to be yours. Do let me, Philip."

His face had darkened.

"Need you insult me quite as crudely as that?" he had said.

His mother and sister, exulting openly in the salvation of Ravensthorpe, made things worse. They were willing to leave the old house to him and Helen, and live themselves in the cottage that had always been used as a dower-house. The great fact was that Ravensthorpe was saved. The fences could be mended, the farm buildings repaired, the fabric of the old house restored, the neglected garden tidied and restocked. Sometimes, after listening to their plans, even though Helen were absent, a gust of anger would seize him.

"Are you aware whose money you're portioning out like this?" he would demand furiously.

"But she'll be a Messiter herself," his mother would retort.

"She's not one yet," he said.

There were times when Helen found him impossible, when it seemed that she could not mention any subject that did not directly or indirectly remind him of her money. It became dangerous to discuss their plans for the future, dangerous even to speak of the past when she had lived in expensive hotels on the Riviera with her mother.

"Yes, my dear," he said once, when she had mentioned quite incidentally a party given by her mother at one of the hotels where they had stayed, "we all know that you both could and can afford that sort of thing, but why rub it in?"

Afterwards he had apologised to her abjectly.

"Forgive me, Helen. I love you so . . . that's why I can't bear it."

The next day there was another scene over the question of the necessary alterations to Ravensthorpe. She had unthinkingly opposed one of his suggestions.

"But, Philip, I think cream-coloured walls would look better."

"As you like," he had replied with a curl of his lip. " 'He who pays the piper calls the tune,' of course."

She had risen from her seat and gone out of the room without a word. Again he had apologised, and their love had seemed to emerge strengthened from the reconciliation.

But it was only a few days later that, after a scene with his mother and sister, he came to her and broke off the engagement.

"It's no use going on with it," he had said. "I'm sorry, but—there it is."

In silence she drew off her engagement ring and handed it to him. Then she said steadily, "I think I have a right to a little more explanation than that, Philip. Why is it no use going on with it?"

He answered her brutally.

"Because I don't know myself whether I'm marrying you for your money or not."

She turned white but answered without a tremor in her voice, "I see. . . . In that case, of course, I agree that it's no use going on with it."

A week after that he had an offer from a speculative builder for an outlying part of the estate, at a price that freed him from his immediate embarrassments and set the estate upon its feet again.

A fortnight later he proposed to Mona Leache, the daughter of a neighbour, and married her within a month.

Helen understood what had attracted him to Mona. She and Mona were as unlike as it is possible for two women to be. Helen was a woman of the world, with the added poise and sophistication that her life in Continental hotels had given her. She was dark and self-contained and slightly disdainful. Moreover, she was only one year younger than Philip. Mona, on the other hand, was little more than a schoolgirl, radiantly pretty, with golden curls and wide blue eyes, patently unsophisticated and childish, and she had worshipped Philip from her babyhood. Hurt and humiliated as he felt himself to be at Helen's hands, he had turned gladly to her warm uncritical adoration. He wanted to forget Helen, put the thought of her out of his life for ever, and Mona seemed the most obvious means of forgetfulness.

And Helen, on her side, had found comfort, temporarily at any rate, in Harold Royston. His kindness had been balm to her bruised spirit, his good looks and fine physique, too, had attracted her, and it had not been difficult to persuade herself that she was in love with him. As to her money, it honestly meant nothing to Harold. "Use it as pocket money," he said casually, and insisted on paying her a generous dress allowance as well as the housekeeping allowance.

She took a cigarette from a box on the mantelpiece and, just as she was striking the match, Philip was announced. She finished lighting her cigarette, then extended her hand casually.

"You're an early caller, Philip," she said lightly.

"Am I?" he said. "I'm afraid I never thought about the time."

"Sit down, won't you? It's nice of you to look me up."

Her hard bright armour seemed impregnable, as if the keenest dart would only glance off from it. The man stood looking at her in silence. He was of average height, with grey-blue eyes, a rather long mouth, and fair hair that receded slightly at the temples. The curves of his mouth showed a latent obstinacy, and there was an elusive suggestion of "nerviness" about him that lay in no particular feature.

"Is Mona quite well?" went on Helen with her nonchalant drawl.

"Yes, thank you."

"Good. Have a cigarette?"

"No, thanks."

She sought desperately for something to say. A pulse seemed to be beating in her throat with such violence that it almost suffocated her. She felt her armour dropping from her and turned away so that he should not see her face.

In a moment he was across the room and was pressing his lips upon hers in a long passionate kiss. When he released her, her face was white, and her breast rose and fell unevenly. She stood holding the back of a chair for support. Then she spoke in a low breathless voice.

"You might have spared me that, Philip."

His face, too, was strained and haggard.

"I had to show you that it's no use pretending."

"Yes," she said slowly, "you're right. It's no use pretending."

"I can't live without you, Helen," he burst out. "I was mad. I've been in hell since I let you go. Listen. You love me. You know you love me. We belong to each other. We've always belonged to each other. If you knew how I'd suffered!"

"You can't blame me for that," she said, with a faint tinge of bitterness in her voice.

"I don't. I was a fool. It was that cursed money. I couldn't bear it. I loved you so. You were giving, giving, giving, all the time. And I'd nothing to give you in return. I couldn't bear it. Don't you understand?"

She was silent for a moment, then said, "Why have you come here, Philip?"

"I had to come. I love you so. I had to come just to see you."

"It's madness. . . ."

"No, it's not. I was mad before. I'm sane now. Helen, you love me. You know you do. It's no use pretending any longer. We can't live without each other."

She could hardly bear to look at his drawn tortured face. Her love for him was like a fire consuming her soul and body. Again the terror of a trapped creature gripped her by the throat. She turned her head away and spoke unsteadily, but with an attempt at lightness.

"Well, what are you proposing? An intrigue? I should have thought you'd have known me better than that."

"I do. And I don't want an intrigue either. Come away with me, Helen. It's all been a nightmare, but it's over. It can be over if you'll let it be. We've been mad—or rather I've been mad—but that's no reason why we should live in hell the rest of our lives. . . . Say something, Helen. It's so simple. It's just you and I. It's been just you and I since the moment we met."

"Aren't you forgetting Mona? And Harold?"

"Do you love Harold?"

"I've married him. And Mona——"

He flung out his hands with a gesture that might have been despair or disgust.

"You know Mona. . . ."

Yes, she knew Mona. Or rather, she had met Mona. She had heard that sweet childish voice that went on and on, babbling inanities, relating lengthy stories of her schooldays, stories of encounters with the mistresses in which she had always come off best, discoursing at length upon her own characteristics ("I'm like that. I'll do anything for anyone I'm fond of, but it's no use trying to force me."). She had understood, not only how the self-centred childishness must once have attracted Philip, but also how intolerable it must have become when the freshness had worn off.

"That doesn't alter the fact that she's your wife," she said, replying to his unspoken criticism.

"She's a child," he burst out bitterly, "and a child who'll never grow up. God knows why—I was mad, I tell you, and that's all there is to it."

"She loves you?"

"In a way. I don't make her happy."

"I don't suppose you do," she said with a crooked smile. "You didn't make me happy, and I was only engaged to you."

"I know I was a beast," he burst out savagely. "It was because I loved you so. I've been punished cruelly."

"And I?"

"Oh, I know. . . . Helen," his voice grew hoarse and tremulous, "when I heard you'd married Royston I—I nearly went out of my mind. Why did you do it?"

"I loved him."

"I don't believe you."

"I thought I did."

"Royston! He's a pompous——"

"We won't discuss Harold, please," she interrupted sharply.

He set his lips.

"Why not?"

"For one thing, he's my husband and——"

He interrupted impatiently.

"You weren't in a normal state when you married him, just as I wasn't in a normal state when I married Mona. I was half mad with anger and humiliation and I only wanted to—forget. It was the same with you. It isn't fair that we should suffer for the rest of our lives for what we did when we weren't responsible. Oh, why are we talking and talking like this? We love each other. There'll never be anyone else for either of us. There's nothing even to discuss. It's—so simple."

She had turned her head away again.

"It isn't simple," she said in a low voice. "It was simple as long as there was only you and I."

"We can go back to that time."

"We can't. That's the tragedy of it. We can't go back to that time. It can never again be just you and I. We threw away our only chance. I'd give anything on earth to have it back—but we can't. It can never be—just as it was. There's Mona and Harold—" She stopped suddenly then added—"and there's Pen."

"Pen?"

"Penelope . . . Harold's daughter."

"Oh, that!" He made a gesture dismissing Penelope, Harold's daughter.

"You're talking for the sake of talking," he went on. "Listen to me, Helen. I want you to come away with me. Now, at once. This afternoon. Write a note for Royston, and I'll send one to Mona. We must burn our boats behind us. There's only one thing that counts, and that's our love. We love each other and belong to each other. Nothing else matters. You know that really. You're just making futile objections because you're frightened of facing things. These people are all shadows. They don't matter. After to-day we'll never see them, never think of them, again. We'll go abroad. My mother and sister can run Ravensthorpe. I've loathed the place ever since it came between us. There'll be just you and I—as there always has been, and as there always will be."

She was silent, gazing in front of her with tightly set lips. He put his hand on her arm.

"Helen . . ." he pleaded.

She shrank away from him with a sharp intake of breath.

"Don't touch me, please."

He obeyed, withdrawing to the mantelpiece, where he stood watching her.

I can't bear it, she was thinking desperately. There's no way out. I wish I could die.

Even when she married Harold she had known that she would never love another man as she had loved Philip. But she had looked on her love for him as over and done with. What she had not realised, had not realised indeed till this afternoon, when Philip stood on the threshold looking at her, was that she still loved him, loved him with a stronger, deeper passion than she had felt before. She knew that if he were to take her in his arms again now her last resistance would vanish.

"Well?" he said at last.

"I don't know," she answered still in that low far-away voice. "It's all so complicated."

"Helen, if only you'd see! It isn't complicated at all. It's the simplest thing in the whole world. If I thought you'd ever regret it—— Look at me, Helen."

With a painful effort she forced her eyes to meet his, and as she did so a sudden trembling seized her body, a sudden exultation her spirit. Yes, he was right. It was all quite simple. They loved each other, and their love was the only thing that mattered. She wasn't trapped, after all. There was a way out. They could go back to the time when there had only been the two of them. They could leave all this behind. How strange it was that she hadn't realised it before! She seemed to speak gently, reassuringly to the woman who had sat opposite Harold at lunch this morning with terror and despair at her heart. It's all right, she seemed to say. It's not too late. You can get out.

"You'll come with me?" he said.

She nodded.

He started forward as if to take her in his arms, but she put out a hand to hold him off, though his very touch seemed to fill her whole body with sweetness and her longing for him was almost more than she could bear.

"Not here," her lips said soundlessly.

He rose to his feet. His face was very white.

"We mustn't wait any longer," he said, speaking slowly and with an effort as if his emotion were choking him. "Let's go at once. I'll wait for you. How soon can you be ready? Never mind about packing. Just put on your hat and coat. We'll go to London to-night. You can do all the shopping you want there. We can cross to France to-morrow. What's the matter?"

The swooning softness had left her eyes. Her body was tense and rigid.

"Phil, I've suddenly remembered. I can't go with you to-day."

"Why not?"

"It's old Mr. Royston's birthday."

"Well?"

"I can't spoil it."

"What on earth do you mean?" he said slowly.

"Harold's grandfather. Old Matthew Royston. He's ninety-five to-day. He's having us all to dinner to-night."

He stared at her.

"I'm afraid I still don't understand," he said. "What has that got to do with us?"

"Nothing, I suppose, in a way. Only, it would spoil it for him, for everyone, if I went away with you to-day."

His face had hardened.

"Helen, you're incomprehensible. You tell me one minute that you love me enough to come away with me, and the next that you won't come because it's the birthday of an old man of ninety-five, who means nothing at all to you and whom you're never likely to see again."

"I suppose it does seem like that to you," she said slowly. "I'm sorry. After all, Philip, what difference does one day make?"

The familiar look of obstinacy had come into his face, tightening the corners of his long nervous mouth.

"It makes all the difference. If you loved me as I love you, then other people like these Roystons"—his tone was angrily contemptuous—"would mean nothing to you."

She laid her hand on his arm.

"Philip," she pleaded softly, "don't let's quarrel over the Roystons. If we do, it only proves that I was right, after all, that we can't go back to the time when there was only you and I. You say that it shows that I don't love you, if I won't come with you now at once. Doesn't it show that you don't love me if you won't wait for me one day?"

He put his hands on her shoulders and gazed down at her, devouring her hungrily with his eyes.

"You promise it will be only one day? You swear to me on your honour that you'll come with me to-morrow?"

"Y——" she stopped suddenly. Her eyes slid away from his, and he felt again the bracing of her shoulders under his hands, as if she were trying to resist the influence of his touch.

"Phil . . . I've just thought of something else. I want you to wait till Pen goes back to school."

He stared at her incredulously, and she went on quickly, "It would spoil the holidays for her so utterly. And—I'd promised to take her up to Town for a day. I want—just to do that."

He dropped his hands from her shoulders.

"Why?" he said tonelessly.

Her eyes looked through him, beyond him.

"I want to have it to remember. I want her to have it to remember. Phil, I'm sorry. You—don't understand, and I can't explain."

"There's nothing much to understand," he said coldly. "It seems fairly simple. You thought you loved me, but you've discovered that you don't."

"*Phil!*" She clutched him urgently, a hand on either arm. "Don't be so cruel. You know I love you. Look at me."

They stood again in silence, their eyes fixed on each other, and though neither moved it seemed as if their two beings flowed into one. She stirred at last, breaking the spell.

"Well?" she said.

He spoke unsteadily. The sweat stood out on his brow.

"I'm sorry. It's only that—I can't bear to think of your belonging to that fellow for another day even."

"I don't 'belong' to him," she flashed proudly. "I belong to no one but myself."

"You're going to belong to me."

"No, I'm not. I love you with all my heart and soul, but I'll belong to myself till I die."

In the silence that followed suspicion seemed suddenly to descend on him again.

"Helen—I'm not going to make a fuss again. I'd wait for you till the world's end, and you know it. But—well, I *can't* understand it. That you should put a schoolgirl's treat, an old man's birthday, before your love for me. I——"

She had turned to the window.

"Look!" she said suddenly. "He's coming."

"Who?"

"The old man. And there are two people with him. I don't know who they are."

Chapter Nine

GASTON cleared the lunch things, moved the old man's chair to the window, and went away, closing the door quietly behind him. The little yellow cat still slept upon the hearthrug. Again the sunshine seemed to creep into the old man's thin frame, warming his bones to their marrow. His thoughts went back over the morning. Hope had been to see him. . . . She had stood in this very room in her white crinoline with a wreath of roses in her dark hair. Hope. . . . The sweet excitement surged over him afresh. He had dreamed that Hope was dead, but, of course, she wasn't dead. She had been to see him. She had stood in this very room. . . .

He turned his head to look down upon the garden. It was—different somehow. It reminded him of dreams he had had in his boyhood, dreams of landscapes bathed in some unearthly glamour of which the memory would thrill him for hours after he awoke. The garden hadn't been like this yesterday or even this morning. It had been an ordinary garden—lawn, flower-beds, trees—the garden he had looked out upon for years and had long ceased to consider as anything but a natural part of his surroundings. Now suddenly it had become new, as if it had just been created for the first time beneath his eyes. New and strange and unutterably lovely—so lovely that he caught his breath in wonder. For a moment he couldn't understand it, then he remembered. He had met Hope last night. That was why the whole world was different. He was going to see her this afternoon. She had said, "Come to-morrow. You won't forget?" He would see her again in a few hours' time. Ecstasy swept over him, the humble, innocent ecstasy of first love. Then he looked down at his hands upon the arms of the chair, yellow, wizened, an old man's hands. He raised his eyes from them to the garden. Charlotte was crossing the lawn, wearing a gardening hat and a pair of gardening gloves. Charlotte, an old woman, his daughter. She began to cut the flowers that were to decorate the table for his birthday party to-night. He relaxed in his chair with a long quivering sigh. He was an old man. He was ninety-five to-day. It wasn't Hope who had been to see him this morning. It was Beatrice. Beatrice and Stephen. But Beatrice had brought Hope back to him. He didn't know how or why—but he knew it was true. Beatrice wasn't Hope, but she had brought Hope back to him. He went slowly across to the book-shelves and took down one of the volumes of modern poetry that he had begun to read lately.

> The light became her grace and dwelt among
> Blind eyes and shadows that are formed as men.
> In wild wood never faun nor fallow fareth
> So silent light, no gossamer is spun
> So delicate as she. . . .

That was Hope, of course. The man who wrote that had seen Hope as she was when she stood in his room this morning. No, that was Beatrice. He must try not to confuse people. Lately he had been rather apt to confuse people, though he had been quick enough to cover up his slips when Catherine was there. Catherine mustn't find out that he confused people. He must try to get it right. Hope was dead. It was Beatrice who had been to see him this morning. Then she had gone away, and Richard had come. Richard was clearer. One couldn't confuse Richard with anyone. He had sat on that chair, his thick-set figure looking neat and trim and compact as it always did, and had complained about the traffic in Danesborough. The traffic in Danesborough, he had said, was growing worse and worse. It was quite impossible to cross the street with any feeling of security. It was criminal to have taken off the speed limit. This morning he had had to wait five minutes before he could cross High Street, and then he had just missed being knocked down by a lorry coming round the corner at a breakneck speed. Something ought to be done about it. He had nearly written a letter to the local paper about it himself last week.

The old man chuckled as there came to him a mental picture of Richard sitting at his desk, writing the letter to the local paper, tearing it up, writing another, tearing it up, writing another . . . till by the end of the morning the waste-paper basket would be full of torn-up letters to the local paper about the traffic in Danesborough, and Richard would have worked himself into a nervous fever.

"How many did you write, Richard?" he said, his blue eyes twinkling behind the bushy white eyebrows.

Richard hastily changed the subject and began to discuss the weather, which somehow seemed to lead to the noise of Danesborough streets. That, too, according to Richard, was growing worse and worse. Motorists, said Richard, should not be allowed to sound their horns when coming through the towns. If they drove with due care there would be no need to. The old man had another mental picture of Richard—this time hovering on the door-step of his lodgings, dreading to leave its peace and quiet for the bustle of the streets.

"You should have been a snail, Richard," he said. "Then you could have taken your house about with you."

Richard smiled perfunctorily, and there was a short silence. The old man broke it by saying abruptly:

"Did you know Stephen was here?"

"I knew he was coming to-night."

"Well, he's here now. He's been to see me this morning with Beatrice."

A worried look came over Richard's face.

"You know, father, I still don't think it was wise of you to invite her."

"You were always a fool, Richard," said the old man dryly, "but I thought you were a fairly broad-minded fool. It's news to me you've joined the Pharisees."

Richard waved the suggestion aside with horror. His pale face had flushed slightly.

"No, it's not that. Of course it's not that." He turned his kind, gentle, rather anxious grey eyes upon the old man. "It's—the others. The women, I mean. Margaret and Helen will be all right, of course, but the others—Isabel, Milly, Lilian."

The old man's brows drew together in a quick scowl. He understood what the boy meant. Even as a child Richard could never bear to see anything suffer. Without any open discourtesy the Royston women could, of course, show Beatrice that they considered her as belonging to another and unrecognised world. Then he remembered the shining remoteness of the sweet pale face, and his brow cleared.

"They can't touch her," he said exultantly.

"How do you know?" said Richard, and added, "It won't be pleasant to watch them trying to, anyway. You know what Isabel can be like. And even Milly. . . ."

The old man's eyebrows swooped together again. He seemed to see hounds with open mouths and gleaming fangs hunting a white faun through the thickets. Yes, how did he know they couldn't touch her? He felt less sure now that she wasn't actually there before him. And suddenly it seemed to him that the white faun was Hope. He saw her dark eyes wide with fear, her sweet lips parted in agony. He brought his fist down heavily on the arm of his chair.

"By *God*!" he said.

"What's the matter, father?" Richard said, starting forward anxiously.

"They won't try it in my house," said old Matthew in a strange choking voice. "I'm damned if they'll try it in my house."

"Of course they won't, father." The effect of his words had terrified Richard. "I didn't really mean it. Of course they won't. Don't worry about it, father."

"That's all right, lad," said Matthew in his ordinary tone.

For a moment he had thought that his anger was going to bring on an attack of his "indigestion," but the breathlessness that had come upon him passed.

"Enid's a good sort," went on Richard reassuringly.

The old man gave a short laugh.

"Aye, but she's what's known as a good woman, and they can be as cruel as hell."

Then Catherine entered and dismissed Richard rather summarily, saying that it was nearly father's lunch-time. Richard, who had never outgrown his childhood's awe of Catherine (Catherine as the eldest had been somewhat of a nursery tyrant, and Richard as the youngest had borne the full brunt of it), hastily took his departure, turning at the door to complain, in his prim but harassed voice, of the way people littered the street with their 'bus and tram tickets.

"It makes the whole place look so untidy," he said. "Why can't they put them in the boxes provided for them?"

"Write to the papers about it," chuckled Matthew, his good-humour returning as suddenly as it had gone.

While he ate his lunch, the old man's thoughts turned to what Richard had said. Margaret and Helen would be all right, of course. It struck him suddenly how much alike those two were. Or rather, Helen was like Margaret, as she had been before she had let life enclose her in that ice-cold detachment. Odd that so many men unconsciously choose as their wives women who remind them of their mothers. He had done so himself. His memories of his mother were faint and uncertain, but he knew that Harriet had been like her. He had never loved Harriet—never even pretended to love her. But she had been a good wife to him. She had kept his house in order, guarded his interests, brought up his children carefully. On his brief visits home, it had not been unpleasant to return to a well-organised household and a quiet Victorian wife, who spoke little, obeyed his wishes, and closed her eyes to everything in him she disapproved of.

The door opened, and for a moment it seemed to him that he had just returned from one of his trips abroad, and that Harriet was coming in to welcome him.

"Well, Harriet," he said. "Everything gone on all right?"

But it was Catherine who stood looking at him, her eyes bright and watchful, a faint gleam of triumph in their depths. He tried to cover the slip.

"I've been asleep," he said, "dreaming of your mother."

But the triumph still gleamed in her eyes. She knew that he had not been asleep. He was getting queer. She'd suspected it for some time.

"Now, father," she said in the brisk voice that always irritated him, "you must rest this afternoon."

His eyes glinted at her beneath their white overhanging brows.

"What did ye say?" he demanded with ominous distinctness.

Hastily she corrected the offending word.

"You ought to rest this afternoon," she said.

He felt strangely tired. He wanted to rest this afternoon. If she had not said that he must rest, he would have rested as a matter of course, but her authoritative tone roused his obstinacy. She hadn't got her claws into him yet, though she might think she had. That had been a slip about Harriet, but there was plenty of fight left in him.

"I'm not going to rest this afternoon," he said shortly. "I'm going out."

"Where?"

"I'm going for a walk."

"Where to?"

"Is that your business or mine?"

"It's mine. I'm responsible for you, and I can't allow you to——"

His old eyes flashed blue fire at her.

She stopped.

"Get out," he said, "before I teach you who's master in this house."

She went out, cowed and shaken. The old man's anger left him as soon as the door had closed on her, and he chuckled, feeling exhilarated by the little scene. That would show her all right!

The yellow cat woke up with a gasp, and he knelt by it, stroking its head and crooning over it tenderly, reassuringly.

"It's all right, Puss. It's better now, isn't it? You'll soon be well. . . . There, there. Gaston!" he called.

Gaston came out of the bedroom, where he had been polishing the furniture.

"I'm going out."

"Where?" demanded Gaston.

"To hell with your questions!" snapped the old man. "You're as bad as Catherine. I'm going for a walk. You can have the afternoon off. You needn't be back till this evening, in time to help me dress for the party. Hurry up, man. Get me my hat and stick." Again excitement had seized him, for suddenly he knew where he was going. He was going to the White Swan, where Stephen and Beatrice were staying. And he was going to take Beatrice round with him to the whole lot of them—to Margaret, Helen, Isabel, Milly, and Lilian. She would enter their houses under his protection. And they would be civil to her, or he would know the reason why. And then to-night all would be well. They would have seen what store he set by her, and they would not dare to slight her.

Gaston brought him his hat.

"Take the cat into my bedroom, Gaston," he said. "It'll be safer there."

He set off down the stairs. Half-way down he suddenly forgot where he was going and why. He only knew that it was something to do with Hope. Then he remembered the vision he had had of open-fanged hounds in pursuit of the white faun. Again he seemed to see Hope's dark eyes wide with terror. He must go to her quickly, quickly. . . . He started forward, but by the time he reached the hall, he had remembered that he was going to the White Swan to see Stephen and Beatrice. Through the open door of the dining-room he could see the long mahogany table, its extra leaves inserted, covered by a fine damask cloth. The places were laid, and Catherine was putting a big bowl of flowers in the middle.

"Margaret will sit on your right hand, father," said Catherine, seeing him in the doorway, "and I'll be at the other end."

"I'll have Hope next me on my right," said the old man, entering.

"Hope?"

"Beatrice."

The bright watchful eyes were fixed on him.

"You said Hope."

"I'll say what I please," snapped the old man, and went on, "I tell you I'll have Beatrice on my right hand."

"Beatrice?"

"You're not deaf, are you, Catherine?"

The colour stood out in patches on Catherine's face.

"You can't possibly give—Beatrice the place of honour at your party."

"Why not?"

"I want Charlotte at my end to help me, so Margaret must sit on your right. She'd be most hurt. . . ."

"Ye know quite well that Margaret doesn't give a damn where she sits, or whether she comes at all. I wouldn't care if she did, either. Beatrice sits at my right hand."

"I won't countenance this, father."

"Ye can stop away, then. The whole lot of ye can stop away and I'll have dinner alone with Stephen and Beatrice. Will that suit ye?"

Catherine had drawn herself up to her full height, crimson-faced, majestic.

"Father, you say you're the master of this house. Well, it's the duty of the master of a house to protect its women from any contact with impurity and——"

"Who taught ye that?" said the old man. "James?"

Then he went out, chuckling. He walked down the drive, out by the big iron gates, and set off along the country road that led to Danesborough. The sun poured down on the beech trees and fell in golden splashes on the roadway beneath. And again that strange unearthly glamour seemed to inform everything around him, as if the whole world had just been created anew. He quickened his footsteps eagerly. She had told him last night to come to-day. "Come to-morrow," she had said. "You won't forget?" How adorable she had looked, with her tiny waist from which the crinoline swept out like a great bell, with her sweet shy smile and the rosebuds that clustered round her small shapely head! "Come to-morrow," she had said, "You won't forget?" And he had said "*Forget!*"

He hurried on still faster, then turned to see Gaston following. Even as he turned Gaston tried to slip into the shelter of the hedge, but the old man raised his hand and beckoned.

"What are you following me for?" he said angrily, when the man came up.

Gaston's one eye met his undismayed.

"I am not following you," he replied.

"What are you doing, then?"

"I am going for a walk. You gave me the afternoon off."

"I tell you you're following me. What do you think you are? My nurse or my servant?"

"I am not following you," persisted Gaston stubbornly. "I am going for a walk."

"Get off with you!" said Matthew, raising his stick with a threatening gesture. "I tell you I won't be followed."

Gaston fell back and again began to follow the old man. The old man pretended not to see him, but he felt a secret relief that he would not have acknowledged to anyone at the thought that Gaston was near him. He had been walking too quickly, perhaps. He felt that strange breathlessness that usually preceded his "indigestion" attacks. Suddenly one of them was on him. The pain of it seemed to leap out at him like a wild animal, mauling and choking him. Gaston was at his side in a moment, holding a small flask of brandy to his lips. The pain passed, and they sat down together on a low wall by the roadside till the old man had got his breath back.

"It wasn't anything," he panted at last. "Just a touch of indigestion."

"I know," said Gaston. "I'll get something for it."

"Bismuth's what they give for it," said the old man casually.

"I'll get some bismuth," said Gaston.

"If you tell Catherine——" began Matthew.

Gaston shook his head. "I will not tell her," he said.

"Why should you, anyway?" went on Matthew.

"Just a touch of indigestion. Everyone has indigestion."

"Yes," agreed Gaston and added again, "I'll get some bismuth."

The two old men sat there in the sunshine. Matthew realised suddenly that he was very tired. He had been hurrying somewhere—he'd forgotten where—and it had tired him. It was good to rest like this in the warmth of the sun. He was growing old, of course. He was ninety-five to-day.

"If I were dead, Gaston," he said suddenly, "what would you do?"

"I would try to go to Italy," said Gaston. "I like Italy. It is warm in Italy. But," he added, "it takes a lot of money to go there."

Matthew chuckled, thinking that Gaston would be surprised if he knew how much money he would have when he, Matthew, died.

He rose slowly to his feet.

"Well," he said, "I must be going on."

For a moment he searched painfully in his memory for his errand, then he remembered it. He was going to the White Swan to see Stephen and Beatrice. He was going to make sure that the women of his family treated Beatrice properly at his party to-night.

The first straggling shops of the town were now appearing. He went into a dairy and bought a sixpenny carton of cream for the little cat, slipping it into his coat pocket. Then he entered a florist's and bought an armful of roses. He felt rather doubtful about them as he paid for them. Shouldn't it have been some other flower? But what other flower? White jasmine ... that was it. No, roses were right, after all. She had worn rosebuds in a wreath round her small dark head.

It seemed a long way to the market-place, where the White Swan stood, overlooking the quiet cobbled square. It was some time, of course, since he had walked from Greenways into Danesborough.

The news that old Mr. Royston himself had come to visit his grandson caused a flutter in the bar and kitchen of the little inn. Mrs. Slaggit, the landlady, came in person to receive him, hastily slipping a clean apron over her soiled one, and escorted him up to the red parlour, which she had set aside as a sitting-room for the visitors. It was a clean enough room, though the smell of furniture polish and of the mignonette that stood in a vase on the mantelpiece fought unavailingly against a faint but pervasive odour of stale tobacco smoke and spirits. Red brocade curtains hung at the window, red plush chairs were ranged round the walls, on the wallpaper faded red roses climbed up a dim silver trellis. A writing-desk stood by the door beneath an engraving of the Monarch of the Glen, and between the windows was an ancient harmonium, with both pedals missing, that supported a pile of out-of-date reference books. Above the fireplace an engraving of Mr. Gladstone presided grimly over two elaborate equestrian groups in bronze and a clock in a case of Derbyshire spar that had stopped ten years ago at twenty-three minutes past eleven.

"Mr. Royston to see you, sir," announced Mrs. Slaggit.

Beatrice turned sharply from the window where she was standing with Stephen, and came across the room with outstretched arms.

"*You!*" she said in glad welcome. "How dear of you to come!"

Her voice reached him over the years with that indescribable bell-like sweetness that no other voice in the world had ever had, with that strangely childlike inflexion that somehow tore at his heart. The little room faced north, and the sunshine that had poured down in the street outside did not find its way here, but to the old man it was as if he had stepped from cold and darkness into radiant warmth and light.

He put down his armful of roses on the table.

"I've brought you some flowers," he said, "and I want you to come out with me. I want to take you to see the others."

Chapter Ten

DAPHNE sat curled up on the window-seat of her bedroom, craning her neck to look down the road. It was only a quarter to three, and Pen wasn't supposed to be coming till three. Still—Pen was generally early for appointments. She was always so afraid of keeping people waiting, so breathlessly eager not to cause trouble to anyone.

Daphne's mother was giving a bridge party, and already the guests were arriving—well-groomed, well-corseted, well-dressed women, the members of Danesborough's smart set. They met at someone's house nearly every day for bridge and gossip. They went up to London at regular intervals to buy their clothes and see the latest plays. The Collins, who despised Danesborough and its doings, made fun of them, but for all that they were as well dressed as the friends of the Collins who came down from London every week-end and drank cocktails and whisky at the Collins' little bar. The members of Danesborough's smart set did not drink cocktails or whisky. They drank tea—with lemon instead of milk, because it seemed more sophisticated—but they spent as much on their clothes as the Collins' friends and were as quick in catching up a new fashion. And, even if they had not seen everything that was "on" in London, they had the jargon at their fingers' ends and could talk as if they had.

Somehow Daphne still hadn't accustomed herself to seeing these people in her home.

In the old days it had been so different—just Mummy and Daddy and she and John and Biddy. They hardly ever had people in, because it was so jolly with only themselves. When Daddy was away at his office, Mummy seemed to be waiting all the time for him to come back to her. She would change into her prettiest frock for his coming home—instead of keeping it for going out in as most people did—and be waiting at the front door as soon as he opened the gate. John used to tease them and say, "Haven't you two finished your honeymoon yet?" Somehow it was difficult to believe that Mummy was the same person now. She was so smart and hard and restless. She didn't seem sad, as you'd have thought she would be. She talked a lot and laughed a lot and was always going out, or having people in, and that, of course, was the strangest part of all, when you remembered the old Mummy, who had only wanted Daddy and her home and children. She had even changed in appearance. She used to be quiet and placid and rather plump. Now she was thin and fidgety and bright-eyed, and her voice, which had been low and gentle, had become high-pitched and slightly shrill.

Daphne would often think of the old days and compare them wistfully, perplexedly, with these, but she shrank from thinking of the day—early in the summer holidays—that divided them, like a black abyss dividing a warm sunny landscape from a stretch of bleak desert. Even now she wasn't quite sure what had happened. Her memory of it was like a confused nightmare, the sort of nightmare that you daren't try to remember. Setting out in the yacht—she and Daddy and John and Biddy—all laughing and talking together, teasing Biddy because she said she'd seen a sea serpent . . . the sudden squall . . . Daddy and John struggling with the sails . . . then all of them in the water . . . a glimpse of Daddy with Biddy in his arms . . . of John wrestling with an enormous wave . . . then nothing till she woke up in bed and heard them whispering and knew that Daddy, John, and Biddy had been drowned.

"Where's Mummy?" she had cried, but Mummy had gone to London for the day to do some shopping, and no one had been able to get into touch with her. At last she came back, and Daphne heard them telling her, heard her sharp agonised cry, heard her "Which did you say was saved?" then the despairing moan, "Daphne . . . Oh, my God!"

Daphne still heard that despairing moan. Some unerring instinct had told her what it meant. Mummy wouldn't have said it just like that if it had been John or Biddy. John was the only son, sturdy and handsome, with Daddy's brown eyes and jolly smile. Biddy was the baby, the latest born, roguish and dimpled, quick and loving and deliciously quaint. Daphne had always known that she was less dear to her parents than the other two, had known it without resentment, because she admired John and loved Biddy almost as much as they did. Beneath her anguish in their loss was an odd sense of guilt, as if somehow she were to blame for having been saved instead of John or Biddy. She thought that Mummy had the same feeling, that she never looked at her without saying to herself: If only it had been one of the others! That anguished "Oh, my God!" seemed to stand between them, so that they could not see each other clearly. She had gone back to school soon after the funeral, and, when she came home at the end of the term, it had been to find Mummy like this. She had come home determined to try to make up to her for everything she had lost, for Daddy and John and Biddy, and she had found that she didn't want her at all. Sometimes she had a horrible suspicion—a suspicion she tried not to face—that Mummy would rather she had been drowned, too. Mummy wanted to forget altogether, and Daphne's presence kept reminding her.

The shrill tinkle of voices rose from the drawing-room downstairs.

"Yes, it's his birthday to-day. He's ninety-five. Isn't it wonderful? . . . We're all going there to dinner to-night. Family gatherings are generally ghastly—aren't they?—but this is rather an occasion." Then in a lowered voice Mummy said something about "My brother . . ." That was Uncle Stephen. There was supposed to be a sort of mystery about Uncle Stephen. People never mentioned him when she or Pen or Pippa were there, but they knew what it was. He was living with someone who wasn't his wife, which, of course, was a terribly wicked thing to do. Daphne stood gazing dreamily in front of her, thinking about him. Her memories of him belonged to the old happy days. He used to come to nursery tea with them and let them search in his pockets for pennies, and he always took them to the pantomime at Christmas. He had a funny, slow, kind smile and very big hands that were much gentler than other people's smaller ones. It was hard to think of someone who'd taken you to the pantomime and given you pennies as wicked. And she remembered that once he had paid for a street-sweeper's little boy to go into hospital to have his legs put straight. It was so puzzling when wickedness and goodness got muddled up like that. Daphne had never seen the woman he lived with. She must be very beautiful. ... Wicked women were always beautiful. She probably looked like Cleopatra. And Daphne saw her quite plainly, with green slanting eyes and red hair and jewelled breast-plate and long trailing robes and bracelets all up her arms. Then she realised that she couldn't possibly be dressed like that at great-gran's party. But still—she was sure she'd have green eyes and red hair. It would be rather thrilling to sit at the same table as a wicked woman. Aunt Anthea had been wicked, of course, but not till after she left Uncle Paul. And Aunt Anthea certainly hadn't looked like Cleopatra. She had been pretty and slender and vague and untidy, her fair hair always tumbling about her face, her clothes put on anyhow. She was always forgetting things and losing things and being late and not listening to what people said, and she had a lovely laugh like a waterfall in a wood. She generally ran instead of walking and went through the High Street without a hat and sat in the garden in a kimono drying her hair in the sun where people could see her from the road and didn't care what anyone thought of her. Aunt Catherine used to look very grim whenever she was mentioned. She said that she did not support Uncle Paul's dignity and that she knew of several people who had stopped having Uncle Paul for their doctor because they disapproved of Aunt Anthea. Aunt Catherine had been glad when she left Uncle Paul and then later wrote to tell him that she was living with someone else so that he could divorce her.

Daphne glanced at her watch. It was ten minutes to three. Pen was generally very early, but she wasn't going to be very early to-day.

She stood up and carefully smoothed down her dress in front

of the looking-glass. She'd crumpled it a little by curling upon the window-seat. How leggy one always seemed at the beginning of the summer holidays! This dress had been quite long last summer. She examined the hem. It would easily let down. She'd ask Cook to do it for her. Cook was very good about doing things for her. Last holidays, when she was in bed with a feverish cold, Cook often used to come up and straighten her bedclothes and put eau-de-Cologne on her forehead. Of course, before—it happened, Mummy used to fuss round all day when one of them was ill, running up and downstairs, bringing iced drinks and fruit and sitting by the bedside, reading aloud. But last holidays Mummy hadn't even seemed to know that she was ill. In a way it was as if her real mother had died, like Pen's. Only she hadn't a stepmother as Pen had. She'd hate to have a stepmother. She wondered if Pen hated it. Pen never talked about Aunt Helen, but she hardly ever talked about anything. Aunt Enid called her "little Sobersides." It was terrible when Aunt Enid called you things like that—it made you curl up inside—but she was a good sort, and it had been nice of her to ask them to join her hockey team when they left school. Leaving school would be rather fun in a way. It would mean that one was really grown-up. She went over to the mirror on the dressing-table and studied her reflection carefully, wondering if she were pretty. Life, of course, would be much more exciting if one were pretty. She was rather like Pen, she decided, except that she had more colour and her hair was more golden. Pen's paleness and straight figure made her look very distinguished. She took up her hand-mirror and studied her profile dispassionately. No, on the whole, she didn't think she was pretty. Biddy had been lovely, with deep blue eyes like violets and thick curls that looked as if the sun were shining on them even on a dark day. And she was always laughing—a rich, deep, baby chuckle, whole-hearted, delicious. In the early morning she used to come to Daphne's room, and they used to have games together in bed, Daphne making hills and earthquakes of her knees and Biddy rolling down them and laughing. Often now in bed in the morning she would imagine Biddy's coming to her and she would put her knees up and down and almost feel

Biddy's soft, warm little body rolling about. Sometimes it seemed so real that she was surprised that Mummy didn't hear Biddy's laughter in her room next door.

And John. . . . Daphne used to imagine him coming in his pyjamas to sit on her bed and talk to her, as he often did in the old days, and that, too, was so real to her that often she seemed actually to see him—his serious young face, his untidy hair, his hands stuck down deep in his pockets. She would tell him how Mummy had changed and ask him what she ought to do about it.

"You can't do anything, old girl," he always said. "Just carry on."

However tired she was when she went to bed she could never settle down to sleep till she had had a pretend game with Biddy and a pretend talk with John. Somehow it seemed so cruel to shut them out as Mummy did. And nearly always at night she left her bedroom door ajar, so that the dream-Biddy could come in if she felt frightened of the dark. Biddy often used to be frightened of the dark and creep across the landing to Daphne for comfort. She had done it the night before—it happened.

"But Biddy," Daphne had said, "you ought to be brave."

"I *am* brave," Biddy had replied. "I mean, I'm part brave and part frightened. I mean," she had explained further, "I'm brave of lions and brave of dragons, but I'm not brave of the dark."

Often now Daphne would half awake from sleep in the night and seem to feel the warm baby figure climbing into her bed. She would hold up the bedclothes and murmur, "Come on, Biddy darling."

She never told anyone of this dream game. She had another dream game, too, one of which she was secretly ashamed. It was a dream in which Mummy wanted her and they comforted each other, and Mummy talked to her about Daddy and John and Biddy and didn't go white and stony when they were mentioned.

"But I've got you, darling," Mummy would say in that dream. "I couldn't bear it if I hadn't got you."

When she was away at school that dream seemed so real that she almost believed it. She talked to her friends as if it were true.

"It's hateful having to leave her for the term," she would say, "because I'm all she's got left, and we simply can't bear to be away from each other."

She invented reasons to account for Mummy's not writing to her, saying that she had hurt her wrist and that the doctor had said she mustn't use it, or that instead of writing she kept a diary and gave it her on the first night of the holidays. But she knew that they didn't really believe her. Still—the dream generally became so real to her during the term that when she came home she couldn't understand what had happened just at first, and she would soon begin to long for the term time again so that she could go on pretending. After Christmas she would be at home all the time. The thought of it suddenly frightened her. Would Mummy grow really to hate her?

"I can't bear it if she does," she said aloud, and suddenly seemed to see John, his untidy hair sticking up all over his head, grinning at her.

"Keep smiling, old girl," he said, "and just carry on."

She grinned back.

Then she glanced at her watch again. It was five minutes to three. She went to the window and looked out. Pen wasn't in sight yet. She might as well get her things ready for to-night while she was waiting. It was going to be rather a rush changing between the tennis party and great-gran's dinner. She took her evening dress down from the wardrobe and laid it on the bed, together with her evening slip and stockings. Then she took from a drawer the present she had bought for great-gran—a leather note-case and pocket-book combined. He probably had dozens of them already. It was so difficult buying presents for old people. By the time you were ninety-five, of course, you had everything that you could possibly want. A sudden vision of great-gran's face came to her, and she wondered what it felt like to be as old as that. He generally looked as if it were rather a joke. She wondered if anyone really knew him. He seemed to live right away from everyone, somewhere behind the bushy overhanging eyebrows. His eyes gleamed out from them—shrewd, humorous, slightly cynical.

They were all just a little afraid of him, but no one knew why. She tried to imagine herself ninety-five years old, with children and grandchildren and great-grandchildren. But perhaps she wouldn't marry. Lots of women didn't. Aunt Charlotte hadn't married, and neither had Aunt Enid. Right down at the bottom of one's heart, however, one rather hoped that one would marry. She didn't remember her great-grandmother. Great-gran must have been in love with her, of course. She tried to imagine great-gran as a young man in love, but it was quite impossible. She couldn't imagine him as anything but a very old man, with a lined wizened face and eyes that twinkled disconcertingly behind white bushy eyebrows.

The clock struck three. She went to the window again and looked out. Pen still wasn't in sight, but Aunt Lilian was coming down the road, and turning in at the gate. Aunt Lilian was a newcomer to the family, like Aunt Helen. Uncle Paul had married her after he divorced Aunt Anthea. She was as unlike Aunt Anthea as anyone possibly could be. She was slow and dignified and silent. She had high cheek-bones, a smooth, rather sallow skin, big dark velvety eyes, and very full red lips. Some people said that she was beautiful, but others called her plain. Daphne always felt shy with her and never knew what to say to her. She made no effort to put one at one's ease, treating one generally as if one were not there.

Pen was awfully late—at least late for Pen. It was two minutes past three now. Daphne decided to go down the road towards Uncle Harold's and meet her. She took up her tennis racquet and ran lightly downstairs. Mummy and Aunt Lilian were standing in the hall.

"I didn't know you were having a party," Aunt Lilian was saying in her deep voice. She wasn't really fat, but she made Mummy look terribly thin. Mummy's bright green dress seemed to hang on her as if she were just a pole. Mummy always wore very bright colours now, though in the old days she had worn dark colours because Daddy liked her best in dark colours.

"It's only a little bridge afternoon," said Mummy. "I wish you'd join us, but you don't play, do you?"

"No. Well, I won't keep you, but, if you haven't made any other arrangements for to-night, shall Paul and I call for you in the car to take you up to Greenways?"

"Oh, my dear, how sweet of you! I'd forgotten it for the moment. Do come into the drawing-room a minute. . . . You know everyone, don't you?" She turned to the others with her bright, restless smile. "You all know my sister-in-law, don't you? I've just been telling them that grandfather's ninety-five to-day and having the whole family to dinner. It's a real occasion, isn't it, Lilian?"

The sombreness lifted for a moment from Lilian's face.

"It's rather sporting of the old man, but Paul thinks he'll find it too tiring. He's looked very frail lately."

"Oh, he's as tough as a piece of leather," said Isabel lightly, thinking that Lilian was taking a too proprietary attitude towards the old man, considering that she was only an in-law, and a recent one at that.

Someone saw Daphne in the hall and screamed out.

"Hello, darling, I didn't know you were back."

Daphne, entering, glanced at Isabel, but as usual Isabel's eyes slid away from hers.

"I only came back yesterday."

"And where are you off to now?"

"A tennis party at the Rectory."

"Oh yes. Mrs. Harte was ordering the cakes for it in Pollit's this morning. Adam's home, isn't he?"

"I suppose so. The colleges always come home before we do."

"He's finished at college now, I believe. I don't know what he's going to do. I've heard that his father's so disappointed with him for refusing to go into the Church that he won't raise a finger to help him. Of course it *is* disappointing. The Church is so *safe.*"

"How sweet you look in that yellow dress, Daphne!" said Mrs. Hacket, a diminutive woman with assertive manners, whose husband was on the staff of the Danesborough Grammar School. "Her colouring's just like Biddy's, isn't it, Isabel?"

Mrs. Hacket had come this afternoon determined to make some reference to Biddy. It was absurd the way Isabel wouldn't mention any of them. Someone ought to take the bull by the horns and force her to. Mrs. Hacket considered that her husband's position on the staff of the Grammar School made her an authority on all matters of culture. She had a vague smattering of Freud and could talk very glibly about repressions and inhibitions, and she had come to the conclusion that it was her duty to break down Isabel's inhibition for her.

But Isabel said "No, *no!*" with a quick intake of her breath, not so much denying the likeness as pushing the thought of Biddy aside. There was a gleam of terror in her bright glancing eyes. Mrs. Hacket decided not to try to break down her inhibition again. The woman looked almost insane. The others all began to talk at once, tiding over the awkward moment. A strange nightmare feeling descended upon Daphne. She murmured something about "three o'clock" and hurried out of the house, down the little drive, and into the street.

Yes, there was Pen, running round the corner. She wore her pink dress with a white hat and a white belt.

"I'm *so* sorry I'm late," she said breathlessly.

"It's all right," Daphne reassured her.

Out in the bright sunshine the nightmare feeling was leaving her.

"How nice you look, Pen!" she said. "That's a new belt, isn't it?"

"It's not mine," said Pen. "It's Helen's. She lent it me."

"Oh," said Daphne, hoping that Pen was going to talk about Aunt Helen, but Pen went on, looking at the drawing-room window, which could be seen from the road:

"What a lot of people in your house!"

"Yes. Mummy's giving a bridge party." Daphne hesitated, wondering whether to say that they had both been terribly disappointed that the Rectory tennis party came on the same day, because Mummy had been so looking forward to having her at home for the bridge party. But it was no use saying things like that to Pen. She would pretend to believe it, but she wouldn't really, and then it would be spoilt for Daphne. Now that she was out of the house in the bright sunshine, she could almost believe it herself. Almost. As long as she didn't say it to anyone. ("Darling, I'm so sorry you have to go out your first day like this," Mummy had said. "But never mind. We've all the rest of the holidays, and we'll have a lovely time together.")

"Aunt Lilian's there, too," she said. "She called to say that she and Uncle Paul would give us a lift to great-gran's party to-night. I've got him a notecase. It seems terribly dull, and he must have hundreds."

"I've got him a letter weight. It's so difficult to get presents for old people. They have everything already."

"I know. I think it must be dreadful to be old and to know that everything that was going to happen to you has happened, and—— Look! Here's Uncle Paul."

A car drew up at the side of the road, and Paul Royston smiled at them from the driver's seat.

"Can I give you a lift anywhere?" he said. "I suppose you aren't going my way, though. I'm going home to lunch."

"You're late, aren't you?" said Pen.

"I know. A doctor shouldn't have a stomach at all. I've had four unexpected cases this morning."

He was a tall spare man with a pleasant rather tired face. He stooped slightly, as if from bending over innumerable sick-beds, and had a habit of pursing his lips, as though afraid of letting out professional secrets. He reminded Daphne of both Uncle Richard and great-gran. He had Uncle Richard's kind eyes, but, instead of the timidity that lurked behind the kindness in Uncle Richard's, was a faint spark of the shrewdness that twinkled behind great-gran's bushy eyebrows.

"Aunt Lilian's at our house," volunteered Daphne. "She called about your giving us a lift to-night. It's awfully nice of you."

"Don't mention it," he said with mock politeness. "The pleasure will be ours. And where are you off to now?"

"The Rectory. There's a tennis party."

"Oh yes. I saw great preparations. I had to go round there this morning. That little pig Cressida only got home from school yesterday, and she's given herself stomach-ache already with eating green apples." He pursed his lips. "Don't tell her I said so, though.

She'll probably pretend it's something much more dignified. Adam was marking out the tennis court. He's quite a young man-about-town nowadays, isn't he?"

"Is he?" said Daphne. "I've not seen him for ages. He was away from home last holidays and the holidays before."

"Well, I won't keep you. We'll all meet at the family beano to-night. By the way, your Aunt Enid's just on ahead. I suppose she's going, too?"

"Yes, and Pippa. We're going to call for Pippa now. We're horribly late, I'm afraid."

"So am I. Good-bye."

"Good-bye."

They hurried on to Pippa's.

Chapter Eleven

PIPPA hated being called Pippa. Facetious people, meeting her in the street, said "Pippa Passes," or asked her if all were right with the world. Occasionally she tried to persuade her acquaintances to call her by her real name, Philippa, but they never did so for longer than a day. She had by now resigned herself to Pippa with that faintly smouldering resentment with which she had resigned herself to most things.

She was sitting in her bedroom, sewing up the hem of her tennis dress, where her heel had caught in it the last time she had worn it. It was a creased and somewhat soiled dress of blue cotton. Pippa had wanted to have it washed this week, but mother had said that it would do to wear another time. "But it's dirty," Pippa had protested. "It's not dirty enough to wash," mother had replied firmly. "We have a large enough ordinary wash without you putting in extra things like that." Mother seemed to think it waste of time to wash anything till you could hardly see it for dirt.

Pippa looked at her watch. Twenty minutes past two. More than half an hour before Daphne and Pen would be here. She must iron the dress when she had finished mending the hem, then perhaps it would look better.

On the bed lay her evening dress ready for tonight. She had been stitching on to it the spray of artificial flowers that they had bought this morning in Barrat's. A sudden wave of anger surged over her. It was so hateful being poor. Pen and Daphne would be wearing smart evening dresses of ankle length, and she would have to wear that old white alpaca that she'd had for her confirmation two years ago. It had long sleeves and only reached a few inches below her knees, though it had been let down as far as it would let down. It pulled across her chest, too, and had that horrible yellow look that white gets when it has been washed over and over again. And, of course, it was badly ironed, the sash pressed into zigzag creases and the front looking as if it had been rough dried. Mother had ironed it. "Here it is," she said when she'd finished. "It'll do. . . . I haven't time to do it any better."

To Pippa that "It'll do . . ." was like an irritant applied to an old wound. Since her early childhood she had heard mother saying "It'll do" like that, whenever she couldn't be bothered to finish something properly. It summed up in one short phrase the slovenliness, the "anyhowness," the lack of care and method, that lay like a blight over the whole house. Ever since she could remember, Pippa's attitude to it had been one of sullen, ineffective resentment. Occasionally she made blundering attempts to fight against it, but generally she surrendered to it without resistance. It was something too strong to be resisted.

At first, of course, she had taken her surroundings for granted, but disillusion had been swift and complete when she went to school. On her second day there she had overheard two mistresses obviously talking about her.

"She's appallingly dressed, isn't she?" one of them had said, and the other had replied, "Yes. At least her mother might darn her stockings and sew the buttons on her cardigan. Just *look* at those safety pins."

Pippa had glanced down at her small person. Holes in stockings were wrong, then. And so were safety pins instead of buttons. It was quite a new idea to her. Then gradually had come that sense of humiliation that was to be her most familiar companion through her school-days. The looks of faint disgust on the two mistresses' faces heralded it. People despised her because she had holes in her stockings and safety-pins instead of buttons. Other girls, she began to notice, did not have these things. They were sent to school fresh and dainty, darned and brushed and cleaned and polished. There was, indeed, a sort of competition among the mothers as to which could send the best-turned-out child to school. Pippa's mother did not enter the competition. She could not even get hers off to school punctually. She never knew what the time was, because she never could remember to wind up the clocks.

"Pippa, you'd better get up. . . . I don't know what the time is. . . . Goodness, you'll be late. . . . That's nine o'clock going. . . . You'll have to do without breakfast. Anyway, the porridge is burnt. Here's a piece of bread. You can eat it on the way to school."

Or sometimes—again owing to Milly's chronic ignorance of the time of day—she would arrive before the school doors opened and would have to wait outside in the cold and rain for ten or fifteen minutes.

Her neglected, badly groomed little figure continued to irritate the staff.

"Pippa, your *nails*! They're simply disgusting. Doesn't your mother ever clean them for you? . . . Well, you must learn to do it yourself, then."

"Pippa, have you brushed your hair this morning? It's like a bird's nest. Go to the cloak-room at once and brush it. You really *mustn't* come to school in this state."

"Pippa, don't come to school in those stockings again. Your heels are right out of both of them . . . and will you please ask your mother to brush your coat."

The other girls would look at each other and smile. . . . Pippa had the pride of the over-sensitive, and several times a day the iron of hot angry shame would enter her child soul.

Milly remained unmoved by the messages that Pippa duly brought home.

"Well, I haven't got any more darned just now. I've been so busy. . . . You'll have to wear them another day, at any rate. The holes hardly show."

The staff sent courteous notes. Would Mrs. Chudleigh please see that Pippa's shoes were mended? Both soles were through, and the child was coming to school with wet feet every day.

"How they *fuss*!" said Milly placidly.

They sent her home from school with streaming colds and once with a stye in each eye that prevented her from reading.

"I'd never noticed," said Milly, still unperturbed. "Why didn't you tell me if you weren't well?"

Pippa grew up sullen, aggressive, "difficult," cherishing a bitter sense of aggrievement against life in general. Her one consolation was that she was clever. She took a secret exultant pride in her cleverness. They could sneer at her as much as they liked (they did not, of course, sneer at her as much as Pippa imagined they did), but she could beat them all at lessons and examinations. She felt especially bitter towards her cousins, Daphne and Pen, attributing to them feelings of complacent superiority because they went to expensive boarding schools instead of the local day school and had pretty fashionable clothes to wear, while she wore her shabby school uniform all through the holidays. She imagined that they spent most of their time together discussing the inadequacy of her clothes, the dinginess of her home, and the general awfulness of her parents, and finding an unending source of amusement in these things. In order to show them that she knew all this but did not care, she avoided them whenever she could and was as ungracious as possible when she was obliged to meet them.

She would have been amazed had she known that, although she was one year younger than Pen and two years younger than Daphne, they stood in awe of her.

She broke off her cotton and, going over to the long mirror of her wardrobe, held her dress up against her figure. It was new this summer, so it wouldn't be so bad when it was ironed. It was grubby, though. Perhaps if she just scrubbed the back of the collar with her nail-brush. . . .

She laid it over a chair and began to study her reflection. Her hair was very straight and of an unattractive shade of red, her eyes were hazel, her lashes colourless, and her dull skin thickly covered with freckles. It was a type of looks she particularly disliked, and she often wished despairingly that she had been plain in any other way. Mark, her brother, was like her, but somehow it wasn't so bad for a boy. He didn't mind being called Ginger and Carrots, and didn't get annoyed when people put their hands on his hair and then pretended that they had burnt their fingers. Leslie, her younger sister, was pretty, with long dark hair that twisted easily into curls, a pink-and-white complexion, and heavily lashed blue eyes. The family had always been divided into two camps—Pippa and Mark in one, Leslie with their mother and father in the other. Leslie was their parents' favourite. She was proud of the position and had devised innumerable ways of turning it to account. Before she was three she had discovered that reporting the misdemeanours of Pippa and Mark brought her praise and reward. Retaliation on the part of Pippa and Mark could also be reported and resulted in their further punishment. In the end, she found, she scored. Moreover, there was quite a lot to be got out of both mother and father if you went the right way about it. Father especially. You climbed on his knee and called him "Daddy darling" and ran to get his slippers and played with his hair and said that you wished it was Sunday every day so that he could always be at home, and he brought you presents—sweets or toys or games. He never brought presents for Mark or Pippa. You called yourself "Daddy's little daughter," ignoring the sight of Mark pretending to be sick behind his chair, and he would let you take pennies—or sometimes even sixpences—out of his pocket. He never gave Mark or Pippa any money except their pocket money, and he was always stopping that. He often said that if they would only model their behaviour on Leslie's—little girl though she was—he would be more pleased with them and they would find themselves better off.

"I'd rather not have a penny of his beastly money," said Pippa passionately, "than smarm over him for it as that kid does."

And Mark said, "Same here!"

Pippa never remembered a time when she did not dislike her father. She felt for her mother a half-affectionate contempt, but she actively disliked her father. She disliked everything about him—his stout clumsy figure, his harsh voice, his round red face, always faintly blue about the jowl, his pompous bullying manner. He shouted orders in his home like a drill-sergeant and expected to be instantly obeyed. He nagged like a woman when anything went wrong. He made scenes over the most absurd trifles, merely to give himself the enjoyable feeling of being master in his own house. Though Pippa was sixteen and Mark fifteen he would box their ears if anything they said or did annoyed him. He sometimes flew into grotesque rages and hit out at them savagely while they dodged his blows as best they could. Mark, who disliked him even more than Pippa did, could give exquisitely funny imitations of him in his rages, but beneath their amusement was a harsh unchildlike bitterness. Though Leslie was no fonder of their father than the other two, her methods ensured that he never hit and seldom scolded her.

Despite his irascible temper, Arnold Chudleigh was a deeply uxorious man, and after eighteen years was almost as much in love with his wife as he had been when he married her. It was, perhaps, a sort of inverted vanity that made him close his eyes to her faults. She was his choice and therefore perfect. His own standards of comfort were not high, and he saw little wrong with her methods of housekeeping. And she, on her side, was in love with him. She admired his assertiveness, accepting without question his dogmatic pronouncements on all subjects, even those about which he obviously could know nothing. Her conversation was always freely sprinkled with "Arnold says . . ." or "I'll ask Arnold." When he came home, tired and cross, and scolded her about some slight household matter, she behaved with flattering docility, weeping at his anger, apologising for her fault, receiving his forgiveness with humble gratitude. He always enjoyed comforting her after he had made her cry. In his conflicts with Mark and Pippa she invariably supported him, reproaching them for "upsetting your poor father who works so hard for us all."

She thought herself very happy in the possession of a good husband and three nice children (though Mark and Pippa were very naughty sometimes), and considered that she did her duty by them all to the uttermost. She was not unlike Charlotte in appearance and possessed her power of seeing all her surroundings through a rose-coloured haze.

Pippa laid down the dress and took her white canvas shoes out of the wardrobe. She had cleaned them, but the sole of one of them was worn right through. It was that wretched asphalt playground at school. It simply tore rubber soles to rags. And it was no use asking for a new pair. It would be a long time before father would pay for anything else for her.

There had been another row last night. Mark had come into the dining-room, leaving the door open, and father, who was sitting near the window, flew into one of his sudden tempers. "Leaving that door open with the draught blowing straight on to me!" he had shouted in his harsh rasping voice. "You'll go in and out of that door ten times and shut it after you each time and see if that'll teach you. Go on!"

Mark had looked at him and gone out of the room, closing the door. They had waited for him to return, Pippa hot and breathless with anger. But all they had heard had been the sound of the shutting of the front door. Leslie, agog with excitement, had crept out to reconnoitre. "He's gone out," she reported shrilly. "He's gone out. He's walking down the street."

"I'm glad he has," Pippa had said exultantly.

His face livid with rage, her father sprang at her, hitting out wildly. She dodged him round the room, shielding her head with her arms, then ran upstairs, where she locked herself in her bedroom and did not dare to come down again that night. Mark had returned later, and the performance had been repeated. She heard her father's voice raised in hysterical fury, heard the scuffle that meant that Mark was dodging his blows, the flight upstairs, and the locking of his bedroom door.

Then mother had come up and cried. "Behaving like that to your father after all he does for you!" she had sobbed reproachfully.

"*What* does he do for me?" Pippa had flashed.

"He works hard for you all day."

"*Works!*" Pippa had echoed contemptuously.

"Aren't you going to apologise to him?" her mother had continued.

"No," said Pippa. "And he can't make me by saying he'll take me away from school now, because I'm leaving, anyway."

Her father enjoyed receiving apologies, and generally could force one out of Pippa by threatening to take her away from school. Despite its frequent humiliations, Pippa loved school. There was beneath her quick sharp cleverness something of the real scholar's passion for learning. She felt in herself powers and capabilities that had as yet hardly been tapped. But her father had sent in notice for her to leave school at the end of the term and had entered her name at the local "secretarial college." She was to have a three-months course in shorthand and typing there and then go as a typist to Derrick and Sanders', where her father was managing clerk.

"And you're lucky to get it," he had added when he told her. "Lots of girls would give their eyes for a nice steady job like that. I hope you'll try to show me a little gratitude for all I've done for you."

Pippa had given him a long, slow, bitter look. That unchildlike bitterness was beginning to show in every aspect of her. It lurked in the corners of her crooked sensitive mouth, it gleamed from her sharp bright eyes, it rang in the defiant tones of her voice. So she would spend the rest of her life as a typist working with second-rate girls in a second-rate office under her father's hectoring rule—she to whom the gates of new and glorious worlds of scholarship were just beginning to open. . . . It made it worse that she had just passed her matriculation with honours in English, and that both the English mistress and the head mistress had wanted her to stay at school and work for a scholarship to college. The very thought of it had set her soul aflame, but her father had seemed actively to resent the suggestion.

"Putting ideas into the girl's head," he had grumbled, "as if she wasn't difficult enough already! All this fuss about a college education! I never had one and look at me."

Pippa had given him again that long, slow, bitter look. Reluctantly, she had relinquished her dream. It was no use trying to fight. One had no weapons. One could only hate life for being so unfair.

She roused herself from her reverie with a little shake. It was quarter to three now. She had better get on with things. The holes in her shoes wouldn't be noticed as long as she was playing, but when she wasn't playing she would probably be sitting on the grass with the other young people, and she knew by experience how hard it is to sit on the grass and not show holes in the soles of one's shoes. Leslie had a new pair and, though Leslie was only twelve, they took the same size, but Leslie wouldn't lend them to her. Conscientiously Pippa had protected Leslie from the humiliations that had beset her own path at school, darning her stockings, brushing her clothes, grooming her person, but Leslie had naturally found these attentions unwelcome, and relations between the two sisters had never been cordial. She would just have to do the best she could about the shoes. She must sit with her feet curled under her, so that the soles didn't show.

She began to brush her hair with quick fierce movements, as if her whole thin body were full of a nervous energy that must find vent in the slightest action. She frowned savagely at her reflection in the mirror as she brushed. If only her hair weren't that particular shade! It was red—plain ungarnished red. You couldn't call it auburn, however hard you tried.

Adam Harte would be there this afternoon, of course. She stopped brushing and stared dreamily into space, seeing again his pleasant blunt-featured face with the honest, puzzled, grey-blue eyes and well-formed mouth.

Pippa had never been friendly with the Rectory children. Mrs. Harte, the Rector's wife, had been one of the Monkton-Staffords of Devonshire and had always considered it regrettable that Danesborough contained so few of what she called the right people. She had allowed her children to associate with Penelope and Daphne. To Pippa she had been less cordial. Like the other two she was a great-granddaughter of old Mr. Royston of Greenways, but she had always been badly dressed and badly behaved, with a disconcerting habit of staring you out of countenance. And the home the child came from was really appalling. Mrs. Harte had called there once for a subscription, but had never repeated the visit.

Even before she went to school, Pippa's sharp eyes had seen the distinction drawn between her and her two cousins by people like Mrs. Harte. She had accepted it stoically, defiantly, carrying off the situation with childish bravado, talking about "those soppy little

Harte kids", though she had once cried herself to sleep on the night of the Rectory children's party to which she had not been invited.

But this half-term something had happened that she had kept hidden in her heart ever since. She had set off for a long tramp over the hills outside Danesborough, and had met Adam Harte. He was home from college for a week-end and was also setting off for a long walk. Pippa was a good walker, and they had tramped together over the hills and had tea at a little inn in the valley beyond. Adam had railed against the smugness and self-sufficiency of Danesborough. Pippa had agreed with him. Then they talked about books and discovered that they had read and liked the same authors—modern and, for the most part, somewhat revolutionary.

"And I bet no one else in this blighted hole so much as knows they exist," Adam had said savagely.

They discovered that they had many opinions in common. They both hated performing animals and the Zoo.

"When you think of the lives they live in the jungle," Adam had said indignantly, "how they prowl about all day long and are hardly ever still a minute, the utter boredom they must feel sitting in little cages behind bars all day simply doesn't bear thinking of. It must be a mental torment, far worse than any physical suffering could be. And performing animals! Even when I was a kid I felt sick with shame to see an elephant balancing upon a stool."

"I've always felt that, too," said Pippa.

"No one else does here, I bet you anything. . . . They say 'How sweet!' 'How clever!' '*Sweet*'!" he echoed venomously. " '*Clever*!' Half the cruelty in the world, of course, comes from stupidity."

After tea they sat on a wall in the valley, and he took from his pocket *The Testament of Beauty*, which he had brought out with him to read.

"Do you know it?" he said.

"I've only read bits here and there. Do read some to me."

He opened at random and read aloud:

'Twas at that hour of beauty when the setting sun

squandereth his cloudy bed with rosy hues, to flood his lov'd works as in turn he biddeth them Good night; and all the towers and temples and mansions of men face him in bright farewell, ere they creep from their pomp naked beneath the darkness;—while to mortal eyes 'tis given, if so they close not of fatigue nor strain at lamplit tasks—'tis given, as for a royal boon to beggarly outcasts in homeless vigil to watch where uncurtain'd behind the great windows of space Heaven's jewel'd company circleth unapproachably. 'Twas at sunset that I, fleeing to hide my soul in refuge of beauty from a mortal distress, walked alone with the Muse in her garden of thought.

She sat spellbound, her eyes fixed dreamily, unseeingly, on the distance.

They had known each other only slightly before that, but by the end of the afternoon their friendship seemed to be firmly cemented.

When they parted Adam held her hand in a tight grip and said:

"It's been awfully jolly meeting you like this. We must see something of each other in the vac."

He had come down from college, she knew, last week, and had had a friend staying with him, so that naturally he had not been able to write or come to see her. But they would meet again this afternoon.

Pippa had learnt in her sixteen years of life not to expect too much. But her youth was ardent and unquenchable. Despite its many hard lessons it still leapt up eagerly in answer to any call. And this call had been clamorously urgent. When Adam held her hand in his so firmly and said, "We must see something of each other in the vac.," she had known, in a sudden illuminating flash of knowledge, that she loved him.

She hid the knowledge away from her, pushing it down into the most secret corner of her heart. But it was there, and sometimes it seemed to escape her control and fill her whole being with an almost blinding radiance. Sometimes his name rang in her heart like a sort of refrain ... Adam ... Adam ... Adam. And she was going to see him again this afternoon. ...

She must iron her dress now. She slipped on her dressing gown, took up the dress, and went downstairs.

She had cleared away the lunch things before she went upstairs, leaving her mother to wash up, but everything was stacked about the kitchen as she had left it, and her mother stood by the window reading the newspaper. She looked slack and shapeless in her large soiled overall. Her hair was coming down, and her face wore that look of stupid placidity that always exasperated Pippa. A mingled smell of burnt stew and sardines hung over the house. Milly had planned to have stew for lunch, but had let it burn and so had opened a tin of sardines instead.

"I'm just going to press this dress," said Pippa shortly.

"All right," said her mother, without raising her eyes from the paper.

"Where's Leslie? I thought she was going to help you with the washing up."

"I don't know. I think she's gone out."

"It's nearly three. . . ."

"I know. It hardly seems worth while doing it before tea-time now. I'll do it all together after tea—or after supper. . . . There's been an awful murder in West Ham."

"Has there? Do you know where the ironing blanket is, mother?"

"I think Leslie put it in the cat's basket. . . ."

Pippa rescued the ironing blanket from the cat's basket.

"The iron isn't in its place, either."

"The murderer has a glass eye, so they ought to be able to find him all right. . . . What do you say, dear?"

"The iron isn't in its place."

"Oh no . . . I had it on Monday. Now where did I put it?"

"Mother, Daphne and Pen are coming for me at three."

"Well, they can wait for you a minute or two, can't they? What's the hurry, child? There's all afternoon. . . . I don't know what you want to iron the dress for, anyway. It looks all right to me."

"Oh *mother*! It's dreadful. I *must* iron it."

"All right. Don't get so excited. Oh yes, I remember about the iron now. I used it to prop the scullery door open. It may be there still."

"It's here. . . . Under the mangle."

"There, you see. I knew it was somewhere about. Why don't you have more patience? . . . There's been another of those smash-and-grab raids in Regent Street."

In silence Pippa began to make preparations for ironing her dress.

"Oh, Pippa," said her mother suddenly, "I wish you'd see if you can fix that big gas ring on the cooker. It seems all stopped up again."

"Mother, I haven't *time*."

"Well, I'll finish your dress for you if you'll see to the gas ring. I don't seem to be able to fix those gas rings, and I'll want to boil some water for washing up."

Pippa shrugged, handed over the iron to her mother, and went into the scullery. Depression had descended still more heavily upon her spirit. Even if she became really friendly with Adam, she could never ask him here. . . . Over and over again that had spoilt her school friendships. She had asked her friends to tea, and when they came everything had seemed so dreadful that she had never been able to look at them afterwards without remembering the dreadfulness of it and thinking that they were remembering it, too. And so she had begun to avoid them, and that was the end of the friendship. It wasn't only that the whole house wanted doing up, though it certainly wanted it badly enough. The paper hung down in festoons from the ceiling of the hall. The white paint had worn off the skirting boards and stair-case till the bare wood showed through. In all the rooms the wall paper was faded and torn, splashed with ink, stained with grease. The chairs sagged, and the worn upholstery of many of them revealed bare springs and stuffing. But that was not the worst. Anyone might be poor, though they were not really as poor as they seemed, and a better manager than mother would have made things look quite nice. The worst was the trail of dirt and untidiness that lay over the whole house. A faintly musty smell pervaded every room. There was a dull film of dust over all the furniture. Nothing was ever in its right place. Piles of garments waiting to be mended or sorted stood about on chairs, and there were generally cups and saucers on the mantelpiece. In the scullery this squalor was seen in its most concentrated form. The faintly unsavoury smell that haunted the other rooms became in the scullery a definite suggestion of un-cleaned sinks, of decaying food, of foul dish and floor cloths. The walls were spattered with the marks of boiling fat. Bits of food and refuse lay in corners on the floor. All the panes of the window were cracked and in one was a hole, stuffed with a bit of rag that had been there ever since Pippa could remember.

A wave of helpless anger surged over her. She did her best, but it was no use. She took out the gas-ring, found that the holes were stopped up by food that had been allowed to boil over, cleared it out as best she could, and returned to the kitchen.

Her mother stood by the table, the paper outspread on Pippa's dress. She was reading it and holding the iron motionless on the skirt.

"It says here that there are more than seven thousand people killed in motor accidents in a year," she said.

"*Mother*!" cried Pippa, starting forward.

Mrs. Chudleigh hastily moved the iron. On the spot where it had rested was a large brown mark.

"You *beast*!" said Pippa in a choking voice. "You've burnt it."

"*Pippa*!" expostulated her mother. "How *can* you speak to me like that! I'm sorry I've burnt it. I can't think how it happened. I was being so careful. I'd only just rested it there a second and——"

But the pent-up fires of Pippa's resentment broke out suddenly. She burst into angry tears.

"It's not only that," she sobbed. "It's everything. It's all so *hateful*. It's a beastly house. Everything in it's filthy. I can't even invite anyone to it. I haven't any friends and I never will have. You spoil everything. Everything. I hate it all. I——"

"*Pippa*!" said her mother again, dismay and amazement in her smooth round face. "Stop talking like that at once. You *wicked* girl! I'll tell your father every word you've said when he comes home to-night."

"Yes, tell him," sobbed Pippa, now beyond her own control or anyone else's. "And tell him I hate him. I hate him and I hate you. You've spoilt everything ever since I can remember, and now you've spoilt this afternoon."

Milly sat down abruptly on the nearest chair and began to cry.

Leslie, open-mouthed, open-eyed, appeared suddenly at the kitchen doorway.

"Listen to this wicked, ungrateful girl," sobbed Milly. "After all we've done for her!"

Leslie listened with relish.

"What have you ever done for me?" demanded Pippa hysterically, her voice coming in strangled gasps. "You've never done anything for me. I'm sick of being told to be grateful when I've nothing to be grateful for."

"Oo, isn't she awful?" put in Leslie, watching the scene with ecstatic enjoyment. "What ever'll Daddy say when he hears about it?"

"I'll never be able to wear it again, and it's the only decent dress I've got. I can't go, that's all, and you don't care. . . . You don't know what it means to me, and you wouldn't care if you did. I'll run away. I'll kill myself. I'll——"

There came a knock at the front door.

Leslie ran to it and, with a skill born of long practice, reconnoitred through the letter-box. Then she came running back.

"It's Daphne and Pen," she announced.

Chapter Twelve

PAUL ROYSTON swallowed the last mouthful of an excellently cooked savoury, then leant back in his chair and lit a cigarette.

Lilian was the ideal doctor's wife as far as housekeeping was concerned. She never complained of his irregular hours, and, however late he came in, there was always a perfectly prepared meal ready for him. The household machine ran smoothly on oiled wheels. When without cook or housemaid, Lilian would quietly take over the duties herself, and the work would be done more quickly, more efficiently, than it had ever been done before.

It was strange to look back upon the days of Anthea's régime. His lunches then seemed to have consisted chiefly of cold meat and tepid potatoes, or, failing that, bread and cheese. Anthea, sweet, vague, untidy, and heart-rendingly lovely, laying her cheek caressingly on the top of his head as he sat hacking his way through a piece of cold leatherlike steak:

"Darling, aren't I dreadful? I did mean to get a proper lunch for you but I forgot. That was left over from yesterday. It wasn't very nice even yesterday, was it? Is it too, too horrible now?"

"But what have you had?" he would say anxiously.

"Oh, I had something about half-past eleven. . . . I forget what."

She was the vaguest creature he had ever known, but somehow her vagueness had delighted him. Her loveliness and charm shed a sort of glamour over everything—even the ill-prepared meals she gave him.

She was so adorable that whatever she had a part in was perfect in his eyes. She couldn't keep good servants, of course. Though they liked her, they couldn't put up with her vagueness. She gave orders and forgot that she had given them. She promised to see to household matters and didn't remember one of them. She had no idea of time. She got up when she felt like it and had meals when she felt like it. (As far as Paul could make out she seemed to live chiefly on biscuits and chocolate.) She did everything on the impulse of the moment. Once when the moon was full she had coaxed him out to an all-night picnic in the valley beyond Danesborough, and he had been fit for nothing the next day. She seemed to be able to exist without sleep or food. It was partly the result of her upbringing, of course. Her father had been an eccentric genius of an artist who had spent a Bohemian existence, moving erratically from one European capital to another. He had adored his daughter and had shielded her carefully from the darker side of his Bohemian life, but he had instilled into her none of the minor but useful Philistine virtues, such as method and punctuality, having indeed none to instil. Paul had met her in Paris, and they had fallen in love with each other at once. He still believed that, had it depended on the two of them, the marriage would have been a success. To him her grace and loveliness would always have atoned—and richly atoned—for the discomforts of her ill-ordered *ménage*. The unconventionality that set Danesborough by the ears was to him the waywardness of a beloved child. But, of course, it didn't depend on the two of them. It depended upon Danesborough and its highly respectable citizens, his own family among the chief. And Danesborough lost no time in weighing her in the balance and finding her wanting. She omitted to ingratiate herself with her husband's important patients. She treated everyone alike with an off-handedness that Danesborough found exasperating in the extreme. Socially she was a complete failure. She accepted invitations and forgot them, she invited people to her house and was not there to receive them. She had inherited from her father a passionate love of beauty, and she would let everything else slip from her mind while she watched the shadows lengthen over the old-fashioned garden or the first pale stars appear in a faintly flushed primrose sky. ("Darling, I *am* so sorry. Yes, I knew we were going out. Yes, I remember now that I promised to be dressed by eight, but it was such an unbelievably beautiful sunset that I simply forgot everything else. . . . I suppose we shall be frantically late now, shan't we? Let's not go. Couldn't you just ring them up and say we can't go?")

She had early alienated his family. Shortly after his marriage he had invited them all to tea—Aunt Catherine, Aunt Charlotte, Aunt Margaret, Uncle Richard (the old man, of course, never went out to tea), Isabel, Milly, and the rest of them. He was nervously anxious for the affair to be a success and had helped Anthea with all the preparations. When he left her after lunch she was just going into the town to get some *petits fours*. When he came home at tea time the whole family was assembled in the drawing-room in an ominous silence, and Anthea was missing. The housemaid said that she had not yet returned from the town. In sudden anxiety, Paul telephoned the local hospital, but there had been no accident. Tea was brought in, and Aunt Catherine poured out, grim, outraged. Aunt Charlotte, fidgeting nervously, had kept up an incessant murmur: "I'm sure she'll be here in a *minute*. . . . It must just be that her watch is wrong. Mine was five minutes fast all last week. . . . Why, here she is," whenever anyone passed the gate. "Oh no, it isn't she. But I'm sure she'll be here in a minute."

At six o'clock, just as the party was about to break up, Anthea returned. She looked startlingly beautiful, her hair blown about her face, her cheeks flushed, her eyes bright. Her arms were full of heather, bracken, rowan, and long sprays of golden beech.

"I've had the loveliest day I've ever had in my life," she announced.

There was a strained silence, then Paul said:

"Where have you been, Anthea?"

"I've been up on Heathgyl Common," she said. "I was passing the station, and I saw there was a train to Heathgyl, so I caught it, and I've been walking there all afternoon. It was wonderful. I can't tell you how wonderful it was."

Then, of course, Aunt Catherine took command of the situation.

"We were invited to tea, Anthea," she said majestically, "and we have been waiting for our hostess since four o'clock."

Anthea stared with wide blue eyes, surprised, perplexed. Then all the vivid flame of her died away, as she left the world of beauty and freedom that was her heritage, and entered the world of convention in which she always seemed to grope her way blindfold.

She looked from one to another, her glowing harvest still clasped to her breast.

"*Oh!*" she gasped. "I—I quite forgot. I'm so sorry."

"We *quite* understand," said Aunt Catherine, grimly. "It's natural, of course, that you should prefer to go for a walk by yourself rather than meet a lot of dull relations."

As if feeling suddenly cold, Anthea crept nearer to Paul, and he slipped his arm round her reassuringly, though he felt desperately unhappy. They'd never forget it, of course. They'd never give her another chance. . . .

They filed out one by one, Aunt Charlotte pausing to murmur unhappily: "I expect your watch was wrong, wasn't it, dear? These things will happen. . . ."

When they had gone, Anthea stood by the table and let the flowers and branches fall one by one from her arms, her eyes fixed unseeingly in front of her.

"It was dreadful of me, wasn't it, Paul?" she said. "I quite forgot."

He picked up a few pieces of heather that had fallen upon the carpet.

"Don't worry about it," he replied. "It's all over and done with now, anyway."

She turned her eyes to his slowly.

"You aren't angry with me?"

He put his hands on her shoulders and kissed her cold smooth cheek.

"You know that I could never be angry with you whatever you did."

But, of course, all Danesborough knew about the affair by the next morning.

As time went on he realised that his wife formed the staple diet of Danesborough gossip. Her slightest lapses from convention were reported and exaggerated. He felt that she was trying hard but unsuccessfully to fit herself into an uncongenial mould. One hot night the next summer, while she was lying awake by his side, it occurred to her suddenly to go and bathe in the pool up on the hills outside the town. She whispered "Paul!" but he was heavily asleep, so, not wishing to rouse him, she dressed quietly and went out. She walked to the pool, took off her clothes, bathed in the clear icy water, then dressed again and returned, refreshed, to bed and sleep. Unfortunately, someone coming home from a visit to an outlying country house had seen her, and that story, too, was all over Danesborough the next day. Even Anthea began to realise that she was being ostracised. She realised, moreover, that it was affecting Paul's professional position. People did not want to employ a doctor whose wife bathed naked in pools at midnight. . . .

"But, Paul," she said, puzzled, "why was it wrong?"

"It wasn't wrong," he said. "People here don't do it, that's all."

"Why don't they do it?"

"Search me!" said Paul.

So remote and wild and elfin did she seem that he had no idea that the attitude of people around her troubled her at all. He was amazed, therefore, when one morning she suddenly announced that she was leaving him.

"It's not you, Paul," she said. "I love you and I think I shall always love you. It's—this place. I thought I could get used to it, but I can't."

"I'll find an exchange," he said.

"That wouldn't help. It would be the same anywhere. I must go. It's the only way."

She looked so childish, with her wide blue eyes, wistful lips, and white pointed chin, that he treated her as if she were indeed a child, reassuring, comforting, teasing.

"What nonsense!" he said. "You're tired. That's what it is."

"I'm not tired."

"Just go away for a change."

"No. I must go away altogether. I'm doing you harm. I'm doing myself harm, too."

"You absurd little idiot!"

"Paul, I mean it."

"Well, look here. I must dash off now. I've got rather a big round this morning. We'll talk it over again when I come home, shall we?"

She said nothing.

When he came home she had gone. He had vainly tried to trace her; then, several months later, he had received a letter from her, telling him that she was living with a man she had known before she met him, and asking him to divorce her. He put the divorce through as quickly as possible and had heard no more from her. Till to-day. . . . He took the letter from his pocket and read it again.

"Dear Paul,—I want to come and see you. There's something I'd like to discuss with you. If you'll see me wire to me at once at this address and I'll come to Danesborough by the train that gets in at 6.42.

"ANTHEA."

It had upset Lilian, of course. Lilian had been jealous of Anthea from the beginning. She couldn't understand his love for Anthea, couldn't leave it alone, tortured herself over it incessantly, tried, by every means in her power, to make him disown it. Often he had been tempted to give in to her for the sake of peace, to say that his love for Anthea was completely dead, but then there would come a vivid memory of Anthea, and his loyalty would stiffen itself again to resist attack. He still felt for Anthea what he had always felt, a deep protective tenderness, a yearning pity, as for something small and helpless. He had loved her in the way in which a man should love his child rather than his wife. He loved Lilian as a woman, as his mate and equal, loved her with his body and mind and intelligence, as he had never loved Anthea. But Lilian wouldn't be content with that. She wanted everything. She was passionate and possessive. There was going to be hell to pay over this letter. There hadn't been time to thresh it out properly at breakfast. She had turned white when he gave it to her, and her hand had clenched and trembled as she read it.

"How *dare* she?" she had said in a low voice, and then: "You won't let her come, Paul, will you?"

138

He had shrugged faintly and spread out his hands.

"My dear . . . I can't refuse to see her."

"Of *course* you can refuse to see her. It would be an insult to me."

"I don't see that."

"I suppose I mean nothing to you, then."

"For heaven's sake, don't start that sort of thing, Lilian. You know quite well that you mean everything to me."

"So you say," she said, with a faint sneer, "yet this woman who's dragged your name in the dirt has only to raise her little finger, and nothing—not your self-respect or my feelings—count with you any longer."

"Don't exaggerate the situation," he had remonstrated. "I'm merely going to meet an old friend who may be in trouble."

That, of course, had infuriated her.

"An old friend!" she had echoed contemptuously. "If she is in trouble it's her own fault, and what claim has she on you now? Tell me that."

"The claim of old association," he said, aware that he was handling the matter tactlessly, but obstinately determined not to yield to her.

She gazed at him in silence for a few moments, then said slowly: "I've known all the time at the bottom of my heart that she'd only got to raise a finger and you'd want her back again."

"I don't want her back again," he said shortly.

"If you won't do this for my sake—and I'm learning now how little you really care for me—won't you consider your own position? What will people think of you, married to me, yet meeting this—this woman surreptitiously behind my back?"

"I don't care a damn what they think," he had burst out in sudden exasperation, "and I'm not meeting her surreptitiously behind your back."

At that point the maid had entered to tell him that the surgery was full, and he had gone to his patients. He had not seen her since, but on his way home he had sent Anthea a wire telling her to come and saying that he would meet her train.

He leant back in his chair and sighed. He felt extraordinarily tired. He had been up half the night with a maternity case, and all the night before with a heart case. Sometimes he could snatch a rest in the afternoon, but, though he had finished his round this morning, he must pay several second visits this afternoon. He had a bad pneumonia case and one of rapid tuberculosis and another rather worrying one of blood poisoning. And he must try and look in on old Mrs. Featherstone. She wouldn't last much longer. Pity she'd messed about for so long with quacks before she came to him. . . . Then he must be at the station by six forty-two to meet Anthea's train. And to-night was the old man's party. Why on earth must that come to-day on the top of everything else? He'd like to make time for a chat with old Stephen, sometime, too. They would hardly get a word together to-night with all that crowd. He would try to look in at the White Swan if he could manage it. The brothers never wrote to each other, but they got on excellently when they met. Paul had gone down to the Wiltshire farm, without telling anyone, to see Stephen and Beatrice, and to let them know that he didn't disapprove of them. He had come away feeling faintly envious. There had been an air of extraordinary peace and happiness over the little farmhouse. His thoughts went back to their childhood. . . . Stephen as the eldest had always borne the brunt of their father's temper. If ever he, Paul, had children, he'd see that they had a better time than he and old Steve had had. . . . His heart contracted suddenly. Suppose Anthea were coming to tell him that she had had a child by him. . . . He had clung to that hope after she left him. If by any chance she discovered that she was going to have a child, he might be able to persuade her to return to him. But as the months passed by his hopes waned, to be killed finally by her letter asking him to divorce her. And yet—often his thoughts returned to the subject. She might have had a child and not have let him know lest it should give him a claim upon her. Suppose she were coming to-day to tell him that she had had a child. . . .

The door opened suddenly, and Lilian stood on the threshold. For a moment they looked at each other in silence. He saw that that air of brooding passion that generally hung about her was deepened, intensified. The full red lips were set in a tight line, marring the perfect cupid's bow that they formed when in repose. Her dark eyes held a sombre light. Poor Lilian! She was so tragic, so dramatic, so intense and emotional and—wearing. She lacked a sense of proportion and its dependent sense of humour. The slightest *contretemps* could assume the proportion of unmitigated tragedy in her eyes. Often he did not know what had upset her, only knew that her "mood" (as he always called it to himself) lay over the whole house like a thick black cloud. He would be aware of it as soon as he opened the front door, before he had seen her or spoken to her. There was, however, no doubt what had upset her to-day.

He greeted her lightly, determined to hold off the inevitable scene as long as possible.

"Hello. . . . Sorry I was so late for lunch. And thanks for a most excellent meal."

"I'm glad you enjoyed it."

As she spoke, she went over to the window, drawing off her gloves. Her silk dress showed to perfection the soft curves of her voluptuous figure.

Her appeal to him at the beginning of their acquaintance had been definitely sensual. It was later, when he knew her better, that he came to love her for her sincerity, her integrity, for that simplicity and humility that lay behind the defences of pride that she showed to the world. Life with her had not been easy. She loved him passionately and was jealous of everything that separated him from her, his profession, his outside interests, and, on one or two occasions, his women patients. Even when this attitude of hers exasperated him most, he could not help feeling pity for her. She tortured herself so incessantly and with such exquisite cruelty. And her moods of tender gaiety, of untroubled serenity—most of all her deep passionate love for him—made up to him for everything.

But he must go carefully to-day. The sombre light of her eyes and the tragic lines of her mouth warned him of that. . . . He must go carefully, but he was determined—doggedly, obstinately determined—not to betray Anthea to her possessiveness. The silence between them was becoming significant. He hastened to break it.

141

"I hear you went round to Isabel's," he said casually.

"Who told you?"

"I met Daphne and Pen."

"I went to ask her if she'd like a lift to-night."

"Why didn't you telephone?"

She turned from the window and faced him.

"I wanted to get out of the house."

The implication was obvious and he sheered away from it.

"I suppose she'd like to come with us?"

"Yes. . . . She was giving a bridge party."

"What a racketing life the woman leads! I told her last week that she'd have a breakdown if she wasn't careful."

Lilian was silent. Her silence implied that she wasn't interested in his sister's health and wasn't going to pretend to be.

"Daphne and Pen were going to a tennis party at the Rectory," he went on. "They were on their way to Milly's to call for Pippa."

Lilian's silence implied that she wasn't interested in his nieces' social engagements and wasn't going to pretend to be.

"Aunt Catherine rang up just after I'd come in," he continued rather hastily. "Had a long tale about grandfather getting what she called 'queer.' Wanted me to keep my eye on him, said something about 'power of Attorney.' It's probably just ordinary failing of memory. She said that he'd insisted on coming into Danesborough himself this afternoon and seemed to think that that finally and completely proved him mad. Why on earth the poor old boy shouldn't come into Danesborough if he wants . . ."

Again she made no comment. There was a long silence in which he relinquished his attempt to hold at bay the subject that was in both their minds.

Lilian broke the silence, speaking in a quick breathless voice.

"Paul . . . you won't let—that woman come, will you?"

He braced himself for the fight.

"Anthea? I've wired to her this morning, telling her to come."

She stared at him. Her eyes seemed to grow bigger, darker. The colour ebbed from her cheeks.

"I don't believe it," she said at last, slowly. "I don't believe you'd do a thing like that."

"I have done it," he said. "I considered that I'd no alternative. . . ."

There was another silence, then he burst out:

"Look here, Lilian, don't you trust me?"

"Trust you?" she echoed. "I think I shall never trust you again."

Her whole body was tense. The lace on her deep bosom rose and fell tumultuously.

"I'm sorry you feel like that," he said, "but in this matter I must follow my own conscience."

"Need you talk about your conscience?"

"I suppose not. The word just occurred to me, that's all."

She was silent for some moments, during which she seemed to gather her whole being together under a rigid control. Her voice when she spoke was cold and steady.

"If you let this woman come, Paul, I shall leave you."

He smiled wryly. It would be an ironical stroke of fate if Anthea broke up his second marriage as lightly as she had broken up his first.

"I've already wired to her to come," he said.

"She won't have started yet. You could send another wire."

"I'm not going back on my word. Lilian," he burst out again, with sudden urgency, "you know I love you. . . ."

Her eyes hardened.

"If you love me, stop this woman coming."

"Be reasonable. God knows what the child's gone through. She never had a chance here. Haven't you any pity for her?"

"*Pity!*" Her eyes blazed at him. She spoke through tight lips. "I'd *kill* her if I could. I'd——"

A maid entered the room.

"Please, sir, it's Miss Featherstone on the 'phone. She says her mother's had a turn for the worse, and will you please go at once."

He strode from the room without looking at his wife.

Chapter Thirteen

"AUGUST always seems a dull month in a garden, doesn't it?" said Helen. "The delphiniums were wonderful in June and July, and the Michaelmas daisies are going to be wonderful in September and October, but just at present there's really very little out."

She was walking round her garden with Beatrice; Philip and Stephen were following; and Matthew, who had declined the tour of inspection, was sitting in the drawing-room, watching them from the open garden doors. Both women were keen gardeners. But apart from that common interest they had, from the moment of their meeting, been conscious of a strong attraction between them. Helen was conscious, too, of the bond of love and understanding that united the two newcomers. It depressed her unaccountably, sending a wave of apprehension and despair through her soul.

Philip and Stephen were very silent. Stephen, of course, was always silent, and Philip was obviously on edge. His hands, rammed into his pockets, twitched and fidgeted, and he spoke, when he had to speak, in a jerky unnatural manner. Helen knew that he was furious at this interruption and anxious to get rid of the intruders as quickly as possible. She, on the other hand, was using every means in her power to prolong the visit. It wasn't just that she wanted to put off the moment when she must again face the issues of her love for Philip. It was that she wanted to rest her spirit for a little time in the serenity of the woman beside her. Serenity, a tender, radiant serenity, seemed to emanate from her very being, and in it Helen's spirit found shelter, as a bruised and battered bird finds shelter from the storm outside, in a lighted room. Only when the two visitors exchanged a fleeting look, did that odd wave of depression—was it fear or envy?—surge over her.

They stopped to examine a group of white phlox, and the two men joined them.

"They smell so lovely just about dusk," said Beatrice. "Have you noticed?"

Helen smiled. "Yes. You could find them blindfold by their scent," she said, and added, "I expect you have a wonderful garden in Wiltshire."

"There was none when we went there," answered Stephen. "Beatrice has made one out of a wilderness."

The words, of course, held a deeper meaning than the obvious one, and their eyes met again in that quick fugitive glance of understanding.

Helen looked at the other woman. . . . Yes, she would make a garden out of a wilderness. . . .

"I love gardening," Beatrice was saying. "It spring-cleans one's mind, somehow. After a day's gardening, I'm covered with dirt outside, but I always feel as if my inside had had a good wash."

"She does too much," said Stephen. "She isn't strong."

He turned to Philip.

"Are you interested in gardening?"

"I know very little about it," replied Philip shortly.

Helen and Beatrice moved on again, followed by the two men.

"Tell me about your farm," said Helen.

"It's just a small stone farm-house," said Beatrice, "and the stone has that warm golden tint that comes with age. The tiles on the roof are golden, too—or rather, orange—with lichen. It's covered with climbing roses, and I've made an old-fashioned garden—hollyhocks and larkspur and pinks and canterbury bells and mignonette and marigolds. . . . I love the names of flowers—don't you?—though Stephen says that they always remind him of the names of diseases. He says that, if you didn't know you'd be quite likely to think that influenza and pneumonia and laryngitis were names of flowers, and that helianthus and campanula and coreopsis were names of diseases. I suppose it's because they both come chiefly from the Greek or Latin."

Helen smiled.

"Do you grow much fruit?" she asked.

"Yes. ... The orchard is lovely in May—a thick roof of pink and white blossom."

"With daffodils in the grass," supplied Helen.

"No. Not daffodils. Sheep. The sheep graze there. I think that's the picture I carry most clearly through the winter—the fresh green grass and the sheep and the whitened trunks of the apple trees and over it all the roof of apple blossom. ... There's a little wood at the bottom of the garden and I've planted bulbs there—bluebells and daffodils and scillas and crocuses and snowdrops. A stream runs through it with tiny ferns on the bank hanging over the water."

"It sounds very peaceful," said Helen dreamily.

"It is peaceful."

"You never get tired of it?"

"Never."

Beatrice had talked more than was usual with her. Though completely lacking in self-consciousness, she was naturally shy, and it always cost her an effort to overcome her shyness. This afternoon, however, she had been aware of some desperate unhappiness weighing upon the other woman's spirit, and she had talked, partly to distract her, as one talks to an unhappy child, partly to extend to her that tacit sympathy that can so often underlie a superficial conversation.

They had finished their circuit of the garden now and reached the open French windows of the drawing-room again. Old Matthew was dozing in his chair. Despite his height, his figure looked strangely shrunken and wizened.

Helen's eyes were fixed on the spot where—was it half an hour ago or in another life?—Philip had held her in his arms. She shivered, feeling that she could not bear to enter the room, and drew Beatrice away for another turn round the garden. The two men stayed by the open door, watching them.

"Mr. Royston looks tired," said Beatrice. "To-night will be rather a strain for him. He really ought to have stayed quietly at home this afternoon, and not come out."

Helen laughed shortly.

"If he wants to do a thing he'll do it," she said, "and nothing on earth will stop him. Mrs. Moreland's found that out."

"I think he—didn't want you all to meet me for the first time to-night," said Beatrice.

I wonder which of us he was frightened of, thought Helen, with a wry smile.

"Have you seen Paul yet?" she asked.

"Not to-day. He rang up and left a message saying that he'd try to get round to see Stephen before to-night, but that it's a particularly heavy day for him. He's been down to see us in Wiltshire, you know."

Good for Paul! said Helen to herself. Aloud she said:

"Would you let me come down some time?"

"Why, of *course*. I'd love it."

Helen laughed nervously.

"It sounds so peaceful. . . . If ever I feel—desperate, may I just descend on you?"

"I'd love it. I really mean it."

"I wish Pen had been here. You'd like her. She's Harold's daughter, you know. But you'll see her to-night. . . . How many of the family have you actually met?"

"I saw Mrs. Moreland and Miss Royston at Greenways," said Beatrice, "and we went to Mrs. Lessing's this afternoon and saw her and her daughter. Miss Lessing was just going out."

"Enid? Oh yes. She was going to the tennis party at the Rectory, I suppose. She was here to lunch. I was horrid to her. I generally am horrid to people. I wish I weren't, but—it's dreadful living in a small country town surrounded on all sides by one's husband's relations."

Beatrice smiled slowly.

"I'm sure it must be. . . ."

Old Matthew woke up and came across the lawn to them. He seemed pleased by the sight of their obvious friendliness.

"That's right," he said. "That's right, that's right. ... Now I'm going to drag these people away."

Philip and Stephen had followed him slowly and in silence.

"I wish you'd stay to tea," said Helen.

"We've no time for that." He turned to Beatrice, bending towards her with an old-fashioned movement that was almost a bow. "You ready, my dear?" and abruptly, "Ready, Stephen?"

They took their leave and went down the path into the street.

"We're going to Isabel's now," he said.

"First of all," said Beatrice firmly, "you're coming across to the White Swan to have tea with us. Isn't he, Stephen?"

"Rather!" agreed Stephen.

"We've no time for tea," began the old man firmly. Then he stopped and said, "D'you want tea?"

"Of course I do," she smiled.

"Come on, then," he said, and the three of them crossed the square and entered the White Swan.

Helen and Philip returned slowly to the drawing-room.

"I thought they'd never go," he burst out impatiently, as he closed the door. "Why on earth did you ask them to stay to tea? Suppose they had done! I felt I was going mad."

Helen was staring dreamily in front of her.

"She's lovely, isn't she?" she said slowly.

"I don't know. I hardly looked at her. No, of course she isn't lovely. A white-haired hag. ... Look here, Helen"—he seized her roughly by the shoulders—"you don't mean what you said about waiting till that child goes back to school. I tell you I can't wait. I can't wait a day. I can't wait a minute."

She turned her eyes and looked at him in silence—a long dreamy look.

"Don't you understand, Philip?" she said at last. "It's—impossible now."

"Impossible?" he repeated slowly. "What do you mean?"

"I mean that I can't go with you at all."

"Are you out of your mind?"

"I don't think so."

"You were ready enough to come with me before those people came. What's changed you?"

"Those people, I suppose."

"That great lout of a farmer and his white-haired hag of a woman?"

"If you like to put it that way."

He struggled silently with his anger and bewilderment. Then he said, with a painful effort at self-control:

"Will you please explain to me what's happened, Helen?"

"I thought you'd have understood," she said. "I thought you'd have felt it, too."

Frowning, he tried to guess her meaning.

"They aren't married," he said, "and they're a couple of boring country clodhoppers—though, of course, she dresses well—but—*darling*," he burst out, "we needn't be like that. The fact that two people who happen not to be married are a couple of deadly bores doesn't prove we'd become like that. . . ."

"Oh, *Philip*," she breathed, "I didn't think you could be so blind. . . . Didn't you see? . . . They love each other."

"That's all right, then," he said easily. "It's worked out all right in their case, and it will in ours. What on earth are you worrying about?"

"Did you see the way they looked at each other?"

"Can't say I did. I was trying to get you to look at me."

"Well, it was—the way they looked at each other. . . . It was—the real thing. And it showed me that ours—isn't. We aren't—big enough, either of us."

He stared at her again in silent bewilderment.

"You surely aren't trying to deny that we love each other," he said at last slowly.

"We love each other in a way, but—it's not the real way. There's no trust behind it. It's physical love, and when it dies, as physical love always dies, it will leave—nothing."

He started towards her, but she put out a hand to hold him off. "Don't try that again," she said in a low steady voice. "It wouldn't be any good."

His arms fell to his side.

"You're afraid," he said. "You haven't the courage. You've seen those two—the old chap having to cart them round because he thinks that otherwise the virtuous female Roystons will refuse to sit down at the table with them to-night—and you suddenly realise what it means. You're afraid. Can't you understand? There'll be none of that sort of thing for you. We'll go right away; we'll start a new life. Harold would divorce you, wouldn't he?"

"Oh yes," she said, with a short, hard laugh. "Harold always likes to do the correct thing."

"And I'm sure that Mona will divorce me. We'll be able to marry. There's nothing, nothing to be afraid of."

"I'm not afraid—of that."

"What are you afraid of, then?"

"I'm afraid of you—and of myself. You failed me once——"

"My God!" he burst out angrily. "Will you never let me forget that?"

The door opened, and the housemaid entered with the tea tray. They stood in silence while she set it on the low round mahogany tea-table—Helen gazing out of the window, Philip glowering at the empty fireplace. The girl glanced with furtive interest from one to the other before she withdrew.

"Well?" he said shortly, as the door closed.

She put a hand to her head. "I've forgotten what I was saying."

"You were reminding me—not for the first time"—he said bitterly, "that I let you down. You're not exactly generous, are you?"

"I suppose not. . . . We made a mess of things. And we're still the same people we were then. What happened once can always happen again. It's what I said before. We're neither of us—big enough."

An ugly sneer came into his face.

"I suppose that the plain truth is you want to have your cake and eat it. You're in love with me, but you want to continue a respectable matron of Danesborough. Well, I suppose that it can be managed."

She threw her hands out in a little hopeless gesture.

"I thought you understood about that. You don't trust me. You didn't trust me before, and you'll never trust me. There's no real love without trust."

"By heaven," he burst out angrily, "why must you take our souls up by the roots and examine them like this? Can't you see? In all this there's only one thing that matters, and that is that we love each other."

"We love each other," she agreed slowly, "and we can't be together for five minutes without quarrelling. We quarrelled all the time we were engaged. We were quarrelling when those people came in this afternoon. We're quarrelling again now. What sort of a hell would our life together be—tied by a physical passion and with no real understanding at all?"

"You're damnably prudent and long-sighted all of a sudden," he sneered.

"Well, one of us has to be. . . . We rushed into an engagement that lasted a month. Our marriage would be wrecked on the same rocks, and we couldn't get out of it as easily as we got out of our engagement."

He was silent for some moments, then said quietly:

"You were willing enough before those Roystons called."

"I know."

He came nearer her. His anger and bitterness had left him. He looked pale and unhappy.

"Look here, Helen," he said, "what chance of happiness lies before you as Royston's wife?"

"I don't know," she answered. "None, perhaps. But he can't hurt me as you can hurt me, and that's something."

"It's no use talking to you," he said abruptly. "You must have gone mad. It's the only explanation I can think of. I'll come again, and hope to find you saner."

"Don't come again, Philip."

"Good-bye. . . ."

He went out, and she heard the front door close after him.

She looked down at the untouched tea tray and remembered the girl's furtive glances. Mechanically she poured a little tea into each teacup and emptied the rest upon the garden bed that ran beneath the window. Then she crumbled a little bread and butter on to each plate. No need to let the whole of Danesborough know that Philip Messiter had been making love to her.

Chapter Fourteen

THE oldest part of the Rectory was a square, Queen Anne building, on to which wings had been built, spoiling its original proportions but giving it a rather attractive, rambling appearance. The garden, picturesque and haphazard like the house, was shut away from High Street by a mellow sun-baked brick wall, which seemed to have enclosed, as well as the house and garden, a certain air of leisure and repose that belonged to the days when they were made.

The tennis party was already assembling on the lawn, and the Rector and Mrs. Harte were receiving their guests under a large copper beech. The copper beech overhung the tennis courts and was much admired by people who had never tried to play tennis beneath it. The Rector, who did not play games, would not allow it to be "mutilated," but the young people regularly, if surreptitiously, broke off as much of the overhanging branches as they could reach.

The Rector was a tall, good-looking man, with an elegant figure and a charming smile. Charm, in fact, was the quality he chiefly cultivated, and it had certainly so far served him well in his career. Danesborough was commonly regarded in ecclesiastical circles as one of the stepping-stones to a bishopric. The town was, on the whole, proud of its rector. He had a good presence, a facile eloquence, and such beautiful manners that no social function ever seemed quite complete without him. He had, moreover, the rare and valuable gift of making unimportant people feel important while he was talking to them. This was, perhaps, especially useful as a sort of offset to his wife's gift for making the most important people feel wholly unimportant while she was talking to them. Mrs. Harte could never forget that she was one of the Monkton-Staffords of

Devonshire, and, though Danesborough was vaguely proud of her noble origin, it resented her patronising manner. This manner had carefully graduated degrees. With parish assemblies it was frigid and long-suffering and she addressed them collectively as "people" ("Good afternoon, people," or "Tea in the parish room, people"). Sometimes she addressed them as "good people", but there was felt to be a subtle distinction, "good people" denoting a lower social grade than "people." She called the mothers' meeting "good people" and the Sunday School teachers "people."

She was appropriately aristocratic-looking—her face just a little too long, her features just a little too straight, her carriage just a little too upright.

Neither of her two daughters was quite as handsome as the mother, though, oddly, the younger, Cressida, who had inherited her patrician cast of countenance, was exasperatingly promiscuous in her acquaintances, while the elder, Alicia, whose features were of an almost plebeian bluntness, shared her mother's exclusive outlook and imitated her aristocratic manner to perfection. The younger boy, Dorian, was at that stage of adolescence when the sleeves of his jackets never seemed quite long enough, his voice varied between a treble squeak and a bass roar, and his manner between boyish high spirits and the dignity of extreme old age. The elder boy, Adam, was a pleasant unassuming youth, who always looked embarrassed and slightly ashamed when he had to listen to his mother patronising his father's parishioners.

His face this afternoon wore a rather sulky expression as he strove to tighten the ancient and permanently sagging tennis net.

Cressida lay in a deck chair, covered by a rug, a cushion behind her head. It was a hot day, and the rug was wholly unnecessary, but Cressida had put it over her in order to heighten the suggestion of invalidism that she intended her appearance to convey. To a small band of contemporaries whom she had persuaded her mother to allow her to invite to the party, she was describing Dr. Royston's visit to her that morning, throwing out veiled but none the less ominous hints.

"I saw him look at mother after he'd tested my heart. They

didn't mean me to see the way they looked at each other, but I've known for some time that my heart was a bit wonky. I get awfully out of breath when I've been running, and that's always a sign. . . . He looked very serious when he tested my lungs, too, and, of course, I know my lungs aren't very strong. I perspire sometimes in the night, and that's a sure sign of lungs. . . . I had terrible pain last night. That was why they sent for him. Heart and lungs together, of course, are *dreadfully* painful. I don't suppose that I shall be going back to school next term. I shouldn't be surprised—one doesn't like to say this, but I couldn't help seeing the way the doctor looked at mother—and somehow I've always had a sort of *feeling* that I shan't grow to be very old."

Dorian passed them and tweaked Cressida's hair.

"What do you think of this kid," he said to the group, "getting collywobbles with eating green apples the first day she comes home and having to have the doctor to administer castor oil?"

Cressida blinked through her spectacles, but the expression of her long thin face remained inscrutable.

"Dorian's a dear," she said, when he had passed. "I particularly asked him to tell people that, because I do so hate a fuss. Poor Dorian's awfully worried about me really. . . ."

But somehow the atmosphere was spoilt, so, throwing aside the rug and sitting up straight, she began to tell them about a mistress at her school, who, she said, was really the head of a famous international gang of crooks. Cressida herself had discovered this, and as yet had said nothing about it to anyone, because she meant next term to appeal to the mistress's better nature and try to reform her.

"What about that girl at your school who had been captured by bandits in China?" asked one of the group.

"Oh, her!" said Cressida vaguely. "She's all right."

"I thought you said they'd cut her ears off."

"Yes, they did. I mean, she's all right except for that. She's got false ones, and she can hear quite well with them."

Cressida had a fertile imagination, but an unfortunately short memory, so that she was frequently being asked for the sequel to adventures whose beginnings she had completely forgotten. Her mother had told her that she might invite a school friend to spend part of this summer holidays with her, but Cressida, though she would like to have had a holiday companion, had decided not to avail herself of the permission, as she could not remember to which of her friends she had represented her mother as a Russian princess (with various thrilling details of her escape during the revolution) and to which she had represented her as a secret service agent in the pay of the Jugo-Slavian (Cressida had chosen that country because she liked the sound of it) government. Then there was the everyday life of the Rectory—a pleasant enough life, but neither so picturesquely elegant as Cressida had described it in certain moods, nor so picturesquely poverty-stricken as she had described it in others. On the whole Cressida thought that it would be safer to keep her home life and her school life quite separate. So she had blinked behind her round spectacles and said: "Thank you, mother dear, but I'd rather just spend my holidays with you. If I had a friend staying with me I couldn't see as much of you or help you as much as I'd like to."

She said this with great unction, thinking that it ought at least to be good for a new tennis racquet, her need of which she had mentioned frequently in her mother's hearing.

Mrs. Harte was touched, but not to the extent of a new tennis racquet. Cressida had this afternoon, therefore, taken Dorian's, leaving her old one in its place, thinking, without much real hope, that perhaps he would not notice.

"There's Miss Lessing," said another of the group. "My sister's in her hockey team. She says she's a jolly good sort."

They all turned to look at Enid, who had just arrived and had taken her seat on a basket chair near them. She was gazing unseeingly in front of her, unaware of their scrutiny.

If only Stephen and that woman hadn't come. . . . It had all seemed so simple before Stephen and that woman came. She gave her head a little determined shake. She must just forget Stephen and the woman—Beatrice, her name was, and somehow it suited her. She must pretend that she hadn't seen them. Then it would be all right. . . .

"I saw her grandfather this afternoon," said another member of the group round Cressida. "He was walking down the road quite alone, and then when he was outside our house he seemed to turn faint, and I was just going out to see if I could help him when that funny old servant of his came along. . . ."

Cressida said nothing. It was suddenly she, not her friend, who had seen the old man turn faint. She had run out to help him. She had supported him into the house. She had bathed his brow with eau-de-Cologne. He had said: "Thank you, my child. If I'd had a little daughter like you I might have been a better man now. . . ."

Next week he died, and when his will was read everyone was surprised to find that he had left all his money to Cressida Harte. She was very generous with it. She gave a large sum to her mother, with only a slight reference to the tennis racquet. She bought for herself a house like Buckingham Palace outside and like the Strand Palace Hotel (where she had once had tea with her godmother after a pantomime) inside, and occasionally had members of her family to stay with her.

"My sister says that Miss Lessing is a simply marvellous centre-half," one of the girls was saying. "She says that it's a picture to see her tackling and passing."

"I'm going to be centre-half next term," said Cressida.

"But what about your heart?"

"Oh, that!" said Cressida casually. "Well, I'm probably going to have some treatment that will put that right."

Enid woke from her day-dreams with a start as she saw her three nieces approaching. Pippa looked plainer than usual—her freckled face flushed and blotchy—but much better dressed. The white silk tennis frock she wore was fresh and dainty and better cut than Pippa's dresses generally were.

She smiled and waved to them, and they came to her across the lawn.

"Hello, Aunt Enid."

"Hello, infants. How nice you look, all in your best bibs and tuckers! Is that new, Pippa? I've not seen it before, have I?"

Pippa's freckled sullen face did not lighten.

"It's not mine," she said shortly. "Daphne lent it to me."

"Pippa's had got scorched," broke in Daphne with her little nervous laugh, "so I ran back for one of mine."

Pippa preserved an ungracious silence.

Pen glanced uneasily from one to the other. It had been dreadful at Pippa's. There had evidently been some sort of a scene, and both Pippa and her mother had been crying. Pippa had looked furious as well as miserable. She had faced them stonily in the dusty little dining-room and said that she wasn't coming. At first she wouldn't say why, then Aunt Milly had entered, wiping her eyes and sniffing, and said that Pippa's dress had got a bit scorched in the ironing, but the mark hardly showed at all and she didn't know why Pippa was making such a fuss about it. At once, before anyone could stop her, Daphne had run off home for a dress.

"I don't want it. I shan't wear it. I'm not going, anyway," Pippa had called after her, but by that time Daphne was at the gate.

Pippa and Aunt Milly had then gone away, leaving Pen to wait alone in the dusty little dining-room, with Leslie standing in the hall and staring at her through the crack of the door. Once Pen said:

"Come in and talk to me, Leslie," but Leslie did not answer or move, and the unblinking eye continued to be fixed on Pen through the crack.

There was always something terribly depressing about Aunt Milly's house. It smelt of cabbage water and dust, and there always seemed to be traces of the last meal about.

After a few minutes Daphne came back, breathless with running, carrying a dress box in which she had packed a clean white silk tennis frock.

Pippa had then appeared, still sulky and red-eyed, protesting again at first that she didn't want it and wasn't going, anyway. Finally she had yielded and thanked Daphne in a half-ashamed fashion and gone upstairs to put it on. She hadn't spoken at all on the way here, and Pen and Daphne had kept up an uneasy, self-conscious conversation about nothing in particular, because it seemed so dreadful for the three of them to be walking along saying nothing. It was always difficult to know what to talk about to Pippa. If they talked about their schools, she thought that they were showing off, and if they asked her about hers she thought that they were patronising her. Still—here they were, and Pippa was just beginning to look a little less sulky.

Cressida Harte got up from her chair and began to walk across the lawn. No one seemed to be taking much notice of her, so, remembering once more the doctor's visit this morning, she put on a rather ostentatious limp, using her tennis racquet as a walking stick. . . .

"Hurt your foot, Cressida?" called out Enid in her loud hearty voice.

Cressida turned to her with a brave little smile.

"It's not—terribly serious," she said. "I mean, I hate making a fuss about things, don't you? I had to have the doctor this morning, and he says that it won't be really serious if I take care."

She passed on, limping. They watched her in silence. Then Enid said: "Poor kid!"

"We met Uncle Paul on the way," said Pen slowly, "and he said he'd been here to her. He said she'd got stomach-ache with eating green apples."

"But how could that make her limp?" asked Enid.

They gazed after her retreating form. It still limped, showing indeed every appearance of acute pain bravely endured. Suddenly Dorian appeared on the lawn.

"Hi!" he called to her. "You've pinched my racquet, you rotten little skunk!"

She brandished it over her head.

"All right," she challenged. "Come and get it."

With that she began to dodge lightly in and out of the trees, leap over the flower beds, and run fleetly round the lawn.

"It must have been only stomach-ache," said Enid. "She's a queer kid."

Adam lifted his flushed face from his struggles with the tennis net, and accosted his younger brother and sister in authoritative tones.

"Stop mucking about, you young fools, and come and help with this."

Dorian joined him obediently, but Cressida, adopting a haughty manner, said: "I think I'd better go and help mother receive," and proceeded to make her way with slow dignity over the lawn to where her mother and Alicia were receiving the guests.

Adam, in looking up from the net, had caught sight of Pippa standing by Enid's chair.

"Here! See what you can do with it," he said to his young brother. "I'm sick of the thing."

Pippa's heart began to beat rapidly as he approached. His whole face had lighted up when he saw her. He *did* love her. . . . Oh, how glad she was that she hadn't stayed at home after all! Her pride suddenly abased by her love, she felt even glad that her mother had scorched her dress, because this dress of Daphne's was nicer than any of hers. Her eyes brightened, a tremulous happy smile played round her usually sulky mouth. She looked, for the first time in her life, almost pretty.

As his hand clasped hers and his eyes rested on hers, a wave of exultant happiness swept over her. This thing had happened to *her*, not to Pen and Daphne, though they were so much prettier and more attractive. Beneath the exultation was a strange humility. Everything hard in her seemed to be softened. She wanted to be kind to people, to comfort those who were unhappy, to try to make up somehow to all the people to whom this miracle had not happened.

"Would you like to see round the garden?" he said, including them all in his invitation, as she realised, of course, that he must.

"Take the infants," said Enid. "I'm old enough to be allowed to be lazy."

She laughed loudly and rather harshly as she spoke.

They wandered off towards the kitchen garden, leaving her lying back lazily in her chair.

She closed her eyes, trying to summon again the memory of the moment when Max Collin had taken her in his arms, trying to recapture with it the feeling of reckless excitement that had possessed her, the conviction that what she wanted to do was not only inevitable but necessary. If only Stephen and—But she must forget them. . . .

The guests were arriving in a thick stream now. It was rather a heterogeneous gathering, as Mrs. Harte had used the opportunity of her children's tennis party to invite everyone in the town to whom she owed an invitation of any sort.

Mr. Somervell, the headmaster of the Grammar School, was shaking hands with Mr. Harte. He was a small man with an over-pleasant manner and a large pale face that wore always a faintly deprecating smile. He had been appointed to his post twenty years ago on the strength of an almost phenomenal success in coaching boys for classical scholarships. He was a brilliant scholar and a fine coach of brilliant boys. He had a flair that bordered on genius for discovering a potential classical scholar in a messy, inky, Fourth Form urchin. Once discovered, the potential classical scholar was allowed no peace. He was coached in season and out of season, he was guarded, protected, sheltered from the cold blasts of other interests as if he had been a sensitive hothouse plant. He was, in fact, taken prisoner, body and soul, till the time when his name should be triumphantly inscribed on the Classical Scholarship board in the big hall.

For the rest, Mr. Somervell spent most of his time evading—always with that faint deprecating smile—the responsibilities incidental to his position. There was about him a sort of inherent slipperiness that made it impossible to tie him down to anything. He would make any promise demanded of him, relying upon his ingenuity to extricate himself afterwards. He had long since ceased attempting to reconcile his various and conflicting statements. He knew that his staff despised him, but he did not mind this as long as they performed their work satisfactorily and bolstered up his sagging credit by winning good results in the examinations. One of his guiding rules was to avoid what he called "unpleasantness," and no one had ever succeeded in provoking a scene with him. When he had to dismiss one of his staff for incompetence he would give a specially eulogistic testimonial, and explain that the dismissal was entirely due to a reorganisation of the time-table. He was anxious to keep on good terms with all the parents, but he singled out the sons of the more prominent citizens for preferential treatment, and his detractors said that his caning of the mayor's son and of the son of the small station tobacconist were very different affairs. To do him justice, however, he disliked administering corporal punishment, and even the station tobacconist's son came off fairly lightly.

A certain nervousness invaded the diffidence of his smile as he appeared on the Rectory lawn. So might Daniel have looked on entering the den of lions. The place was probably full of parents who would approach him and ask him how their boys were getting on. He had an unusually poor memory for both names and faces, and he felt particularly nervous to-day because of an unfortunate mistake that he had made last week. Meeting a man of local importance, whose son, he knew, attended the Grammar School, he had told him how well the boy had been doing lately, only to discover that the boy had been away all the term through illness.

He glanced around and heaved a slight sigh of relief. No governors here, at any rate. A few prominent citizens, but no governors. In a small country town like Danesborough it seemed impossible ever to go out without running into one of the governors. Mr. Somervell was well aware that there were two parties on the Grammar School board of governors, one of which frankly regretted his appointment and was in favour of demanding his resignation, the other of which considered that the tale of classical scholarships, added yearly to the scholarship boards, amply compensated for his incapacity in other departments. He was aware, too, that the latter party was rapidly diminishing.

His wife was shaking hands with Mrs. Harte. Mrs. Somervell was a majestic woman with an assured and somewhat arrogant manner. She was the daughter of a bishop and, till the arrival of the Hartes, had been considered the social arbiter of Danesborough.

Mrs. Harte, however, did not think much of bishops as bishops, though she fully expected to be the wife of one. Her standard was the simple and absolute one of birth, and Mrs. Somervell's father, despite his bishopric, had been the son of a provincial draper.

To watch the two women meet like this and greet each other on the sunny lawn suggested the clash of two mighty armies. The air around them was thick with battle, though all Mrs. Harte said was, "*How*-do-you-do, Mrs. Somervell? So *glad* you were able to come," and all Mrs. Somervell said was, "*How*-do-you-do, Mrs. Harte. ... How beautiful the dear Rectory looks to-day!" Mrs. Somervell was taller and more majestic, but on the whole Mrs. Harte came off victor. Her air of sublime indifference conquered even the majesty of Mrs. Somervell.

Cressida had wandered over to an old lady, who was sitting alone at the further end of the lawn. Cressida generally found old people appreciative audiences. She enjoyed playing the angelic child to them and bringing out quaint sayings that she had carefully prepared beforehand. Moreover, she always had a vague hope that one of them would be so touched as to leave a fortune to her when she died, and old people, of course, might die at any minute.

She took her seat by the old lady and gazed up at her, making her eyes as big as possible.

"I always sink," said Cressida with the slight lisp that she generally assumed when about to give utterance to a quaint saying, "that sweet peas are more like faiwies than any other flower, don't you?"

The old lady bent to her, cupping her ear in her hand.

"What do you say, my dear?" she asked.

Cressida blinked at her inscrutably and was silent. As an expert in quaint sayings, she knew that they do not bear repeating. The old lady's eyes remained fixed on the child's face. Cressida's bilious attack had certainly robbed it of its usually healthy glow.

"You don't look very well, my dear," she said.

Cressida's coltish form took on an invalid droop, and again she smiled her brave little smile.

"No," she said. "I don't feel very well."

"But what's the matter, my dear?" said the old lady in a tone of deep concern.

Cressida considered the rival merits of heart, lung, and sprained ankle, finally rejecting them all. She had, she felt, in the course of the afternoon, already abstracted from each whatever thrill it was capable of yielding. She cast round for some other inspiration, and remembered suddenly Dotheboys Hall in *Nicholas Nickleby*, which she had been reading last term. She assumed an air of heartrending pathos.

"Well . . . of course I only got back from school yesterday," she said in a small, suffering voice, "and I never do feel well at school."

"But why not, dear?" said the old lady solicitously.

"I'm always hungry there, for one thing," said Cressida, stretching her eyes to the utmost and dropping the corners of her mouth to give her face a hungry look. "We never have enough to eat, and—well, they aren't very kind to us, either."

"But, my dear," said the old lady, much distressed, "do your parents know about this? How are they unkind to you?"

"No, I've never told mother and father, because I don't want to worry them," said Cressida, "and—well, they're unkind to us in such lots of ways." She dismissed the régime of Dotheboys Hall as being too crude for her purpose, and continued: "If we don't get every one of our lessons absolutely right one day we have nothing but bread and water to eat and drink all the next day."

"But, my *dear*," said the old lady again, now shocked as well as distressed, "for growing girls that's most *unwise*."

"Yes, I know," agreed Cressida pathetically, "but don't tell father or mother about it, will you? I do so hate worrying them."

Chapter Fifteen

MR. SOMERVELL had been buttonholed by a vivacious little matron in a pink frock and a large black hat. His pale puffy face wore its usual deprecating smile and his small eyes darted furtively about, as if in search of some way of escape.

"I'm Mrs. Davies," she began eagerly. "I don't suppose you remember me, do you, Mr. Somervell? There are so many of us worrying parents, aren't there?"

"Of *course* I remember you perfectly, Mrs. Davies," he said courteously.

She was a parent, anyway. It was something to know that. He remembered an occasion—it had happened about ten years ago, but the memory of it still turned him hot and cold—when he had told a woman who spoke to him at a party that her son had improved very much this last term, only to discover that she was not married. He had an uncomfortable suspicion that the story was still repeated against him in the town. Davies . . . Davies. . . . He tried hard to remember Davies. He certainly wasn't one of his classical protégés. He knew all of those, could have described each one down to the last hair, but the rest of the school was a vague blur to him.

"Do tell me," continued the vivacious little woman, smiling up at him from under the large hat brim, "how is Tony getting on? *Really*, getting on. Now don't try to soften the blow. I know he's a little pickle, and I know he got into *terrible* trouble last week for carving his name on a desk—the little monkey!—but do tell me—*honestly* now—if you think he's going to be any good."

"Little" was a help, of course. He must be one of the younger boys. He might even have caned him last week for carving his name on a desk. Davies ... Davies. ... If only he hadn't such a wretched memory! She might be a friend of one of the governors' wives. ... He must be careful not to make any obvious slip. These stories got so wretchedly exaggerated as they spread about the town.

He laughed with a fair imitation of heartiness.

"Oh, Tony will turn out all right, Mrs. Davies. You needn't worry about him."

Mrs. Davies clasped small, daintily gloved hands. "I'm *so* glad to hear you say that, Mr. Somervell, because you must have had such a lot of experience with boys, and you must *know*. ... Now, do tell me, what do you think he ought to *do*? When he leaves school, I mean. He seems to have no particular bent, does he?"

He felt on easier ground now.

"That will come, that will come. ... I never believe in hurrying these things. They can't be forced, you know. There's plenty of time yet."

"Of *course* there is, Mr. Somervell. How wonderfully understanding you are. ... I suppose I mustn't monopolise you any longer, but I *have* so much enjoyed this little chat with you, and Tony will be quite flattered to hear how well you remember him."

She passed on, smiling. He heaved a faint sigh of relief, then glanced across the lawn to where his wife sat—majestic, sublime, invulnerable. She was so firmly encased in her armour of self-sufficiency that she never perceived any of his uncertainties or blunders. He was headmaster of Danesborough Grammar School. The matter, in her eyes, began and ended there. She did not admit even the possibility of any criticism of him. He looked ahead into the future with that feeling of apprehension that the future always gave him. Oh, well ... he would be able to retire in about five years' time. On the other hand there was to be a "full dress" Board of Education inspection next year, at the thought of which he felt unpleasant qualms somewhere in the pit of his stomach.

Suddenly he saw two girls walking across the lawn. He wasn't sure of their names, but he knew that they belonged to the Royston family, and that encouraged him, because it was so easy to remember the Roystons. They stood out so prominently against the background of Danesborough. He approached them and raised his hat.

"How's your father?" he said to Penelope.

"He's quite well, thank you."

"Fine boy he was. . . . I always remember his taking the part of Henry V. at his last Speech Day. Splendid actor!"

"He always enjoys acting," said Pen, then flushed faintly, as if afraid that the words might seem to have a double meaning.

"And your uncle Paul? Good, solid, hard-working boy, he was, and an excellent doctor now. Does one good to see boys profiting by their education like that." He hesitated. There'd been another brother, he remembered, but he had a vague idea that he'd gone off the rails. Turned out a bad lot. Better not mention him, anyway. . . . "Your great-uncle Richard was before my time, of course," he went on, "but he certainly had the lion's share of the honours in his day. . . . How's old Mr. Royston?"

"He's very well," said the prettier of the two. The other looked pale and sulky. "It's his birthday to-day, you know. We're all going to have dinner with him to-night. He's ninety-five."

"Splendid!"

He smiled again, raised his hat, and went on, holding his flabby figure a little more upright, his self-respect partially restored. He'd really remembered those Roystons wonderfully well. . . .

Cressida, having tired of the rôle of Smike, slipped from her chair, smiled sweetly at the old lady, and ran off to join her brother at the tennis net. The old lady gazed after her in a bewilderment that gradually changed to indignation. Really, the things the child had told her (Cressida had rather let her imagination run away with her towards the end of the recital) couldn't *possibly* be true. It was *outrageous*. . . . She remembered now hearing someone say once that Cressida Harte was a most untruthful little girl. Her indignant eyes followed Cressida as she leapt up to the lowest branch of the copper beech and hung there swinging. . . .

Adam had first manœuvred to walk in front with Daphne, leaving Pen and Pippa to follow, and had then managed to escape from Pen and Pippa altogether and take Daphne to the stable, where he was showing her a new litter of kittens.

He knelt on the stone floor and handed two of them up to her. She stood holding them in her arms, smiling down at them. The mother cat watched, anxious but trusting, from the straw-lined box.

"They're rather nice, aren't they?" said the boy. "We're going to try to find homes for them all, so that we needn't drown them. I think it's so hateful drowning kittens."

"Yes, isn't it?" agreed Daphne. She was looking at the box where the other kittens tumbled blindly about their mother. She could see Biddy quite plainly . . . bending over it, taking out the kittens one by one and stroking them, holding their soft warm bodies to her cheek. She almost heard the delicious gurgle of baby laughter. . . . On the lawn she had seen John helping Dorian with the net . . . going indoors with him to fetch out more chairs for the visitors. . . .

She replaced the two kittens, in the box and, bending down, began to stroke the gaunt sinuous cat. It stood up, arching its back against her hand, purring loudly.

"You stroke it, Biddy. . . . From its head to its tail, you know. This way."

Biddy could never remember which way you stroked cats.

She had taken off her hat, and the sunlight poured through the dusty window on to her honey-coloured hair and smooth soft cheek.

The boy, standing beside her, watched in silence. It was nearly a year since he had last seen her, and in that year he or she or both of them must have changed completely. Or had she been even then as lovely as this, and had he been utterly blind? The first sight of her this afternoon had made him feel for a moment shaken and bewildered. He had not noticed her till he had crossed the lawn to speak to Pippa Chudleigh. He had been glad to see Pippa there.

He and Pippa had had such a jolly afternoon together that Saturday in the early summer when he had come home for the week-end and had felt so unutterably fed up with life. It had been wonderful to find that there was someone in this smug little town who shared his interests and enthusiasms. But, of course, it was only the sort of friendship that one had with another man. He had felt towards her, indeed, exactly as he felt towards his college friends. It was finding her here in Danesborough that had surprised and delighted him—Danesborough, where everyone seemed so hidebound by convention, so intolerant of all that was new, so scornful of intellectual interests. Then, just as he was shaking hands with Pippa, Daphne had turned and looked at him. His heart had missed a beat, and an odd wave of mingled joy and terror had surged over him. Despite his bewilderment he knew what had happened to him. He had fallen in love—irrevocably and for ever. . . . His bewilderment was now leaving him, and in its place was a new strange purposefulness that he had never known before.

Daphne put back one of the kittens that was trying to climb out of the box, and rose to her feet, moving a strand of hair from across her eyes.

"Hadn't we better go back to the garden?" she said. "They'll be wanting to start the tennis."

"They can start without us," he said.

From the distance came Enid's loud brisk voice: "Thirty-love."

"It's all right," he said. "They've made up the first set. . . . We needn't go yet. . . . Let's sit down here."

They sat side by side on one of the dusty packing cases that were piled about the disused stable—packing cases in which the Rector's library had been transferred to Danesborough eight years ago.

"Won't it dirty your dress?" he said anxiously.

"No. . . ."

Her voice was, as usual, low and gentle, her blue eyes met his unflinchingly, yet he felt that she was suddenly ill-at-ease, that something of the disturbance of his spirit had communicated itself to hers. She sat beside him, silent, motionless, yet she made him think of a bird fluttering in the first unreasoning terror of capture.

"I've come down from college for good," he said abruptly.

"I know," she said in her sweet slow voice. "What are you going to do?"

"That's what I must talk to you about," he said. His young brow was set and frowning, his voice urgent, business-like. "You see, my people want me to take Orders. My godmother's a very religious woman, and she's offered to pay all the expenses—theological college and everything—and a relation of my mother has a living in his gift. There's an old man in it now who's agreed to hang on till I'm ready before he retires—so, you see, they think it so obvious. And they won't help me any other way. They think I'm just being—difficult. It's a career ready made, free of charge, as it were, and if I don't take it they think I can just stew in my own juice. After all, there's not much money, and there's Dorian and the girls to think of. In a way one sees their point. . . ."

"Yes . . ." she said. She spoke rather breathlessly and there was a question in her voice.

He continued as if with an effort.

"But—if you—I want you to tell me—if you'd like me to, I will."

She turned her head and looked at him. His face was pale and set. Body and soul he was surrendering himself into her keeping. She went pale, too, but her eyes did not falter.

"No," she said in a low, steady voice. "I don't want you to."

"I must get to work and find something else, then," he said.

Not a word of love had passed between them, yet both knew that he was speaking of their joint future.

The cat craned up her neck to look at them over the top of the box. A kitten climbed up to the edge, then tumbled over backwards.

Daphne's eyes were fixed unseeingly in front of her, and she spoke in a jerky unnatural voice.

"You remember about—John and Biddy, don't you?"

"Yes."

"I—often—pretend they're with me. I can almost see Biddy now, playing with the kittens—and I imagined John outside helping

Dorian." She stopped as abruptly as she had begun. She had never told anyone else about John and Biddy. Before this afternoon she had thought that she would rather have died than tell anyone. Telling him was like tearing out her heart. But she had told him because she wanted to tear out her heart for him. She wanted in her turn to surrender herself, body and soul, into his keeping.

"I understand," he said quietly.

The tenseness of her slender frame relaxed. Again they looked at each other, the two young faces set and stern, as though some momentous decision had been taken. Neither moved. . . .

Then Dorian's voice rang out in the distance.

"Where's that blighter Adam got to?"

Daphne rose in a slow dreamlike fashion, as if moving in her sleep.

"We'd better go back to the others."

Then went back silently, side by side. They had not kissed or even touched each other, yet each knew that they were vowed to each other till the end of life. Neither of them realised that no words of love had been said. The thing had happened. They just accepted it. There was no need of words.

"Come on, you lazy blighter!" Dorian greeted his brother. "We want to get up another set."

The non-players—mostly elderly ladies—sat on chairs at the end of the lawn, ostensibly engaged in watching the game, really engaged in the exchange of local gossip.

"The butcher told my cook that they've not paid their account for three months. Not that I listen to servants' gossip, of course."

"Of course not. I don't either, but my housemaid was with her, you know, before she came to me, and she says that she half starved her maids. All the food was kept locked up."

"Shocking!"

"Well played!" called an isolated enthusiast.

"Well played!" echoed the gossipers mechanically, throwing lack-lustre glances in the direction of the game, then returning with renewed vigour to their interrupted conversation. The Collins, of course, came in for their share of attention.

"*Fast*, my dear, isn't the word. Her lips the colour of a pillar-box. And that actor *always* there. . . . I don't say that there's anything in it, but he's *always* there. I think it a pity that Enid Lessing sees so much of them nowadays."

"By the way, what do you think of the new Mrs. Harold Royston? She strikes me as being very hard and standoffish. I'm afraid she won't make much of a mother to little Penelope. . . ."

"She behaved awfully badly to poor Philip Messiter, you know. Threw him over for no reason at all. An only child and thoroughly spoilt."

"Do you know what I heard yesterday? Mind you, I don't want this repeated. . . ."

Voices became lower, heads closer together.

"Well hit!" called the solitary enthusiast.

Another group was discussing Mr. Somervell.

"He's very unpopular. . . . His staff hate him. One of them told my husband that he was the biggest liar he'd ever met."

Little Mrs. Davies clasped her daintily gloved hands.

"Oh, I can't believe that!" she said earnestly. "He was so *perfectly* sweet about my little Tony."

A second set was beginning, and Enid, wandering over to a chair apart from the others, leant back and watched the new game absently.

Pippa, who had been her partner (there never seemed to be enough men at these affairs), had disappeared. Pippa was a fairly good tennis-player as a rule, but this afternoon she had played abominably. Once Enid could not help whispering: "Buck up, Pippa! What on earth's the matter with you?" After that the child had played worse than ever, serving continual faults and missing every ball, looking furious and utterly wretched all the time. . . . What a queer kid she was! It had been a rotten game. It was hard enough playing at the copper beech end of the Rectory tennis court, even at the best of times. No grass grew there, the players slipped about on moss or bare earth, and very few balls escaped the overhanging branches. Occasionally a ball would remain lodged in them, and the game would be stopped while they all tried to shake it down.

Oh, well—Enid dismissed the game from her mind and turned to face the problem that confronted her. Max ... Stephen ... Beatrice ... She didn't really understand why the two visitors had suddenly made her love for Max seem shoddy and unreal. Frantically she argued with herself.

"You can't back out now. You've practically promised. It's too late to back out." ... "It's not too late." ... "But it's what you've always wanted. You know it is. Right down at the bottom of your heart you've always wanted it." ... "But not like this. ... Not this way." ... "It isn't as if you didn't love Max, as if you were just doing it out of curiosity or for a sensation. You do love him. Remember what you felt when he kissed you this morning. ... Why, even the *thought* of him ..." ... "But you know how it will end. You saw that girl this morning. She loved him. ..."

Mr. Morrow, the curate, was making his way across the lawn to the vacant chair beside her. She smiled at him as he sank into it and mechanically assumed her breezy manner.

"Perfectly marvellous summer it's been, hasn't it?"

"Hasn't it!"

He turned to her and added slowly: "I want you to be the first to know. I'm going at the end of next month."

"Leaving Danesborough?"

He nodded.

"But why?"

He smiled slightly.

"I've got to my fourth Arundel print. Flemming said I'd go at my fourth Arundel print."

"Flemming? Oh, he was here before you, wasn't he? I remember him."

"Yes. He went at his third Arundel print. He told me that I'd obviously got a little more patience than he had, but that I'd probably go at my fourth."

"What on earth are you talking about? *What* Arundel prints?"

"The Rector bought several dozen of them at a sale some years ago. He's given them as peace offerings ever since."

"Peace offerings?"

"Yes. . . . You see, he can't bear anyone else to have the slightest credit for anything to do with the Parish Church. He takes all the credit for things he's had nothing at all to do with. It would be disloyal to tell you this, of course, if I weren't definitely going and—well, there's another reason, too, why I want you to understand exactly how things are."

She was still staring at him in amazement.

"But what on earth have Arundel prints got to do with it?"

"Well, you see, when he's done something mean, he always feels uncomfortable about it, and he sends you round a little present to make things all right. And the little present, of course, is always an Arundel print. Naturally, as he's got several dozen of them put away in the attic. And, of course, they're quite jolly things. Flemming said he felt frightfully bucked and touched when he got the first one . . . but, of course, I was prepared, and after a bit it does begin to get on your nerves."

His eyes rested on the Rector, who was standing talking to a group on the lawn.

His handsome face, elegant figure, and charming smile made him everywhere a centre of attraction.

"One can't dislike him," went on his curate thoughtfully. "He works like a nigger, and he's very pleasant to deal with. As long as he can have all the limelight to himself, he's really an ideal chief."

"Why not let him have all the limelight, then?"

"Heaven knows he can as far as I'm concerned. It's the work I care about, not the limelight. But, you see, as soon as you begin to make a success of a piece of work, and people begin to talk about it and connect it with you, it riles him and he stops the work. I was preaching a series of sermons on Job on Sunday evenings, and people liked them and talked about them, so he took over the evening sermon himself and put me on to the morning. It's—galling in a way. He sent me an Arundel print, of course, after that. It's really rather a jolly one—Michelangelo's Creation of Adam—and I'd like it awfully if it weren't for—well, the reason why I got it. Then I started a service for 'busmen on Friday evenings

174

at the mission church, which is just by the 'bus terminus. He said it hadn't the slightest chance of success, but he let me do it, and quite a lot of them came and people in the town began to talk about it, so he gave me a confirmation class on Friday evenings, and took the mission service himself, but it's not really the sort of work he likes, so he closed it down after a time and said that there wasn't really time for it with the other parish activities. Really made himself believe it, too. Said he was sending the Arundel print that time as a recognition of the good work I'd done for it. There wasn't any reason at all why it shouldn't have gone on. I don't bear him any malice, but I've had enough. Somehow I think one could put up with it if he didn't give one Arundel prints. Anyway, I've got four and I'm clearing out, as Flemming said I would."

She laughed.

"Oh well ... You'll have your four Arundel prints to set up house with when you go somewhere else."

"Five. He'll give me one for a leaving present. He bought three dozen, Flemming said."

"Are you going to warn the next man?"

"No. Far better not. Unwarned he'll probably last out to six or seven. Flemming hadn't been warned, but he wasn't a patient man at the best of times. He admitted as much."

"He's spoilt, I expect," she said, watching the Rector, who was now drawing forward a wicker chair for an elderly guest with his inimitable air of courtliness. "He's so nice looking. Nice-looking parsons are generally spoilt."

He looked at her in silence, gathering up his courage. He had decided more than a week ago to propose to her as soon as an opportunity should present itself, and here was the opportunity. He believed that a clergyman ought to be married, especially a beneficed clergyman, and he fully expected to be given a benefice in the course of the next year or so. The only woman he had ever loved—and, he was certain, would ever love—had married someone else, but he did not intend to remain unmarried on that account. He had thought several times that Enid Lessing would make an excellent clergyman's wife, but, till he gave notice of his resignation of his curacy at the Parish Church, he had not actually made up his mind to propose to her. Then it had occurred to him that he was not likely to discover anyone more suitable and that he had better propose to her before he left the neighbourhood. He admired her, though he did not love her. He admired her largeness and wholesomeness, her hearty honest manner and genial laugh. He admired, too, the classic regularity of her features and her generous proportions. She got on well with young people, which was a great asset to a clergyman's wife, and she was eminently capable and business-like. There was a good humour about her, as large and generous as her frame. "A good sport" everyone called her, and that was what a clergyman's wife should be—"a good sport."

He cleared his throat. "You'll be surprised at what I'm going to say to you, Miss Lessing, but I'm not saying it without serious consideration. I know that it is usual to prepare the ground more, in these cases, but I'm a very blunt man, and it seems to me that two people can't live in the same small town as long as we've lived without getting to know each other pretty well, even if they only meet occasionally, and in the presence of other people. . . . What I want to ask you, Miss Lessing, is this: Do you think you could ever care enough for me to marry me?"

She stared at him in astonishment, and it was the real Enid who assured him—in a breathless, frightened voice, all the heartiness gone from it:

"Oh no . . . no, I couldn't. I'm sorry."

"You mean—you don't want even to consider the question?"

"No. . . ."

"You don't care for me at all? I'm not talking about what people call being in love. I mean—don't you think that friendship and mutual respect and work in common might form the basis of a happy married life? There is no woman—as things are—whom I would rather have as my wife than you."

Again that breathless frightened, "Oh no, no. . . ."

In the silence that followed, Enid's real self, terrified, defenceless, called urgently to her false self to come back to protect her. "Come back and say something for me. I don't know what to say. . . ."

Obediently the false self returned to take up its duties.

"I respect you, Mr. Morrow, more than I can tell you," said the loud assured voice, "but I don't think that's enough for marriage. . . . I feel frightfully honoured that you——"

Mrs. Harte had appeared on the lawn with raised hand.

"Will you come indoors to tea—" She glanced without enthusiasm at the heterogeneous gathering. The word "people" obviously trembled on her lips, but she suppressed it and substituted "everyone."

Chapter Sixteen

SILENCE had fallen in the red parlour of the White Swan. There is a silence that alienates, there is a silence that leaves relationships where it found them, there is a silence that deepens understanding. The silence in the red parlour was of the last kind. None of the three wished to break it. Each found in it a strange satisfaction. It seemed to bring to each of them something vital, precious, unexpected. The old man in particular felt shut away by it into some enchanted place where the discords and annoyances of real life could not reach him.

They had talked freely during tea at the round mahogany table, on whose red fringed cover Mrs. Slaggit had laid her best lace tea-cloth and tea service of Worcester china. Mrs. Slaggit was proud to welcome old Mr. Royston to her house. Despite the fact that he now seldom came into the town, he had somehow impressed himself upon the imagination of Danesborough.

"How's old Mr. Royston?" people would say, or, "Old Mr. Royston was out for a walk this afternoon." They were always conscious of the old man, with his piercing blue eyes, his faintly ironic smile, and his mysterious past, living in the big house just outside the town.

As Mrs. Slaggit, who had changed into her best black silk dress, placed the teapot upon the table, she thought with pride that she would now be able to say, casually, as if it were quite an ordinary thing, "Old Mr. Royston had tea here in the red parlour the other day."

He had greeted her very courteously with a "Good afternoon, Mrs. Slaggit. I hope you are quite well," and she had bridled into portly middle-aged coyness. What a handsome old gentleman he was, despite his ninety-five years! All the Roystons were handsome, of course. There had been a lot of silly talk about Mr. Stephen, but there couldn't be anything wrong, or the old man wouldn't be coming down to have tea with them like this. A sweet lady, too, in spite of her white hair.

She turned her smiling glance to the laden tea-table, said, "I hope it'll be to your liking, sir," and withdrew.

They looked at the array of plates—brown bread and butter, white bread and butter, currant bread and butter, buttered scones, rock-buns, queen cakes, currant cake, sandwich cake, chocolate cake, four kinds of jam, stewed fruit, a large custard tart—then they laughed in sudden light-heartedness. The whole thing had become a delicious adventure.

"It's years since I saw a tea like this," said Beatrice as she took her seat behind the tea-tray.

"There's certainly something about it that warms one's heart," said Stephen.

The two men sat down at the table, and Beatrice poured out. The old man watched her. She poured out as a woman should pour out, as indeed he had known she would, poised and graceful, without fuss or clatter. Her slender hands, moving to and fro among the tea things, reminded him of white birds.

It had always afforded Matthew satisfaction to see a beautiful woman presiding gracefully over a tea-table, and it was a long time since he had seen one.

Charlotte stood up to pour out, chattering and fidgeting all the time. Catherine poured out in an overbearing fashion, making the row of cups in front of her look cowed and frightened, snatching up the milk-jug as if she were going to shake it, keeping a threatening eye upon the teapot. Margaret, of course, could have presided gracefully enough over a tea-table, but Enid always poured out at Margaret's, poured out like the hoyden she was, rattling the tea-cups, banging the spoons, bellowing questions about milk and sugar, whistling between her teeth as if she were grooming a horse.

When they had finished tea, the dishes looked almost as full as before they began, and Mrs. Slaggit, coming in to clear away, shook her head sadly over them.

"Why, you've eaten nothing," she said.

"We've had a most enormous tea," Beatrice assured her.

Old Mr. Royston's keen blue eyes twinkled at her from beneath his bushy white eyebrows, and she smiled at him, smoothing down her ample waist and bridling again into a ghost of her girlhood coquetry. Some of the tales they told about the old man were probably true. He must have been a one when he was young and no mistake. She piled up the large tin tray with practised hands and went out of the door that Stephen opened for her, feeling vaguely thrilled and excited, as if the glamour that held the other three had somehow communicated itself to her. Stephen closed the door, and then that strange dreamlike silence fell upon them. To the old man it was literally like a dream, and in it he wandered from the past to the present, from the present to the past. Sometimes he was a young man, and Beatrice was the girl Hope in the white billowing crinoline with roses in her hair. Sometimes he was an old man, but Beatrice was still the girl Hope. He was conscious only vaguely of Stephen, leaning back in the armchair opposite him, smoking, his eyes fixed on the empty fireplace, but in every nerve he was conscious of the woman who sat gracefully upright in the chair by the window. Hope . . . Beatrice . . . Beatrice . . . Hope . . . the woman in whom there dwelt all the glamour in all the world. Yes, it was stealing into the room, conquering the smell of stale tobacco smoke and furniture polish . . . the faint sweet perfume of white jasmine.

The woman, on her side, was only vaguely conscious of the old man. (What a darling Stephen's grandfather was! She wished she had known him before.) But all her being was conscious of Stephen—as indeed it had been ever since the day she met him. It had been some quality of safeness about him that had first attracted her. She had felt like a ship, buffeted by storms, that suddenly sights harbour. She knew that people generally considered him dull and slow. They had never known the immeasurable kindness, the great-heartedness of him. All her life she had been afraid. Fear seemed to have been born in her—a strange secret fear of life. It had haunted her through her neglected childhood, had deepened into nightmare panic in her marriage, had sunk slowly and tremulously into peace in the shelter of Stephen's tenderness. So real and deep was their understanding of each other that there was little need ever of speech between them. Her only fear now was the fear that dwells always at the heart of love, the fear—or rather the knowledge—that some day one of the two would be left alone. And yet she had a strange conviction that, so united were they, life could not continue in her if Stephen were dead. And, while he lived, nothing could hurt her.

She stirred suddenly, breaking the spell that held the little room. Stephen stood up and went over to where she sat by the window. "There's Penelope," he said, looking out.

The old man turned his head. Penelope ... he remembered her ... a little girl with dark eyes and almost black hair. Harriet was proud of her. But she was ill. Harriet was worried about her. The doctor had been that morning and had said that the bronchitis had turned to pneumonia.

"Don't worry, Harriet," he said aloud.

Then he remembered. He wasn't married. He was a young man, a boy. He was going to see Hope. She had said "To-morrow. You won't forget?" She had come to see him. There she was by the window. Then suddenly the mists cleared. That was Stephen and his wife, Beatrice. Penelope was Harold's daughter, and Harold was his grandson. The little dark-haired Penelope had died long ago. Hope had died long ago. He walked slowly over to the open window and stood there with Stephen and Beatrice, looking down at the market-square. Yes, Penelope and Daphne and Pippa, his great-grandchildren, were walking across it with a young man whom he recognised as the son of the Rector of Danesborough. All four carried tennis racquets.

"They must be coming back from the tennis party," said Beatrice. "Mrs. Lessing said that Penelope had gone to a tennis party."

Suddenly the old man remembered what he had set out that afternoon to do—to introduce Beatrice to the members of his family privately before she met them to-night at dinner. He had taken her to Margaret's and Harold's and Isabel's. There remained Milly and Lilian. And the young people, of course. She must meet the young people. Suddenly Daphne looked up and saw the three of them standing at the window. She smiled and waved her tennis racquet. The old man leaned forward and beckoned. The four stood hesitating.

"Come on in, all of you," he called.

They hesitated again for a moment, then turned and walked towards the inn entrance.

Stephen opened the door, and they came into the little room. Something of youth, poignant, intense, seemed to enter with them.

"This is your Aunt Beatrice," said the old man. "I don't think you've met her before."

They shook hands gravely, shyly. Then Penelope looked round with her sudden childish smile.

"What a darling little ugly room!" she said.

"Isn't it jolly," said the boy, whom Daphne had introduced as Adam Harte. "I've never been in here before."

Penelope looked at the clock.

"I must go," she said. "I told Helen I'd be back early."

"Well, sit down, the rest of you," said old Matthew. He turned to Adam. "Will you have something to drink?"

"No, thank you, sir," said Adam, much gratified by the question.

Matthew's keen blue eyes were fixed intently upon the boy.

"Well, what are you going to do with yourself?" he said. "Going into the Church like your father?"

The boy smiled nervously.

"No, my people want me to, but"—he exchanged a glance with Daphne—"I'm not very keen. They're a bit disappointed about it, of course, because they'd set their hearts on it."

"Well, it's a safe sort of career," said old Matthew dryly. "A clergyman of the Church of England is the only salaried professional man who can't be dismissed for incompetence. If you don't rob the local bank or run away with your neighbour's wife, you're provided for for life, and you need do precious little work for your keep unless you want to. . . . What are you going to do?"

"I—I'm afraid I don't quite know, sir. I must get a job of some sort, of course, as soon as possible."

"What sort of job?"

"Any sort. I think I'd like business. But I don't quite know how to start getting into a business."

"Can't your people help you?"

"They don't want to, because they still hope I'll take Orders. . . ."

"I see."

Beatrice had been watching them. The two rapt young faces told her all that had happened between them this afternoon. Here was young love, with its innocence, bewilderment, and heartrending pathos. Pippa's face, too, told its story—the pallor of her cheeks, the compression of the thin childish lips, the despair in the hazel eyes. Here, too, was love, but love rejected, love in torment.

She interposed suddenly in her low musical voice.

"Weren't you in business?" she said to Matthew.

"I was," he said with a grim smile.

"Haven't you any business friend whom you could ask to take Adam into his firm?"

He looked at her in amused surprise.

Now he came to think of it there were plenty of men, younger than he, still holding the reins of their affairs in their hands, who would take into their firms anyone he recommended for old times' sake.

"I suppose I have," he said slowly. Farley's now. He'd helped young Farley out of a pretty nasty hole once, saved his business from bankruptcy by a loan, which he had allowed to stand over indefinitely, and for which he had not asked interest. Young Farley's gratitude was real enough. He would give a fair chance to any boy he asked him to take on. And Farley's was on its feet again now—a sound reputable firm that any young man would be proud to belong to.

"Will you write to-night and ask them?" said Beatrice, her eyes still fixed on the boy and girl.

Again that odd feeling of unreality had seized the old man, that feeling of moving in a dream. And in that dream Hope—or was it Beatrice? . . . Beatrice? . . . Hope?—had come to ask him to do something for her.

"Of course I will," he said.

The boy had started forward, his face alight with gratitude. The girl's face, too, was shining. The whole room seemed suddenly lit up with radiance.

"I simply can't thank you, sir," stammered the boy. "I swear that I'll make good once I have the chance."

He turned and looked at Daphne, and it was clear that, as they looked at each other, everything and everyone around them faded away. The path they would tread together seemed to have opened out suddenly, plain and straight, before their feet. On that path they would not fail each other or falter.

Suddenly Daphne turned to the old man.

"Oh *thank* you, great-gran," she said, and kissed him impulsively.

"What's it's got to do with *you*?" said the old man, twinkling.

"I hope it's got everything to do with her," said Adam, unsmiling, unembarrassed.

And both of them realised with surprise that those were the first words of love that had been spoken between them.

"I must go," said Daphne; "good-bye."

She wanted suddenly to be alone, not even with Adam. . . .

Beatrice held out her hand, but Daphne threw her arms around her, kissed her, then, after a quick farewell to the two men, went out, followed by Adam.

Pippa hesitated. She didn't want to go with them. She couldn't bear to be with them a moment longer. She felt a dull surprise that you could be hurt as much as this and still go on living. She'd—known as soon as they came from the stables on to the tennis court. There was something in their faces that she couldn't mistake. A sort of panic had seized her. If only one could die . . . if only all one's life didn't lie before one, cold and grey—hour after hour of it, day after day, week after week. She couldn't go on living. She couldn't, she couldn't. . . . Penelope and Daphne had taken for granted that she would come home from the Rectory with them, and she could find no reason for refusing even when Adam had offered to escort them, but the walk from the Rectory to the White Swan—Daphne and Adam wrapped in that strange absorbed silence—had been torment. And now she was trapped in this hideous little room with great-gran and Uncle Stephen and the strange woman with white hair. She wanted to escape somewhere where she could be alone. Somewhere in the dark. It was as if her whole soul and body were raw and flayed and couldn't bear the light. If only one could creep into some dark hole and die. . . .

The woman was speaking.

"It's a quaint little room, isn't it? Would you like to come and see our bedroom? There's a lovely old four-poster bed in it and a patchwork quilt."

Pippa didn't want to go to see the bedroom. She wanted only to escape. But perhaps Daphne and Adam would be still standing in the market-square just outside, saying good-bye to each other. At the thought of meeting them again every nerve in her body seemed to shrink. She never wanted to see them again—never as long as she lived. She would die rather than meet them again. She accompanied the woman down a passage to the bedroom that looked out over the Grammar School playing-grounds.

"Isn't it a lovely old four-poster?" said the woman, closing the door. Pippa looked at it, tight-lipped, her plain freckled face stony, her eyes blank with misery.

The woman sat down on the bed.

"Pippa," she said.

The compassionate understanding in the low voice broke down the child's defences.

She stood for a second, with a working face, struggling for self-control, then dropped sobbing upon the bed.

"I can't bear it," she sobbed. "There's nothing left . . . I thought . . . he seemed . . . I can't bear it. . . ." She stopped, then burst out with sudden vehemence, "It isn't only that. It's everything. . . . If only I could go to college. ... I've got things in me—I know I have. ... I could *do* things if I had a chance ... but I have to go into that beastly office with father. Oh, I wish I'd never been born. I wish I could *die*."

She broke again into a sudden storm of sobbing.

Beatrice sat on the bed by her, not speaking or touching her. She knew that the child's pride would resent the slightest manifestation of sympathy. She waited, silent and motionless, till Pippa stopped sobbing and sat up, pushing her disordered hair from her wet flushed face. "I'm sorry I've made a fool of myself," she said thickly.

"Listen, Pippa," said Beatrice gently. "It's going to be all right. I don't mean about Adam—I mean about the other thing. You'll be able to go to college. Try to get over—Adam. You're brave and you'll be able to. You've got all your life before you."

Pippa turned her tear-stained face to her.

"Thanks for being so decent," she said in a strangled voice. "I'd better go now before I start making a fool of myself again."

She picked up her hat from the bed.

"Need I see great-gran and Uncle Stephen? I look awful, don't I?"

"No. I'll get your racquet for you, and you can slip out by the side door. And, remember, it's going to be all right."

When Pippa had gone she went back to the red parlour, where the two men sat in silence.

Old Matthew twinkled at her.

"Well, you've fixed up Adam Harte's future very snugly. Why are you so much interested in him?"

"Because he's going to marry Daphne," she said, and added, "but it's Pippa I want to talk to you about. She must go to college."

He stared at her, then burst into his deep cackle of laughter.

"You've suddenly started putting the whole family to rights," he said. He turned to Stephen. "Is she always such a busybody as this?"

Stephen smiled at her.

"She's so quiet sometimes for weeks together that one mightn't know she was there at all, then suddenly she'll begin putting something to rights, and it's all finished almost before you know it's begun."

"And what is it now?" chuckled old Matthew.

"Pippa must go to college," she repeated. "Did you know she wanted to?"

Matthew considered. He remembered hearing rumours of Pippa's successes in her school examinations, but the Roystons had never interfered in each other's private affairs, and he knew that Arnold had arranged for her to go into his office. He had never thought of himself—or anyone, but Arnold and Milly—as having any responsibility in the matter.

"I can't say I did. Anyway, Arnold couldn't afford it. But she shall go to college, my dear, if you'd like her to. I promise you that."

"You mean you'll send her?"

"Yes."

She was silent, gazing thoughtfully in front of her.

Then she shook her head. "I don't think you ought to. I think your son ought to send her."

"My son?"

"Stephen's Uncle Richard. I think it's—just what he needs. I think it will make all the difference to him."

Both of them stared at her in amazement. Then old Matthew said, in an awe-struck voice:

"I believe you're right. But he wouldn't take it on. It isn't the money—he's not mean—it's the responsibility he'd shirk."

"But you could ask him," she persisted.

Old Matthew laughed again delightedly.

"She certainly gets busy, this woman of yours, once she starts," he said to Stephen, then suddenly: "Let's all go and ask him now."

"Now?"

"Yes. Now."

A strange sense of well-being had come over the old man. He felt young, energetic, equal to any emergency, any claim. Beatrice's suggestion thrilled and excited him out of all proportion to what it actually implied. Because she wasn't only Beatrice, she was Hope as well. He and Hope together, putting to rights the affairs of the children who should have been Hope's great-grandchildren. . . .

"But—it will be too much for you," said Beatrice anxiously. "You must be tired."

"Nonsense! I'm going now. Come along. Oh, wait a minute. I'll write that letter to Farley, and Stephen can take it to the post while you and I go to Richard's."

Chapter Seventeen

RICHARD laid down the book he had been reading and took up the latest number of the *Connoisseur*, turning the pages over absently. He felt depressed and unsettled. . . . The thought of going out in the evening always depressed and unsettled him. He could not forget it even for a moment however hard he tried. It hung over his spirit like a black cloud through every second of the morning and afternoon.

Ordinarily the evening was to Richard the consummation of the day. He would awake in the morning and see it stretching out through its placid hours of reading, writing, gentle constitutional, to the mellow glow of the evening—the excellent dinner perfectly cooked by Mrs. Perrot, the lingering savour of the old port, and then those three hours of lighter reading (he was just now engaged in re-reading Spenser's *Faerie Queene*), with which his day always ended—those three hours in which the blissful somnolence, induced by the excellent dinner, merged gracefully into the equally blissful somnolence that marked the approach of night. He pictured the scene at his father's house to-night—the large family party seated round the mahogany table, the noise of conversation, the clatter of knives and forks—and his soul seemed to curl up like a sensitive plant roughly touched. Richard hated eating in public. In his eyes, talking during a meal was the desecration of a solemn rite. He never even read while he was eating. . . . He tried to console himself by the reflection that this time to-morrow the whole thing would be over, and he would be looking forward happily, contentedly, to a quiet evening at home. But, though reassuring in its way, the reflection did not serve to lift the heavy weight of depression from his spirit, because, though the party would certainly be over by this time to-morrow, the fact remained that it was not over yet.

He laid aside the *Connoisseur*, took up Malon de Chaide's *Conversion of the Magdalen* (he was now studying the Spanish Philosophers of the sixteenth century) and sat down at his desk, determinedly trying to enjoy the present moment and forget what lay ahead. But he couldn't. ... It was like sitting in a pleasant meadow, trying not to see a bleak mountain that rose threateningly just in front of him. And he still hadn't made up his mind whether to order a taxi or not. Uncertainty about that had been torturing him all day. If it were fine, he would not need one. But if it were wet, he must have one. There were few things Richard disliked more than getting wet. Of course, he might wait till the actual time for setting out arrived, and then order a taxi, if it were raining, but that left it rather late, because in that case everyone in Danesborough who happened to be going out to-night would be ringing up for taxis, and quite often, on similar occasions, he had found all the taxis engaged. He sighed despondently. The situation seemed beset on all sides by insuperable difficulties. He was terribly depressed. It wasn't only going out to-night. It was that, for some reason he couldn't understand, he felt old and lonely and a failure. He had never felt quite like this before, and he wondered why he felt so to-day. Suddenly he realised. ... It was seeing Stephen and his wife at his father's this morning. Milly and Arnold, Harold and Helen, and even Paul and Lilian, always made him glad that he had not married. But Stephen and Beatrice had given him the feeling of having missed something vital, something that would have made life a beautiful and gracious thing. Beatrice didn't in the least resemble Hester, and yet she had somehow brought back the memory of Hester vividly to his mind—Hester, with her brown eyes and silky chestnut hair. A dull ache nagged at his heart. ... Why hadn't he asked her to marry him? He had known from the beginning that she would say "yes." Her love would have glorified his life, but he had shirked the responsibilities that it would have brought into it. He still felt that he had been justified, yet that dull weight of melancholy, that heartsick ache of regret, remained with him.

Beatrice. ... Odd that she reminded him of Hester. He tried to shake off the memory, but even if he succeeded there awaited him the depressing thought of his father's party, the torturing indecision about ordering the taxi. ...

Suddenly Mrs. Perrot opened the door.

"It's Mr. Royston and a lady to see you, sir," she said.

She looked almost as agitated by the unexpected visitors as Richard. Her eyes rested on him, full of solicitude. Poor Mr. Richard. ... Really, it seemed like everything coming at once. She never remembered his father's visiting him before. And on the top of going out this evening! It was so upsetting for the poor gentleman, when all he wanted was peace and quiet and to be let alone.

Old Matthew and Beatrice entered. Matthew closed the door behind him. Richard, flushed with perturbation, shook hands and drew up a chair for Beatrice. She smiled at him—her slow gentle smile—as she sat down.

"Won't you sit here, father?" went on Richard, turning his own deep leather arm-chair towards the old man. Then he drew back a curtain, closed a window, moved some papers from a chair, beat up a cushion, seemed about to sit down, changed his mind, straightened the ornaments on the mantelpiece, picked up an invisible thread from the carpet. ...

Matthew watched him with a twinkle, thinking how like he was to a startled, fluttering hen.

"You didn't expect us, Richard," he said. "I'm afraid we've put you out."

"Not at all, not at all," said Richard nervously as he sat down. "I'm very glad to see you."

"I've been taking Beatrice round to introduce her to the family before to-night ... but we've not come to you for that. You met her this morning, didn't you?"

"Yes," said Richard.

He made a courtly half-bow in her direction as he spoke. His kind, anxious, short-sighted eyes went from one to the other.

"It was Beatrice who wanted to come to you," went on the old man.

That sense of physical well-being still upheld him. And a strange mental clarity had come to him. He wasn't confusing the past with the present any longer. He was an old man, and this was not Hope but Beatrice—not a young girl but a poised woman of the world despite her air of virginity. Her eyes were serene and gentle, but they were sharp enough to see in less than five minutes that Daphne and young Harte were in love with each other, and to decide that they must be enabled to marry, to see as quickly that Pippa's only hope of happiness lay in going to college.

Richard was looking at him, perplexed, questioning, waiting for him to explain his visit.

"You see," said old Matthew, looking at Beatrice with a twinkle, "Beatrice has decided that Pippa must go to college."

Beatrice leant forward and laid a hand on his arm, but without taking her eyes from Richard's face.

"She's unhappy," she said. "It's what she really wants, more than anything else in the world—to go to college. And she'd make good there. I know she would. Just now she's—desperately unhappy. It's dreadful for anyone as young as Pippa to be as unhappy as that."

She stopped, and the old man, looking at her, wondered how much more desperately unhappy she had been with her brute of a husband when she was very little older than Pippa.

"It's just now that her whole life can be made or spoilt," she went on. "It may be too late even in a year's time."

"And so," said the old man, enjoying his son's perplexity, "Beatrice has decided that she must go to college."

Richard looked from one to the other, his bewilderment increasing. "Yes?" he said.

"Your father said he would send her," said Beatrice, "but I thought that you'd like to do it."

For a moment Richard looked stunned, then he stammered, "I?"

"Yes," said Beatrice gently, reassuringly, as one would have spoken to a frightened child. "You see—you haven't any children of your own. That's why we thought you'd like to help Pippa."

He was silent, staring at them helplessly. Children ... he had never wanted children in the abstract, but he remembered how, in the days when he had thought he was going to marry Hester, he had imagined the daughter they would have. He had never imagined a son—only a daughter. She had been as unlike Pippa as a girl could be—an idealised child-Hester, lovely, shy, responsive, understanding him as even Hester had never understood him, so that when he knew that he had finally lost Hester for ever by his dilatoriness and indecision, the child-Hester, whom he had moulded to his heart's desire, had at first seemed to stay with him to console him. She had flitted about this very room. She had sat at his feet on his hearthrug, resting her head against his knee. She had bent over the back of his leather arm-chair, her cheek against his head. Then she had gradually faded like the rest of his dreams. She seemed to return to him now, to look at him, her lips parted eagerly, her hands clasped, pleading. . . .

Then abruptly he awoke to reality. It was for Pippa he was being asked to do this, not for his child-Hester; Pippa, plain, freckled, unlovely, ungracious; Pippa, Arnold's and Milly's daughter, not his and Hester's. . . . He thought of the responsibility that the suggestion entailed, the worry, the anxiety, the fresh claims upon his time and interest, and it was as if an icy blast swept through the cosy little room, dimming its light, turning its warmth to arctic cold, blowing his books and papers into confusion.

"I?" he said again.

His bewilderment had turned to panic. He trembled, and his eyes looked desperately towards the door, as if he were contemplating actual flight.

Beatrice took her hand from the old man's arm and laid it on his.

"She's clever," she said again, speaking still in that low gentle voice. "She deserves a chance. . . . Won't you be the one to give it to her? She might carry on your work, if you'd give her her chance."

Again there was silence. "Carry on his work." There was no work to carry on. He was a failure. He had known it for years in his heart. Of all the things he had meant to do when he was Pippa's age, he had done nothing. His life had been utterly useless. He had thrown away his chances of love, as he had thrown away his chances of fame. Nothing was left to him but the dream child-Hester and—Pippa? He thought of her sharp, clever little face, remembered vague stories he had heard (he had taken no interest in them at the time) of her quickness at lessons, her success in examinations. Suppose she were to—justify him. There was about her none of that indolence that had lain like a canker at the heart of all his ambition, all his ability. Suppose that, given her chance, Pippa were to make good, to carry on the torch that had slipped from his inert fingers. He would, in a way, have redeemed the long mistake that his life had been. He didn't want gratitude, but—this warm, lighted, book-lined room that did its best to shut out loneliness, didn't always succeed. He saw Pippa there, her plain, clever little face aglow, telling him of the work she had done last term, of the work she was going to do next. . . . And suddenly the child-Hester seemed even more of a ghost than she had been before—a sentimental meaningless little ghost.

He was always ill-at-ease and embarrassed in the company of his great-nieces and great-nephews. He knew that they made fun of his ordered routine and his indecisions. Pippa wouldn't feel like that about him if it were he who had "given her her chance." There would be a sort of—friendship between them. He thought of it shyly, humbly, and something of warmth crept into his heart.

Then he pulled himself up sharply. What on earth was he thinking of? Had he avoided responsibility all his life to be caught by it at last? He had won peace—at a price. Was he going to hazard it now, just because this woman of Stephen's talked to him with her hand on his arm, just because the ghost of his child-Hester turned treacherously into Pippa before his eyes?

"No," he said with sudden decision. "I couldn't possibly."

"You're well enough off, Richard," said the old man, dryly.

"It's not that. It's nothing to do with money. It's——" he sought for words to explain. "I'm too old to take on responsibilities of that sort."

"You know at the bottom of your heart," said Beatrice, "that if you don't do this you'll regret it all the rest of your life."

He was silent. She was right, of course. It could never be now as if he had not been asked to do it. All the rest of his life he would be worrying over it, wondering if he ought to have done it, wishing he had done it ... worrying ... worrying. ... And then suddenly the ghost of the child-Hester and Pippa seemed to vanish, and he saw the ghost of himself in the days of his ambition, his belief in himself, young, eager, athirst for knowledge—like Pippa. The boy seemed to be pleading for another chance. Or was it only Pippa, after all? Pippa, pleading for herself ... the boy pleading for himself in Pippa ... Pippa, his own youth miraculously reborn. ...

Suddenly all his indecision seemed to fall from him. Even his usual nervousness vanished. He spoke in a slow resolute voice:

"Very well. I'll do it."

"You'll pay the fees," said Beatrice, "and take an interest in her work and help her in any way you can?"

"Yes."

"And—to be really happy and really to do her best, you know, she ought to have enough pocket-money and nice clothes. Will you give her an allowance as well?"

"I'll give her whatever you say."

"You needn't have any of the worry of the details. Your lawyer will see to all that, won't he? Why not write to him and then it will be off your mind?"

Stephen entered the room suddenly.

"Oh ... here you all are."

"It's all right, Stephen," said Beatrice. "Uncle Richard's going to send Pippa to college."

A warm thrill shot through Richard's heart at the "Uncle Richard." He felt that she wouldn't have called him that if he hadn't promised to send Pippa to college. And Pippa, too. ... At the thought of that possible friendship with Pippa—that sharing of Pippa's vivid enquiring youth—the warmth glowed, expanded.

"Good for you, Uncle Richard," said Stephen. "You won't regret it. I always liked young Pippa."

"He's going to write to his lawyer now."

"But what about the parents?" said Stephen. "Hadn't Milly and Arnold better be consulted?"

The three looked at each other and laughed. A pleasant feeling of conspiracy and fellowship had seized them.

"We'd quite forgotten them," said old Matthew. "Ring up Arnold, Stephen. Richard always stammers on the telephone. Be as tactful as you can. I don't suppose that's saying much."

Stephen grinned and took up the telephone. "I want Mr. Chudleigh. . . . Oh, is that you, Arnold? It's Stephen speaking. I'm at my uncle Richard's. I'm speaking for him. He's asked me to ring you up. . . . Yes . . . Uncle Richard. . . . He's interested in Pippa. . . . Yes, Pippa. . . . I mean, he's heard how well she's done in all her exams. . . . He'd very much like to be responsible for sending her to college . . . if you and Milly consent, of course. . . . Well, having no children of his own he's naturally interested in his nieces and nephews, and Pippa's certainly got the brains of the whole bunch. . . . Oh, yes, he'd undertake everything. . . . He quite realises that you can't be expected to go on providing for her in any way once the girl's old enough to earn her own living. . . . Oh yes, he quite realises that. . . . He'd provide for her entirely. . . . Yes, he realises that it will be a great sacrifice on your part. . . . Of course, the girl's earnings would have made a great difference to the home. . . . Oh yes, he quite realises that, Arnold. . . . No, no one's mentioned it to her, of course. . . . The whole thing depends on your giving your consent. . . . Yes, I'll tell him. . . . I'm sure you won't regret it. . . . Good-bye."

He hung up the receiver.

"With a suitable show of reluctance and in the manner of one nobly conferring a favour, brother-in-law Arnold gives his consent," he announced.

Richard was at the writing-table, writing his letter to the lawyer. Already he felt the stirrings of his indecision, and he wanted to get the matter finally settled before it had him in its grip. He knew that he would torment himself incessantly in the future as to the wisdom of the step, but, having definitely taken it, he knew that he would never go back on it.

Beatrice turned to old Matthew.

"Oughtn't you to be going home now?" she said, "I'm sure you ought to rest before dinner. Let Stephen get you a taxi."

Matthew shook his head. He remembered the object of the expedition, and that it was not yet fulfilled. He must take Beatrice to see Lilian. He had meant to take her to see Milly, too, but he knew that that was now unnecessary. Milly would be immensely pleased and flattered that Richard had singled out Pippa for this favour. She had always looked on Richard with respect, taking his work seriously, refusing to make fun of him as the others did. It was Stephen who had rung up Arnold about it, and therefore she would assume that Stephen was somehow involved in it. She would not be likely to risk alienating him or Richard by any discourtesy to Beatrice.

But Lilian? He remembered having caught a look on her face more than once when someone inadvertently mentioned Paul's first wife in her hearing—a look of almost venomous hatred. He could not expose Beatrice to a look like that. He decided suddenly to go there himself first to see how the land lay, to make it quite clear to Lilian that Beatrice was to be treated with respect, and then to take Beatrice to her. He knew Lilian least of his granddaughters-in-law. She could be difficult—he was sure of that—and he didn't mean her to be difficult with Beatrice.

He rose slowly.

"I'm just going along to Paul's," he announced. "It's only a few yards. . . . I'll be back within half an hour."

Chapter Eighteen

"Where are you going, Paul?"

Paul, half-way downstairs, turned at the sound of his wife's voice. She had come out of her room and stood on the landing, looking down at him.

"I'm going to the station."

"What for?"

"To meet the six forty-two."

"Just come up here a minute. . . . I must speak to you."

Her voice sounded strained and unnatural.

He went slowly upstairs and followed her into her bedroom. There she closed the door and stood leaning against it. Her red lips were tightly set. Her great eyes smouldered angrily. She was going to take it hard. . . . Well, on almost any other subject he would have yielded for the sake of peace, but he couldn't yield over this.

"You're going to that woman?"

"I told you that I was going to meet Anthea's train."

"If you do I'll never forgive you. . . . Never, as long as I live."

Her voice broke on a high note. He was tired, and his frayed nerves shrank from the prospect of a scene.

"Don't be a fool, Lilian," he said shortly.

The smouldering fires in her eyes blazed out. Her breast was rising and falling unevenly.

"I know I'm a fool. I've been a fool long enough. I was a fool ever to believe you loved me."

Beneath her anger was something desperately hurt and frightened.

He felt a quick pang of pity for her and, making an effort to conquer his irritation, spoke in a tone of schooled gentleness.

"You know perfectly well that I love you. But that doesn't mean that I have no obligation to anyone else, Anthea has a certain claim on me——"

"What claim?" she countered passionately.

"Perhaps I don't mean claim, exactly, but she was my wife."

"She left you of her own accord."

"I know."

"You think she wasn't to blame for that?"

"God knows who was to blame for that."

She gave a short breathless laugh.

"So you want her back already? Perhaps you'd like to have the two of us? Or have you quite finished with me? Shall I withdraw and wait till you're tired of her and it's my turn again?"

He made a little gesture, half of weariness, half of exasperation. She always seemed to force a scene on him when he was too tired to cope with it.

"I've told Anthea that I'll be there to meet her train, and I'm going to be there. . . . Let me pass, please."

She still stood in front of the door, holding it closed. Every line of her body seemed to quiver with anger.

"You're going to bring her here?"

"I won't do that if you don't want me to, but I must hear what she has to say to me. We could go anywhere to talk."

She laughed again—that short, breathless, angry laugh.

"And let the whole of Danesborough see you walking about the streets with her! Why shouldn't you? Your brother's trailing about all over the town with his woman."

His face darkened.

"Leave that out of it, please," he said curtly.

"Oh yes, you don't care how you drag my name in the mud, but I mustn't insult your brother. Or his woman. Your wife's different. What a fool I was ever to believe you loved me!"

He saw that she was deliberately trying to work herself up into such a state of hysteria that he would not dare to leave her. She had done that once or twice before. . . . He decided to go away at once before she succeeded.

"Let me pass, please," he said again.

"You're going to meet her train?"

"Yes."

She seemed to make an effort to control herself.

"Listen, Paul. She knows where you live, and she can come here. That's enough—don't you think?—for me to let her come here. And if she's anything to say she can say it to you here. But you're not going to walk through Danesborough alone with her."

"Will you come with me then?"

Her eyes blazed at him.

"How *dare* you ask me that?"

He shrugged.

"I'm sorry. I didn't mean to insult you. . . . It's no use talking about it, Lilian. We don't seem able to understand each other——"

She interrupted.

"For the last time, are you going to her?"

"I'm going to meet her train."

"You know that if you do you've chosen finally between us?"

"I know no such thing. . . . Please let me pass."

She abandoned her attempt at self-control and began once more deliberately to give rein to her hysteria. Her voice rose shrilly.

"I wish to God I'd never met you. . . . You've always loved her. You've been meeting her regularly since you married me, haven't you? Haven't you?"

She stopped abruptly. There was the sound of voices downstairs in the hall.

They listened.

"It's my grandfather," said Paul.

They heard the old man's voice.

"Upstairs? . . . No, don't bother. I'll go up to him."

The sound of his footsteps—rather slow and dragging—ascending the stairs. The sound of his knock on the door.

"May I come in, Paul?"

Lilian went from the door and stood at the window with her back to the room. Paul opened the door.

Old Matthew entered. . . . As he entered Lilian wheeled round, showing her flushed, angry face. Paul's face was white and strained.

"What's the matter?" said the old man abruptly, looking from one to the other.

Paul made an attempt to carry off the situation lightly.

"Oh, nothing," he said, with an unconvincing air of nonchalance. "I'm only going——"

Lilian swept across the room to them, her lips set, her eyes blazing.

"I'll tell you what's the matter," she said. "He's tired of me already. He's going to another woman."

Old Matthew looked at her coldly. He hated to see a woman lose her poise. Then he turned to his grandson.

"Well?" he said.

Paul fidgeted uneasily. "It's only that—I heard from Anthea this morning. She said she wanted to speak to me. She's coming by the six forty-two, and I said I'd meet it."

"Naturally—but I don't see what the trouble's about."

His cool acceptance of the situation, his obvious siding with Paul, seemed to destroy the last remnant of Lilian's self-control.

"Of course you don't," she burst out angrily. "You're all of a piece, you Roystons. I've heard some nice tales of you, and here's Paul going off to meet another woman before we've been married two months, and his brother parading his trollop about the town in broad daylight."

For the first time in years the old man lost his temper. He leant forward and dealt her two sharp blows, one on each side of her head, as an exasperated nurse of the old school will box a child's ears. Taken by surprise, she lost her balance, staggered backwards and, falling upon the bed, lay there sobbing with anger.

"You *beast!*" she said, between her sobs. "So that's how you treated your wife. . . ."

"My wife had more sense than to ask for it," he said shortly.

She sprang suddenly to her feet.

"I've finished with you all," she panted, "I've finished with everything. I——"

Before they knew what she was going to do, she was at the window, throwing it open, as if to fling herself out. There was a sheer drop down to a paved path below. Paul started forward, but the old man held his arm in a vice-like grip. He had seen the speculative glance she had thrown at Paul.

"Leave her alone," he said contemptuously. "She'll not do it."

The woman hesitated, then turned from the window, and, sitting down limply on the arm-chair, covered her face with her hands.

In the silence that followed, there came another knock at the door. Paul went to it and took a telegram from a gaping maid-servant. He returned to the room, tearing it open with unsteady fingers:

"It was good of you to say you'd meet me, Paul, but I've changed my mind and I'm not coming after all. I'm going over to Paris by to-night's boat. I don't think I shall come back to England for a long time. I shall often think of you."

His first thought was that it was like Anthea to send a telegram of fifty words where a dozen would have done. He read it through again in silence. A faint smile, half bitter, half tender, played at the corners of his lips. The words seemed to bring her very near—elusive, incalculable, heart-rendingly sweet. He realised suddenly how much he had wanted to see her, how bitterly disappointed he was that she was not coming. It couldn't have been a child, then. Or, if it were, he would never know now. The paper dropped from his fingers on to the floor. Then he looked across the room at his wife. She was watching him, her hands gripping the arms of her chair. The flush had faded from her face, leaving it colourless.

"She's not coming," he said in a dull, lifeless voice, "so we needn't have disturbed ourselves over it."

Lilian said nothing. The old man went across to Paul and held out his hand.

"I must be going now, Paul. I'll see you tonight."

He had meant to prepare the way for Beatrice's visit, he

remembered, but, of course, he couldn't bring Beatrice here now.
. . .

"Good-bye," said Paul, still staring blankly before him.

The old man went to Lilian and held out his hand.

"Good-bye," he said courteously. "I shall see you to-night, of course."

She ignored his hand, speaking to him in a low unsteady voice, her head turned away.

"Good-bye. . . . I shan't be coming to-night. Paul can come alone."

He kept his hand outstretched.

"I'm an old man, my dear. I may never have another birthday. Don't spoil it for me."

"It wouldn't spoil it, my not coming."

"Yes, it would."

She turned her head and looked at him. His blue eyes twinkled at her through their bristling brows—kindly, challenging, teasing, reassuring.

Suddenly she held out her hand.

"You'll come?" he said.

"Yes . . . I'll come."

He clasped her hand in both his for a moment, then went to the door.

"Don't come down with me, Paul," he said.

As the door closed, Lilian laid her head on her arms with a gesture of passionate despair. Paul went across to her and knelt by her chair.

"Darling . . . don't . . . he didn't mean to be a brute. He's an old man. He didn't know what he was doing."

She burst into tears.

"Oh, it's not that," she sobbed. "I don't mind that. It's that—I'm so ashamed, Paul. I've been such a beast. I can't help it, somehow. I love you so much that when I think you love someone else I seem to turn into a devil."

"I don't love anyone else. Not as I love you."

"I know. . . . Oh, Paul, I wish I hadn't been such a beast. When

I think of the things I said to you. . . . I didn't mean any of them. You knew that, didn't you?"

She raised her ravaged face to him.

"I think I did."

"It's only—when I think you don't love me, I—I go mad. I can't bear it. I turn into something hateful. I don't care what I say or do to hurt you. I wish I'd been nice about it. I'd give anything in the world, now that it's too late, to have been nice about it. . . . If ever anything like that happens again, I'll try. I swear I'll try. . . . Paul . . . tell me . . ."

"Yes."

"Did you—mind awfully when you knew she wasn't coming?"

He hesitated. He loved her too much not to be honest with her.

"Lilian," he said slowly, "when two people have lived together and been happy together—whatever happens afterwards—it means something. You can't—forget. . . . Lilian," he went on with sudden desperate urgency, "you *must* understand. I realised this afternoon—there's no possible happiness for us unless you understand . . . I love you as I never loved her, as I never could have loved her, but—she'll always mean something to me. Can't you—understand?"

She spoke in a voice, still choked with tears.

"I'll try. . . . I expect I shall be a beast again, but I will try. I—" Clasped in his arms, she whispered, "Yes . . . when you hold me like this—quite close to you—I do understand."

Chapter Nineteen

CATHERINE came out of the drawing-room as the old man entered the hall.

"Where *have* you been, father?" she said severely. "We've been terribly anxious about you."

"I'm most grateful to you for your solicitude, Catherine," he said politely.

Her eyes slid away from his ironical smile.

"What about your tea?" she went on.

"What about it?"

"Have you had any?"

"I have."

"Where?"

"At the White Swan."

"At the——" Horror deprived her of speech for a moment. "Have you no sense of dignity, father?"

"I have not, thank God," he answered. "Stand on one side, my girl. I want to go upstairs."

She stood on one side and watched him as he ascended the stairs, her lips set firmly. It was so exasperating that the two men whom she regarded as her natural prey (though she would not have used that expression)—her husband and her father—had both succeeded in eluding her, James by the mysterious malady that had so completely changed his beautiful nature, her father by the mixture of mockery, ironical politeness, and little-boy impudence that held her so successfully at bay. One could never tell how he was going to take anything, and it put one at a disadvantage with him. Still, he was beginning to break up. It was only a question of time. She made a final effort to assert her authority.

"Be sure you're ready by eight, father," she said in her brisk, curt tone.

He turned at the bend in the stairs and, looking down at her from behind his long white eyebrows, answered quietly, "I'll be ready when I damn well choose, Catherine."

She returned to the drawing-room, closing the door with unnecessary force.

The old man went on up the stairs, chuckling silently to himself. It always gave him a malicious delight to put his eldest daughter in her place. But behind the malicious delight lurked the ever-present fear. It was a losing battle. Sooner or later she would get her claws into him. . . . Oh, well, he'd fight as long as he had any fight in him, and that would be for some time yet.

When he reached the landing, Charlotte came out of her bedroom, smiling at him affectionately.

"There you are, darling," she said. "We were afraid you'd got lost."

"And where should I get lost?" said Matthew dryly.

"I don't know," she said vaguely, "but people do, you know. One reads of it in the papers."

He passed on, and she smiled after him mistily. Dear old father. . . . So splendid and energetic. Going out for long walks by himself like this. She looked forward to the evening and saw him surrounded by his children and grandchildren and great-grandchildren. It was all so beautiful that it made one want to cry.

Matthew went into his sitting-room and closed the door behind him. Through the communicating door he could see Gaston laying out his dress clothes on the bed. He chuckled to himself again. Gaston had been quick. He had seen him still dogging his footsteps as he came home, keeping in the shadow so as not to be seen. The man was like a fussy mother hen, but somehow his attentions didn't annoy Matthew as his daughters' always did. They amused him rather, especially his clumsy attempts to disguise them, his pretence of being a mere automaton in his service. He must have raced the old man by the back stairs, for he certainly had not entered the house before him.

"Had a nice walk, Gaston?" said Matthew as he closed the door.

"Yes," replied Gaston shortly. "Did you?"

"I did."

"You ought to rest before to-night."

"Rest your grandmother!"

"I have no grandmother," replied Gaston with dignity.

He came into the sitting-room, carrying the little yellow cat.

"I think he must have slept all afternoon," he said. "He is better. You can see that he is better."

Matthew drew out the carton of cream from his pocket.

"Get a saucer," he said.

Together they filled the saucer with cream, put it on the hearthrug, then stood watching the little cat with satisfaction as it lapped and purred.

"That is good," commented Gaston at last.

"Yes," said Matthew. "He must stay here till he's well. Those are my orders, and you can tell Mrs. Moreland so if she makes any objection."

"Yes," said Gaston, and returned to the bedroom.

The old man went over to his bookcase and took out a Bible that was carefully hidden from sight behind a row of French novels. Catherine would have been amazed to learn that he possessed a Bible. She had frequently tried to present him with one—putting it surreptitiously on the table by his bedside—but he had always sent it back to her as soon as he discovered it. He turned to Job and read one of his favourite passages: "But where shall wisdom be found? And where is the place of understanding? Man knoweth not the price thereof; Neither is it found in the land of the living. The depth saith, It is not in me: The sea saith, It is not with me. It cannot be gotten for gold. Neither shall silver be weighed for the price thereof. ..."

He read to the end of the passage. Then, without turning to it, he began to repeat another of his favourite passages: "Where wast thou when I laid the foundations of the earth? Declare, if thou hast understanding. Who hath laid the measures thereof, if thou knowest? Or who hath stretched the line upon it? Whereupon are the foundations thereof fastened? Or who laid the corner stone thereof; When the morning stars sang together, And all the sons of God shouted for joy? ..."

That passage always had a strangely exhilarating effect on him. He would sometimes say it over to himself when he could not sleep.

He replaced the Bible and, taking out the volume of poetry he had been reading that morning, sat down on the chair near the window. In the garden the horizontal rays of the sun cast long shadows over the lawn. The trees stood motionless, sharply outlined against the deep blue sky. There was over everything that strange stillness that ushers in the close of the day.

The feeling of bodily well-being and mental clarity still pervaded him. In spite of his exertions he felt fresh and unwearied. And the past and present were no longer confused in his mind. It was years, he thought, since he had felt so well. He opened the book at random and read:

> She passed as shadows pass amid the sheep,
> While the earth dreamed and only I was 'ware
> Of that faint fragrance blown from her soft hair.

He raised his head and stared dreamily in front of him. It might have been written of either of them. Hope ... Beatrice. ... He felt a slight thrill of pride in the knowledge that he was still keeping them apart. Beatrice, Stephen's love; Hope, his own. ...

He began to think about his dinner party, picturing his family all together round the old mahogany dining-table, and then suddenly the edges of past and present became merged again, because Hope was there. He knew that she would not be there, but somehow he couldn't keep her out of the picture in his mind. She was there in her white crinoline with roses round her small graceful head. The strange sweet excitement that had been with him all day sharpened

to ecstasy, and his heart began to beat with loud uneven strokes.
. . .

Gaston opened the door of the bedroom. "It's all ready," he said. "I've brought your water in."

Matthew rose slowly and went to dress.

They sat round the table in the dining-room, Matthew at one end and Catherine, majestic in wine-coloured satin, at the other. On Matthew's right hand sat Beatrice, wearing a flame-coloured dress that emphasised her white hair and the transparent pallor of her cheeks. When she had entered the drawing-room, tall, pale, exquisite, a sudden hush had fallen over the room. Her dress made the dress of every other woman in the room look provincial and badly cut. She had gone straight up to Matthew, smiling at him affectionately and without constraint.

"Will I do?" she had asked. "I've put on my prettiest frock for you."

"You're lovely, my dear," the old man had said.

Catherine's face had hardened. Shameless, she said to herself, absolutely shameless. . . . Stephen stood behind, smiling proudly at Beatrice's slender loveliness, oblivious of everyone else in the room. If only they would show a sense of proper shame, thought Catherine, one might feel differently to them. It's—indecent. How *could* father let them come? Sitting down at the same table as young girls like Pippa and Daphne. . . . Heaven only knew what harm they would do.

Beyond Beatrice was Richard. Matthew had insisted on that. She was to be fenced round by her allies. Richard was silently enjoying his dinner. He looked a little less harassed than usual. The evening had turned out quite fine, and he had not needed a taxi. He had felt rather nervous about meeting Pippa, but that, too, had been all right. As soon as he saw her he noticed that something of her old mutinous air had left her and that there was about her instead a suggestion of quiet purposeful happiness. She came up to him at once, fixed her direct unsmiling gaze on him, and said, "Thank you, Uncle Richard. I promise I'll try most awfully hard."

No effusiveness, no extravagant gratitude, but again a warmth seemed to steal into the cold places of his heart, and to his surprise and dismay a lump came suddenly into his throat. He took her hand in his and pressed it without speaking. Then shyness overcame them both, and they turned hastily away from each other. The little scene had only taken a few seconds, but the bond between them was signed, sealed, and delivered, and both were aware of it.

Helen sat just beyond Richard. She, too, was rather silent. Oh well, it was over. He had left her, saying that he would come again, but both of them had known that he would not. It was over—finally, definitely over. Further down the table she could hear Harold talking to Enid in his high-pitched, slightly affected voice.

"Of course, I didn't want to stand for it. I'm on quite enough committees in this town already. But they simply wouldn't take a refusal. . . ."

Her brow contracted, and she drew in her breath sharply. Would she ever be able to accustom herself to it, to accept it philosophically and almost with amusement, as some wives did? "Oh, men are all the same. They're just like children." She had often heard women say that, excusing any fault in their husbands from conceit to actual unfaithfulness. Why did she care so desperately? If only she could forget Philip! (She set her lips in a tight line. She *would* forget Philip.) And—if only she could stop snubbing Harold so cruelly! Even now, as she listened, her exasperation was longing to administer the pinprick that would deflate his self-conceit. She must try to conquer her exasperation. Thousands of women had husbands who got on their nerves. After all, Harold was a good husband in many ways. "Men are just like children." She must try to feel like that, to forget that she hadn't wanted a man who was just like a child. She glanced at her mother-in-law's face, cold, beautiful, remote, the lips tight and compressed, the eyes hard and tired, and shivered slightly. Would she grow like that—bitter and joyless and self-contained? Then across the table she met Pen's eyes, shy, adoring, ingenuous. They exchanged a quick smile before they looked away. Something of the weight fell from Helen's spirit. No, she wouldn't grow like Margaret. She would have Pen. . . . She turned to Paul, who was making spasmodic comments on the weather.

"Yes, it's wonderful," she said absently. "So fresh for August."

"It was the wet Spring," he said. "A dry Spring always seems to spoil the whole year."

God, he was tired, tired, tired. It rang in his mind like a refrain. Tired, tired, tired. He had missed two nights' rest, and at the best of times scenes with Lilian left him feeling like a rag. To sleep without being disturbed for a whole night . . . it was like the thought of Paradise. His mind went over his cases. No complications likely to occur in any of them. No babies imminent. But one never knew. Anything might happen. That was the worst of a doctor's life, never being able to count on a good night's rest. . . . He looked across the table at Lilian . . . his eyes dwelling on her smooth olive skin, her full red lips, the soft white curves of her breasts beneath the filmy stuff of her evening dress. Her eyes met his. . . . She did not smile, but her eyes deepened, glowed with a smouldering light of passion, before she looked away. There would be peace after to-day's storm. His weariness would find rest in her love. . . .

He turned to answer a question that Enid had asked him about Cressida Harte.

"No, she hasn't sprained her ankle. At least, she hadn't this morning. She'd got stomach-ache with eating too many green apples. . . . Yes, of course, she'd say anything. She always does. She spun me a yarn this morning about someone's having stolen her essay from her desk last term and having won the prize instead of her. She's got such a way with her that I'd have believed it if it hadn't been the plot of every school story I've ever read."

Enid laughed.

"She's a little devil, isn't she?"

In her mind she was going over the letter she had written to Max Collin. She had turned him down quite definitely. Also she had written to an old school friend who lived at Eastbourne, inviting herself for the week for which Max and Brenda had taken the cottage. There wasn't much fear of her yielding now, but she was going to preclude every possibility of it. . . . There could only have been one end to it—she realised that—but she had to shut out of her mind very firmly the memory of Max's smile and of the thrill that his slightest touch had power to give her. Somehow Mr. Morrow's proposal, ludicrous incident though it was, had helped. It had restored to her her self-respect. No longer need she bear the stigma of the undesired. She wasn't going to Max Collin, she wasn't marrying Mr. Morrow, but she had been desired by two men in one day. She could always remember that. She gazed unseeingly in front of her, thinking of the secret hunger for romance that had always lain hidden behind her matter-of-fact exterior. Well, she was never going to have romance—she could make up her mind to that—but there were still plenty of good things in her life. There would be games for some years yet, and then—oh, there would always be something.

Margaret, glancing down the table, noticed that her daughter was gazing dreamily in front of her, with something in her eyes that she had never seen before—something shy, sensitive, wondering. She felt as startled as if the girl had suddenly struck her in the face. Was Enid—like that really? Had she lived with her all these years without knowing her?

Beyond Harold sat Pippa. She wore the discoloured white alpaca dress with the spray of artificial blue flowers pinned awkwardly on to her shoulder, but for once she was not furiously ashamed of her appearance, bitterly jealous of Pen's and Daphne's daintiness. She shone with an eager radiant happiness. Her eyes looked half bemused by the glamorous vistas that were opening out before her. Knowledge had always been an adventure to Pippa. She was a born student, with a quick receptive mind and a vivid imagination. There was enough of the creative instinct in her to make each piece of knowledge, as it came to her, peculiarly her own. The treasure-house of the ages lay before her. The key was in her hand. She itched to begin work already. She would be going back to school, of course, now, after the holidays, to work for her entrance to college. She must try to get a scholarship. Uncle Richard would be terribly pleased if she got a scholarship—not because of the money, but because it would make him feel proud of her. It would be lovely to be one of the Post-Matric. girls at school. They had long stretches of "free hours" for study—long stretches when you could really get your teeth into something without being jostled from subject to subject, from room to room, every forty minutes by that hateful bell. She simply couldn't wait till next term. She must begin at once. She would start Anglo-Saxon. She had always longed to learn Anglo-Saxon. She would go round to Uncle Richard's to-morrow, and ask him to lend her some books. He was so kind, in spite of his funny ways. . . . She glanced at Daphne, who sat opposite her. How pretty she looked! She would probably marry Adam Harte. Pippa's own feeling for Adam already seemed to belong to another life. To marry Adam would have been to stay in a little sheltered harbour. Instead, she was setting her sails for the open sea of adventure. She would be an undergraduate at college, while Pen and Daphne were still pottering about Danesborough, having coffee in the town at eleven, playing in Aunt Enid's hockey team, going to little tea parties where you always met the same people and talked about the same things. . . . And to think that only this morning she had envied them! She thrilled with exultant confidence in her youth and talent. "I've got things in me," she had said. "I could do things if I had a chance." Her chance had come and she was going to "do things."

Next to her sat Isabel. Isabel, too, was looking at Daphne. Her mind was in a tumult of emotion. She didn't know what had happened to her. She had been standing in the drawing-room before dinner when Stephen and his wife arrived (everyone called her his wife, and it certainly sounded better). At the moment of their arrival Daphne, who had taken her own cloak and Isabel's to Charlotte's bedroom, was coming downstairs. Through the open drawing-room door Isabel had seen her daughter go straight to Stephen's wife. She did not know whether Stephen's wife opened her arms before or after Daphne had started forward to her, but she saw Daphne held for a close short embrace against the flame-coloured dress, the white head bent tenderly over her. At the sight a sharp pang of jealousy had shot through Isabel's heart—a pang that took her completely by surprise. She had not kissed Daphne like that since—since it happened, but the sight of someone else's doing it had sent the blood flaming into her cheeks and set her pulses racing. She couldn't understand the emotion that had seized her. It was jealousy, but it was more than jealousy. The pain at her heart was the pain of something frozen slowly awaking to life. Suddenly every turn of Daphne's head, every expression and feature of her, brought back the memory of Hugh and Biddy and John. Something had broken down the defences that she generally kept so strongly fortified against those memories, and they flooded her soul in wave after irresistible wave. ... Hugh, Biddy, John. ... She wanted Daphne, wanted her desperately—Daphne, who was all that was left to her. She felt as if the accident that had bereaved her of the three had happened yesterday, and the time between then and now had been only a dim uneasy dream in which she had wandered, deprived of the power of speech and volition. But now that was over. She could feel and move and speak. Beneath the anguish that flooded her soul was joy that Daphne was still hers. ... She tried to catch Daphne's eye across the table, but Daphne was gazing in front of her, her eyes starry, her young cheeks softly flushed. ...

At the foot of the table Catherine was keeping a keen watch on guests and servants alike. Gaston was waiting at Matthew's end. It was one of Catherine's many grievances that Matthew always insisted on having Gaston to wait on him at table. The man was enough to take anyone's appetite away. Of course, only the family was here tonight, and they were used to him, so it didn't matter much, but Catherine could never look at Gaston without a feeling of impotent fury. Like Matthew—and upheld by Matthew—he constantly eluded her, seeming almost to mock at her authority. He had disobeyed her flagrantly about that cat to-day. ...

Next to Catherine, and opposite Isabel, sat Leslie. Leslie was Catherine's favourite great-niece. She was polite and nicely behaved. "You're a very lucky little girl to be allowed to come to a party like this, aren't you?" said Catherine. "Yes, Aunt Catherine," said Leslie, demurely. Her sharp eyes were darting to and fro among the guests. ... Uncle Stephen and that woman weren't married, and she had heard mother and Aunt Catherine agreeing that it was shameful of great-gran to have invited them to his party. Aunt Catherine had said, too, that great-gran was "failing," and that really someone ought to have control over him for his own good. Uncle Harold caught her eye and smiled.

"Well, little Miss Leslie," he said. Uncle Harold was always very nice to her, as indeed he was always very nice to everyone, but somehow he seemed to be nice to you more for his own sake than for yours. He seemed all the time to be listening to himself being nice and thinking how nice he was. Leslie smiled at him very prettily, and amused herself by putting out her tongue at him in imagination.

Next to her sat Lilian, and then Daphne. Neither of them was talking. Lilian looked at the old man, remembering how he had come forward to greet her as soon as she entered the drawing-room, how he had bowed low over her hand in that foreign way he had. Nobody watching us, she had thought with a wry smile, would believe that he knocked me down only about an hour ago. Despite his courtliness, there had been no hint of apology in his manner. She tried hard to hate him, but somehow she couldn't. He was an old beast, but there was something rather fine about him. Her great eyes moved to her husband and seemed to grow deeper, darker. How tired he looked! Her heart yearned over him. She had been hateful to him to-day, but she would make up for it. She longed to be alone with him, away from this chattering crowd, to draw his tired head on to her breast. If only this torment of jealousy didn't sweep over her and turn her into a devil. . . . If only she could always feel sure of him. She did when she was sane. But right at the back of her mind was present continually the fear of losing his love, and that to her would be the end of life. Things would be better if she had a child. She wouldn't be frightened, even of Anthea, if she had a child. Please God, she prayed silently, let me have a child, let me have a child. . . . She looked at him again. His face was grey with fatigue, there were hollows beneath his eyes, and his mouth was set in lines of strain. In spirit she was holding him to her breast, kissing his tired eyes. . . .

Beyond Daphne sat Mark and Penelope comparing notes about

their respective schools. Pen and Mark had always got on well together. Mark was like Pippa, but without her sulkiness and ungraciousness.

Then came Arnold, trying to entertain Margaret, whom he admired, smiling his full toothy smile, putting on the arch coy manner that he always deemed suitable to "the ladies." Next to Margaret sat Stephen, and beyond him, on Matthew's left, Charlotte. Charlotte looked round the table with misty eyes. How beautiful it was to see the whole family gathered together like this, all so happy and united and good and affectionate and respected in the town, except, of course, Stephen and that woman, who ought never to have been allowed to come, because there was no doubt at all that the presence of immorality spoilt the atmosphere of family purity. A family ought always to stand for purity. The dear old Queen had insisted on that in her day. But one could forget the presence of Stephen and the woman and pretend they weren't here, or, better still, look forward to the time when her husband should die and they could be married, because, though death is always sad, every cloud has its silver lining. A pity that father was talking to the woman so much and practically ignoring everyone else. It must give quite a wrong impression to the young people. Charlotte broke into the *tête-à-tête* determinedly.

"So wonderful, an occasion like this, isn't it?" she said to Beatrice across the table. "Children and grandchildren and great-grandchildren all gathered together. I'm almost sure that I once read a beautiful poem about a family gathering like this, but I can't remember what it was."

> " 'It is terrible to see three generations
> Gathered together under one roof,' "

quoted Pippa clearly from the other end of the table.

Old Matthew chuckled.

"Great fellow, Pound. I've just been reading him myself."

Pippa felt annoyed. She had wanted to seem modern and daring and highbrow, and great-gran had spoilt it. It wasn't fair of anyone as old as great-gran to know about Pound.

General conversation rose again.

Suddenly the old man knew that the pain was going to attack him. It seemed to give him a second's warning in which to brace himself. Then it sprang like a wild beast, tearing, ravaging. It had never been as bad as this before. Instinctively he put out his hand to Beatrice's and clasped it. She held his tightly, as if aware of his sudden need of her, throwing him an anxious glance. Racked with agony, he managed to smile reassuringly at her. She turned to Richard, who had asked her some question. The pain seemed to pass, and the old man let go her hand. Then—almost at once—it was upon him again, clutching at his very vitals. He seemed to wrestle with it in a tense embrace, clenching his hands, digging his teeth into his lips. He could feel the perspiration running down his forehead into his eyes. Then slowly it faded, leaving him alone in the darkness. No, not alone, for a girl was coming toward him—a girl in a white crinoline with roses in her hair. Her lips were parted, and she held out her arms in welcome.

"Hope!" he breathed.

No one heard him. The conversation went on, rising, falling, rising again. Beatrice turned to him to repeat something that Richard had just said. His blue eyes were smiling down the table, but something about him checked the words on her lips and sent an icy chill to her heart. She laid her hand on his, which hung inertly by his side, then started back as if she had been stung.

"Stephen!" she said.

At the urgency of her voice everyone stopped talking and turned to her.

Then sudden commotion filled the room. They all rose from their seats in panic, some drawing away, some pressing nearer.

The old man's blue eyes still seemed to smile serenely down the table.

www.ingramcontent.com/pod-product-compliance
Ingram Content Group UK Ltd.
Pitfield, Milton Keynes, MK11 3LW, UK
UKHW030703020325
455687UK00006B/60